LOKI'S LAUGHTER

Book Two of the Rune Told Series

John Opskar

LOKI'S LAUGHTER

Book Two of the Rune Told Series

by

John Opskar

With a Bonus Chapter from
Odinsson
Book One of the Rune Told Series

2013
Marble, NC

Copyright © 2013 Word Branch Publishing

All rights reserved. This book or any portion thereof may not be reproduced or used in any manner whatsoever without the express written permission of the publisher except for the use of brief quotations in a book review.
This is a work of fiction. Names, characters, businesses, places, events and incidents are either the products of the author's imagination or used in a fictitious manner. Any resemblance to actual persons, living or dead, or actual events is purely coincidental.

First Edition 2013

Printed in Charleston, SC USA

Cover illustration © 2013 Julian Norwood

Permission can be obtained for re-use of portions of material by writing to the address below. Some permission requests can be granted free of charge, others carry a fee.

Word Branch Publishing
PO Box 474
Marble, NC 28905
http://wordbranch.com
catherine@wordbranch.com

 Library of Congress Control Number: 2013952242
ISBN-13: 978-0615896878
ISBN-10: 0615896871

Dedication:

This one is dedicated to my chosen sons Andrew, Seth, and Tim. Here is to the "Loki" in each of you.

Foreword/Author Note:

Ravens.

Hugin and Munin.

Ravens man, Ravens!

The error is mine, and I admit it. To anyone that previously read the excerpt *Sowilo* from *Loki's Laughter* in any form there are no crows in Alaska, the black birds are ravens. My bad.
Hail Odin!
I need an eye exam, so instead of that, let's have a beer! To Life! I want to thank all of my fans! I am amazed that my books are international, that is why they call it the World Wide Web baby! There are millions of fantastic books out there to read, thank you for picking up this one, this time. You are making my dream come true, hopefully my writing will transport you into a dream as well. I feel I owe it to you to keep writing, because we all want to know what happens. What is going to happen next? How the hell should I know, let's ask the characters?
As readers when we fall in love with the characters in a story and we feel catharsis (being the emotional connection to them verses the purging of the bowels). When we read we are transported into the story, and we live it. We get away from our problems and see the problems the characters have to deal with (sort of demented if you think about it, but at least these are not OUR problems, let the

characters find their way. A toast: To The Characters (are you raising your beverage of choice?)!

I started reading fantasy stories as a form of legal escapism after the death of my father. His name was Paul, and I partially owe my love of Science Fiction to him as I have a memory of him reading Bradbury's *The Martian Chronicles* to me while we were sitting on our "golden" davenport. My father's death plunged me into the realm of the fantastic at age eight, as I no longer wanted anything to do with the real world. My Step-father also named Paul (my mom must have something for that name) helped me understand the real world in a positive way while tolerating the imaginative little geek he accepted and raised as his own "chosen son". Thank you P.K.

Hail Thor!

A shout out to the ingenuity of Johannes Gutenberg, the inventor of the modern printing press. Thank you for allowing us all to read more books. Hail Johannes!

Although I am very happy that my first book *Odinsson* reached publication, I feel that *Loki's Laughter* is a better piece of writing. *Odinsson* helped me learn more of my craft and I'm still learning (thank the Gods). One criticism of my first book is that the beginning plodded along, hopefully this one doesn't have the same flaw.

Even though this is a better piece of literature, it was harder to write. There are difficult scenes, thoughts, issues, which are all parts of life, but that doesn't make them easy to deal with even when writing fiction.

I signed the contract for this book. That meant that I had to write half a novel in two months. Light a fire under my hairy hemorrhoidal hind end! I know that many people write entire novels in a month or less, but when I started thinking: I have a deadline, I'm under pressure, I have to do this, the fun of writing was no longer fun, it was just work, and I have a 104 hour a week "normal" job. I felt like quitting. But I hunted and pecked a few more keys, not exactly like reaching Nome racing the Iditarod but perhaps in some parallel universe...

Here it is! Look Mom, both hands (on the keyboard)!

I raise my cyber-quill to my editor Victor Barrett.

I raise my ethereal mead glass to my publisher Catherine.

Thanks to my wife for "Push"-ing me to keep pounding on the keys. Your understanding and support are things I don't take for granted. Love you.

Hail Freya!

Thank you so much to my "Alpha Readers". Jane Kalkbrenner, without you I wouldn't even be here, thank you so much not only for your work "Alpha-Reading" but for 'taking a big shit'. Jack Pike II: fantasy aficionado, (Dwarves man, Dwarves)!

To reiterate (love that word) My Fans: my fedora is off to you.

Hail Wise Ones!

--John Opskar
Willow, Alaska
Spring 2013

Loki's Laughter

Dedication: 5

Foreword/Author Note: 6

PROLOGUE: PERTHRO 13

SOWILO 16

MANNAZ 26

RAIDHO 33

BERKANO 52

GEBO 62

NAUDHIZ 76

LAGUZ 89

TIWAZ 106

THURISAZ 117

ANSUZ 127

KENAZ 136

URUZ 148

EIHWAZ 152

ELHAZ 158

HAGALAZ 161

OTHALA 174

JERA 178

ISA 189

INGWAZ 195

WUNJO 201

EHWAZ 202

FEHU 211

EPILOGUE: DAGAZ 212

Appendix A: The Runes Simple Meanings 217

Appendix B : Widdershins songs 218

Odinsson 229

John Opskar

PROLOGUE: PERTHRO

The roots were hungry. They thrashed about crying, calling, begging for nourishment.

The three moved as one in an odd dance toward the well. They seemed to skip, walk, and crawl at the same time. They were connected together as if chained. What chained them wasn't steel, and though gossamer it stretched, but didn't break, strands of a web. The web allowed each to move independently and yet not leave the other two. The web was Destiny. Their strange dance ended as they reached the edge of the nearby well.

Each dipped a cup and drew forth water. One of the three walked and gingerly poured her cup out onto a root. The water that came forth glimmered clear and clean like that of mountain streams trickling and burbling over small stones giving life to the animals of the world. As it fell light caught each droplet, and it seemed diamonds were being poured from the cup landing on a maiden's long flowing hair in the autumn wind.

She giggled. Her voice tinkled as bells. Amused she reflected that 'maiden' didn't really fit for an ageless being. Skuld appeared the youngest of her sisters. Her breasts were firm, her pale skin smooth, and her eyes sparkled. Skuld slid her finger along a rivulet of water where it had landed on the root. She licked the water off her fingertip and tasted it.

When the water hit Skuld's tongue images of innocence flashed though her mind. Babies born and fresh fallen snow, parts of nature. The water also tasted of sex. Sex being another natural act. She giggled again, and stroked the ash root as if it were a penis.

Skuld danced a few skipping steps. She did a shuffle-ball-change, and then stood on her tip toes. Holding the pose she cupped her firm breasts and looked at her sister.

Her sister Urdr, laughed a deep hearty full of life chortle at Skuld. Her whole being shook with it, and her cup went flying out of her hand. Her eyes filled with mirth as she watched her cup sail through the air. In contrast to lithe Skuld with her firm tits, Urdr was much rounder, shorter, and her breasts were large like the rest of her. The smile that followed her laughter brought a matured blush reddening her cheeks bringing about the fullness of a countenance both honest and welcoming.

The careening cup's contents splattered on the roots like slush. The liquid from the cup where it landed upon the roots became the color of strong ale and the brown of a fast rushing river in a spring thaw. Its edges a frothy foam resembling the head of the beer and the banks of the river. The brown of the water resonated with a mother celebrating milestones in her children's lives with beer, and the river that of the middle years of the universe.

"Uffda," she said as she patted the roots as if congratulating them. She picked up her fallen cup and let the last of the water in it drip onto her tongue.

"Well we don't want to waste it now do we?" It wasn't really a question. She brushed her hands on her hips and looked at the last of the sisters.

The third sister walked slowly from the well. Her body stooped and hunched over. Her skin gray as ash, tangles of wild white hair fluttered out from beneath a black shawl she wore. Thick ugly veins decorated her almost translucent legs.

The last sister Verdandi knelt on the ground and dug a small hole in the black earth. Into this she poured some of the contents from her cup. This water resembled the living blues and greens of the oceans. The water from the cup filled up the depression in the earth, rested a moment, and sunk into the earth as a coffin lowered into the grave. Verdandi covered the grave with dirt, slowly rose to her feet, clapped her hands, and cackled.

From the cups the three poured the water over onto and into the enormous ash roots that flailed about with serpentine grace like huge blind worms. Even though the roots were white like the bones of dead giant fingers they also scintillated with all the colors of the rainbow.

Everything stilled.

The roots stopped thrashing. They had been fed.

SOWILO

Wasilla, Alaska:

Jari glanced at her temperature gauge. It read -16 degrees. Negative sixteen. That kind of cold demanded respect. When your nose hairs freeze and your extremities shrink instantly. Negative 16 made regular freezing of 32 above a temperature which almost allowed shorts.

Jari donned her bunny boots. White military relics that would withstand -40 and still keep one's feet toasty. She zipped up her outer winter jacket over her sweatshirt. Once the lid was on her mug of coffee thick with French vanilla creamer, she pulled on her gloves. She doubled checked that all her appliances were off.

"Guard the fort," she said to her dog who was part chow, part husky. His name was Gerard after Gerard Butler who she thought dead sexy. She knelt down and scratched her canine behind the ears. Gerard barked and wagged his tail. White, gray, and black Gerard regarded her with longing eyes.

"Hungry?" she asked him. She filled his food dish to overflowing, and poured cold water into his silver water bowl.

"I gotta go," she gave him a pat. Jari shut and locked the door of her trailer. At eight thirty it was pitch black out. The world in the woods silent as if it were four a.m.

She put her coffee in the cup holder and grabbed the snow brush from her backseat. It wasn't windy, so the cold was almost bearable. She began brushing the four inches of fresh snow off her car and scraped the windows, a daily ritual in the winter months. She opened her car door and stuck the key in the ignition whispering a silent prayer that it would start this time.

Dead silence. Frustrated she ripped the keys from the starter.

"Fuckin' old beast," she swore as she plugged in her engine block. Should have plugged it in last night she thought retracing her steps to her trailer.

"I'm home," she announced. Gerard looked up from his food bowl. He didn't seem confused though. Jari petted him again and fished a cigarette out of her purse. She lit the Winston. Winston's always reminded her of her dad; that is why she smoked them. Blessed nicotine.

She went to the freezer and pulled out a bottle of Rich and Rare. Undoing the cap she took a big swig and it sent a fiery sensation throughout her body. She took a much smaller swallow and sighed. She recapped the bottle and returned it to the freezer.

Taking one last drag, she ground her cigarette in the ashtray and headed into the bathroom. She grabbed her toothbrush, squirted some paste on it, and vigorously brushed needing to remove the smell of whiskey from her breath.

"Take two. Don't have any wild sex while I'm gone," she said giving Gerard a pet.

Fifteen minutes later, she locked her trailer door and unplugged the engine block. She sat down in the driver side and placed the key in the ignition a second time. She held her breath and turned the key. Sputter. Sputter.

"Thank you Gods," she breathed when the car rumbled to life. It was well past time to be on her way. She pulled out of her drive onto the winding road that would lead her into town. It was still dark.

A thick layer of snow coated the power lines. The tree branches bowed over the winding road, strained almost to breaking due to the weight of the ice on them. Jari looked at the snow as the road twisted along the course of the river.

Jari's teeth were chattering as she steered her old brown car. The heater wasn't working well; she turned up the defrost. Jari had dressed in layers for the weather, but it still wasn't enough to keep her warm.

"Come on, come on warm up already," her breath came out as a visible mist.

Thin rays of the sun-filtered pink behind the trees as she slowed around a curve. She missed the huge moose by inches as it trotted a little faster to cross the road into a driveway following its mother. The moose was dark in the dim light with a long beard, and snow caked on its nose, a white dot on the black head. The car skidded and fishtailed into the other lane. Luckily there wasn't any coming traffic. Jari regained control, returned to her own lane, and continued onward as her heart thumped from the near accident.

"Do you think you own the road, moose? Yeah I know you do." Jari gripped the wheel harder and concentrated on the road ahead of her. If she was late for work, it wouldn't be the first time. Better to get there alive.

Lighting her second Winston, she tried to crack the window, but it was frozen shut. She exhaled and shivered at the same time. Dad. He had been her world when she grew up. He'd been a man's man, but was lonely after her mother left. He'd taught her how to shoot, hunt, and fish. How to chop wood, ride a four wheeler and a snow machine. They had a lot of fun together before the cancer.

"Dammit Jari, don't cry," she chided herself.

Jari went down a small hill and turned right; the snow on the road crunched loudly under the tires. Five minutes later, the windshield began to defrost at the bottom and worked upward. Jari peered through the clear spot and accelerated to thirty five.

Glass shattered inward and shards ripped into Jari. Her torso looked like a towel decorated with blood splotches where someone had nicked their face while shaving. She didn't feel the pain yet.

She'd failed to see the moose that emerged from the roadside. The little old brown car crumpled like a crushed aluminum can. The sound of metal twisting inward with the impact registered in Jari's ears an instant later.

The distinct smell of gas filled her nose. She unbuckled her seat belt and shoved the door open. Jari tried to exit her vehicle, but her legs wouldn't respond to her commands.

She gripped the edges of her door frame and heaved with all her strength. The pavement came up and her head smacked on the ice covered road. A smear of blood steamed only a second before it froze.

From her position, Jari saw gasoline and other car fluids spreading under what remained of her car. I need my cell phone to call 911, she thought. I don't dare go back into the car though. Jari noticed her chest. Shards of glass stuck out of her like a pincushion. She remembered that her grandmother Florence had a tomato pincushion always bristling with pins and needles. Even in shock her body began to recognize pain, like each piece of the windshield were a pin plunging into that tomato. Her head throbbed from where it had struck the road and some of her cheek skin peeled away from the cold when she pulled her face free.

Her eyes were open, she was still breathing but everything seemed to move slowly as if time had drank surreal cannabis coffee this morning.

"I can't die, who would take care of Gerard?" she wondered.

Jari pulled herself away from the car afraid it would blow. She wasn't wrong. There was a whoosh and the wreckage blazed into an orange inferno. She welcomed the brief instant of heat. Jari kept crawling, pulling her useless legs behind her. Blood streaked the white road with crimson lines where her chest dragged.

Near the shoulder of the road, Jari looked out at the countryside. The sun had risen higher now, and just on the horizon there was a two inch line of gold. Where the fuck had that moose come from anyway?

For what seemed an eternity, she lay by the shoulder. Trees and stark snow were in front of her. The line of gold expanded. Now it was perhaps six inches from the ground to the dark of the sky above. No traffic moved along the road. She heard ravens. There were always a lot of ravens, but right now she wanted nothing to do with them.

"I'm not dead yet you dirty scat suckers!" she screamed.

She knew she needed to move or she would freeze to death. Trying unsuccessfully to ignore the pain she began pulling herself again. Her strength ebbed and she closed her eyes. She pictured her dad as he stood in the kitchen after a shower. Water glistened on his thick black chest hair. He unwrapped a fresh pack of Winston. Her mind flashed to Gerard.

Jari's eyes flicked open, and she began to crawl again.

"I'm coming, you sexy beast," she half laughed and half gritted out as the pain in her chest increased. The fragments were being pushed in further as she progressed.

A little later, she closed her eyes again. The cold stung her raw cheek. The blood trail behind her blackened as it froze. The sun continued to rise. The course of nature continued. The sun would rise and set as babies were born and the aging died.

"Fuck you sun! I'm not old yet!" Jari pulled herself forward again. She heard the noise of an approaching plow truck.

If it hit her at least this might be quick. Not slow and painful like when the cancer ate away at her dad. Quick like a sword decapitating a warrior. 300. Gerard.

"Don't hit me!" Jari screamed holding herself up with her left arm and waving with her right.

The grating seemed to go on forever. The plow came forward and snow flew onto the shoulder as the blade advanced. The fucker is going to hit me; can't the cocksucker see the inferno that was my car? Fuck it. At least it will be quick. Sword slice. 300. Gerard.

Loki's Laughter

"I got to get back to my dog, you stupid asshole plow driver!"

There was a rumbling. Jari felt the road vibrate under her hands. Then there was another sound. A squeaking, followed by a thud and snow crunching.

Jari looked up at the most beautiful woman. Her hair gleamed in the headlights. Was it blonde, red, bronze, copper maybe? Braided, the hair hung between her breasts to her beltline. Jari noticed the woman's eyes were chips of cobalt as she picked her up.

"I'm not dead. Am I? I need to get back to Gerard. I live just down the road," Jari explained.

The woman who drove the plow climbed into it with Jari slung over her shoulder like a sweater. The driver buckled her into the passenger seat, and then got into the driver's side and shut the door. Heat surrounded Jari.

"Don't fall asleep on me. It is not your time yet. Valhalla will wait. Now tell me about Gerard," the woman shifted the plow into gear. Jari couldn't place the woman's accent. German? Scandinavian? Had she just said Valhalla?

"Gerard is the most beautiful man. I mean dog. Well both," Jari fumbled somewhat embarrassed.

"Go on," the plow driver urged.

"I live in the trailer. Gerard is part chow, part husky. My handsome man. The only one worth his salt," Jari said. The woman smelled like pine trees. Maybe she was dead?

"My dad and I used to chop pine trees. Pine burns fast and hot."

The driver shifted gears. The plow moved around her charred car. The driver pulled an old fashioned walkie-talkie and spoke into it.

"Thor, the plow is not fast enough, come meet me."

The walkie-talkie crackled: "Almost there."

Jari again wondered if she'd passed on. Or was she just in shock? She'd clearly heard the word Valhalla and now she heard the plow driver say Thor. Thor! She was probably dead. No if she was dead each breath wouldn't hurt. When she breathed it felt like fire licking her lungs. The sun glinted off the plow's windshield. Wouldn't it be dark if she was dead?

"Did you just say Thor?" she asked.

"I did. I know it hurts, but you need to keep breathing," the woman with the metal colored braid said.

"Is Thor yummy?"

"Most women think so," came the reply.

"Oh what a fuckin' relief. I thought I might be going crazy," Jari said.

As the driver shifted gears again, Jari studied her. She wore a quilted tan vest and a man's long sleeved thermal undershirt. Her lips were full and red, and her cheekbones seemed chiseled and soft at the same time. Her boobs were somehow just right. The woman exuded sexuality and warrior at the same time. Was that possible? Jari thought she needed another whiskey to clear her head.

"Where are you taking me?" she asked.

"To Thor," the woman answered.

"Not much of a conversationalist, are you?"

"Sorry dear. I know that once I drop you off, you are gonna want me to go back and take care of your dog. I will," she answered.

"How did you know I would ask you that?" Jari needed to know.

"Gut feeling, intuition, call it what you like. Thor is likely to talk your head off. Keep looking at him. That shouldn't be hard, but stay awake. You can tell Thor your life story too. He will listen. Be a woman though and make sure he keeps his eyes on the road instead of your tits."

An Alaska State Trooper truck came flying toward them with siren blaring. It skidded sideways and came to a halt. The blue and red flashers shimmered on the white snow. The trooper stepped out and opened the passenger door, then returned to the driver's seat and put on his seatbelt.

The plow driver stopped the plow and gripped Jari. With Jari in hand, she kicked open her door and hopped out. She put Jari down into the trooper truck's passenger seat and belted the seat belt about her.

"Thank you for saving me, could you look after…" Jari broke off with understanding.

"Gerard. Told you I would," the plow driver winked.

The state trooper truck took off without hesitation. Soon the speedometer topped seventy despite the snow and ice on the road. The sun silhouetted all the peaks in the distance. Jari looked at the trooper. She kept looking at him; that is what the plow lady said to do.

"Don't worry I'll get you to the hospital. What is your name young lady?" the trooper asked.

"Flattery will get you nowhere, Trooper," she shot back in response. Perhaps in too harsh of a tone, but her experiences with men hadn't been good. She almost blushed looking at him.

"The life we share is nothing but a song. Good song by Great Big Sea. They are a folk band from Newfoundland, ever heard of them?" he asked.

"No. Look I didn't want to get off on the wrong foot officer. My name is Jari Anderson. I live up the road. I hit a moose, so please give the meat to those on the list. The plow driver picked me up; she must know you…since she radioed you," Jari said as she glanced at his name badge. It didn't say Thor. It said a name…Odinsson.

"Please don't call me Officer Odinsson. My name is Thor," he smiled. Thor pressed the gas pedal and the truck accelerated to something well over seventy. The trees and churches on the sides of

Church Road flew by as they went up one hill and down it, only to climb another.

"Tell me about yourself, Jari?" Thor asked.

"I was born here. Mom left dad when I was fourteen. Dad died of cancer two years ago. I have a dog named Gerard. I'm not married. What else do you want to know?" Jari rattled off.

"Whatever you want to tell me. I have a brother named Loki. Ever heard of him?" Thor asked.

"Only as much as I've heard of you," Jari admitted.

"I have a sneaking suspicion that Loki went into the moose you hit. I think this may be some sick joke that he is playing. I have no proof of this yet, call it a hunch. I am sorry this happened to you. If it was Loki, he had no right to interfere in your life. I will do whatever I can to help rectify this," Thor explained.

"Went into the moose?" Jari wasn't following.

"I think you would call it magic. Don't worry about that right now; try to focus on staying awake. Stay with me Jari Anderson," Thor said.

"I will," she looked at his hands on the steering wheel. They were strong; she thought they might feel good…

"Ever heard of ATF, Alaska Thunder Funk?" Thor asked.

"No. I listen to a lot of country. I like Alan Jackson, Gretchen Wilson, Diamond Rio, Hank Jr., Johnny Cash, Toby Keith, Miranda Lambert, Sugar Land, Patsy Cline, and the Dixie Chicks," Jari answered.

"Check them out sometime, any band with 'Thunder' in their name can't be bad," Thor said.

"You seem a little arrogant, Thor! Slow down, if the moose didn't kill me, your driving will!" she said. She kept looking at him though. He did not look like the pretty boy in the movie, but somehow he was more real (the fact not-withstanding) that she was sitting next to him, and more dreamy at the same time. He had a bushy red beard. His shoulder length red hair under the trooper hat was completely out of place.

"Feisty little thing…" Thor laughed. He took off the mirrored sunglasses and looked at her breasts.

"Keep your eyes on the road," Jari said.

"I am glad you listened so well to my mother," his eyes met hers briefly and returned to the road. What eyes they were. They were blue and full of mischief, and he reveled in it.

When she recovered from the fact that he looked at her tits unashamed and that he had the most gorgeous eyes, what he had said registered. It didn't make any sense; the plow driver looked younger than him.

"She is your mother?"

"You will have a lot of time to talk to my mother. She is amazing isn't she? She puts up with my father, my brother, and me. Did you think my mother beautiful?" he asked as he procured a tin of Grizzly from his uniform pocket and took a big pinch.

"Keep your hands on the wheel," she said even a bit too girlishly for her own liking. Then to take away from that, she said, "I'm not a lesbo. I didn't check out your mother."

"Yes you did. You are a poor liar Jari Anderson," he laughed, he grinned. "She is beautiful; my dad has good taste."

"What sort of sicko are you, Thor?" she spat out.

"You misunderstand me. My mother's name is Freya; she is the Goddess of beauty. If you didn't think she was beautiful something would be wrong."

"Okay truth be told, I thought she was beautiful. Are you happy now? You are infuriating," Jari said.

"That is a good start," he laughed again.

"I think I am dead. I hear Valhalla, Thor, Loki, and now Freya," Jari mused.

"No if you were dead, Mom would have brought you to Valhalla," Thor turned onto the Parks Highway and weaved through traffic.

"It smells funny in here," Jari said.

"That would be essence of goat," Thor replied.

"Goat?" Jari asked.

"Yes. I have two goats and without getting too science fiction on you, they are this truck. Let us say they transformed into this truck like in a fairy tale," Thor answered.

"You are sure I'm not dead? I must look a mess too with my cheek and blood and…"

"Your breasts look fine," Thor said and grinned.

"Did you notice what color my eyes are?" she asked, irked.

"I noticed they are a very fine shade of green," he answered.

They flew past Seward-Meridian and up the ramp onto Trunk. Thor turned left, took them around the round-about and down the drive to the new Mat-Su Regional Hospital. Thor pulled into the emergency entrance. The hospital staff efficiently strapped Jari to a gurney and wheeled her further into the building.

Full daylight had come to The Valley.

MANNAZ

A nurse recorded Jari's vital signs. What the nurse had not done was put her in the normal hospital gown. That worried her. Why didn't they remove her clothing?

A different nurse started an IV. Bless the pain killer, she might live after all? She knew she wasn't dead yet. These were normal doctors; there was no talk of Valhalla going on here. They had asked if she had any religious beliefs that needed to be addressed. She answered no.

A doctor came who didn't speak to her at all, what a prick, she thought. Jari had no idea how long she had been in the E.R. or who dropped her off here. Dreamlike. Now she remembered, it was…Thor. The Norse God of Thunder? These were some killer meds they had her on.

Someone with bad teeth, worse glasses, and a nose like a ballpoint pen cap from admissions floated in front of her. She tried to answer the questions, but focusing was difficult. She closed her eyes, and it seemed as if the Thor ogled her breasts again. Then clouds over Pioneer peak. The snow silhouette of a woman became Freya who mouthed 'I'm looking after Gerard.'

Jari opened her eyes to look at someone new. This someone wore a nice smile, a charcoal suit that fit perfectly, and seemed genuinely understanding, came from financial assistance. Jari let her know that she didn't have insurance but that she would make payments.

Another person appeared. A lab tech who efficiently drew her blood and went away. Then two more people came who wheeled Jari out of the E.R. room to a room to take x-rays. They took their photos and wheeled her back to her E.R. room. Nope she wasn't dead yet.

A different set of people came. They administered some sort of drug. Maybe it was morphine? Blackness. Jari thought she heard someone say 'I.C.U.' Blackness again. The fluorescent lights were intense beyond anything Jari thought possible. She shut her eyes. Gods let this fucking end. Jari told herself she hated hospitals as blessed sleep overcame her.

Jari's eyes flickered open. Shut. Opened again, now where was she? This room was nothing like the last one, which was a good thing. That last room had been way too bright. This room was dim, at least by comparison.

Jari noted that she now wore the customary hospital gown; it wasn't flattering. It wasn't revealing which was a plus as she still thought she felt Thor's eyes on her breasts. Damn that man, and damn him again since she couldn't get him out of her head. Well it was a comforting thought that they had at least cut her blood drenched clothing off and put her in "proper" hospital attire. She disliked the buttons and worried about her ass showing. This was a normal hospital room; did that mean she was getting better or worse? A priest hadn't showed up, that must be a good sign.

Yup, definitely a normal hospital room. Bed that moved, monitors, an IV pole behind her, a TV she could control along with the nurse call button next to her. A curtain separated her room from the hospital corridor. A hideously patterned curtain with blue and brown rectangles and some small orange and yellow lines.

Days passed. How many? She'd lost track. How long had she been here in the Mat-Su Regional Center? She didn't even want to think about the bills. Breakfast would come, followed by the breathing person. A nurse would take vitals, the CNA would get her comfort type stuff, then lunch would come. People from the lab would come and do more blood draws. People would cart her out for X-rays or MRI scans. Dinner would come and then the process would repeat. No visitors came, and loneliness assailed Jari. Gods, she missed Gerard.

She sank into a loneliness worse than after her father's death. Alone like she was in outer-space among the stars and blackness. Loneliness worse than when any asshole "boyfriend" had dumped her or her him. She hoped that whoever this Freya was, she was checking on Gerard like she said she would.

With the loneliness came a cup of boredom, did that mean she was getting better? How long did she fucking have to be here? She had all the stupid TV commercials memorized, not a feat she was proud of. She had watched enough *Burn Notice* to make her puke.

More days passed.

Loneliness.

Boredom.

She slept.

"Your breasts look nice," the voice of Thor. She must be dreaming.

"Fuck you," she answered.

"I see you are feeling better," he answered.

Jari flicked her eyes open and there he stood. Thor. Not in uniform, he wore a gray t-shirt that said HP-AK on it with a picture of a snow-machine. His muscles bulged, and his beard had been trimmed. His hair flowed about his shoulders like a copper avalanche. His eyes gazed at her and his smile was infectious. Despite herself she smiled back.

"I finally got a day off," he said.

"And you came to see me?" She asked.

"Yes, and I brought you something," he said with a mischievous smile.

"You shouldn't have," she said.

"It isn't from me. It's from Gerard," he handed her a box. It wasn't wrapped like a gift; it was just a plain brown cardboard box.

She opened it. Inside was a portable DVD player and two movies. 300, and P.S. I Love you.

"Will you tell him I love him? Is he okay? Is your mother looking after him?" she gushed.

"I assure you he's fine," Thor answered.

"Can you put your hands on my feet so I can see if I can feel them?" she asked.

"Your breasts would be nicer," he smirked.

"I was being serious," she said.

"So was I," he reached forward. He pulled off her tan hospital non-slip socks and placed heavy rough calloused hands on her feet. She could feel her feet! She wasn't paralyzed!

"I can feel my feet! I can feel my legs! I could kiss you!" she said.

"Don't," he said.

"Why not?" she needed to know.

"I'm in love with that girl in that awful movie," he laughed and she knew he was joking. Was he joking about the movie being shitty or being in love? The movie she decided.

Thor did, however, move away from her to sit in the drab green hospital chair under the TV set. She could still feel the tingle of his fingers on her feet though. His hands had been incredibly strong; they had felt as if they were made for battle. The thought was silly to her, but of course they were made for battle, Thor's weapon was that hammer, what was its name again?

"What is your hammer's name?" she asked. She wanted to retract the question because maybe this wasn't THAT Thor. But he made the joke about the movie…

"Mjolnir," he answered without missing a beat.

That was a relief. At least he knew what she was talking about. There sat Thor, red beard, strong hands, the fucking God of Thunder across her hospital room!

"Are you sure I'm not dead?" she asked.

"Your hot feet say otherwise."

"Oh shut up, it wasn't a real question. Now what brings The Mighty Thor to see Jari Anderson?" she asked.

"Gerard said if I didn't bring you his gifts, he wouldn't give me back my hammer." There was a glint in his eyes, he was up to something.

"What, for real?" Jari asked.

"Your breasts, what else," Thor answered. He was looking at them too. Jari crossed her arms over them.

"You're impossible!" she flared.

"So I've been told," he answered.

"You still haven't really answered the question," Jari prompted.

"Maybe I just came to see you," he spread his hands open as an explanation.

"Bullshit. Not buying it," she shook her head.

"Okay. Okay. I come on behalf of my mother," he said.

"What's wrong with my dog?" She hoped he was okay.

"Nothing. My mother has another matter to attend to. I just wanted your permission to look after him," he answered.

She had to think about it for a while. She didn't want a man in her place. He had saved her life though; she could let him look after her dog. What crazy stuff could he do, jack off on her bra? Better if he ran those hands up her legs.

"What does Freya have to do?" Jari asked.

"Suffice it to say that a couple very dear to both of us needs a little help," he answered.

"Well..." she hesitated.

"...I am very good at chopping wood," Thor upped the stakes.

"I guess you can," she allowed.

"Done! I need my hammer back. Gerard thinks the handle is a chew toy," Thor said.

"What about your work?" Jari asked.

"Extensive leave time," he grinned.

"Okay. Will you let me know how Gerard is? I can give you money," Jari said.

"See you in the morning," Thor said.

"Look forward to it. Keys are in my purse," she said pointing to the counter.

"I think I can get in." He touched her feet again, winked, and walked out. She watched him go and appreciated his backside. Her feet tingled. Electricity?

Morning came. Thor didn't. Typical man. However a nurse came and took Jari for a walk. It was shaky, but she could walk. She could walk! Thank the Gods!

Another day passed. The nurses took her for more walks. Her legs were a bit stronger now.

The next day Thor returned wearing a black Harley Davidson jacket.

"Are you ready to go home, Jari Anderson?" he asked from behind mirrored sunglasses. He had a bag in his hands.

"I believe I am, Officer Odinsson," she answered, smiling.

"Good, that would make Gerard very happy. I brought you some clothes." Thor smiled.

Jari dressed in the bathroom glad to be rid of the hospital gown. He had brought her a pair of her panties, leggings, and a pair of her blue jeans. He had been though her dresser. Fuck! He also brought a bra, t-shirt, sweater, and her old black leather jacket which had belonged to her father.

"Now here are the two new items you'll want to wear," Thor said and gave her a dual source heated jacket liner and pair of gloves, both of which could plug in providing extra warmth to cycle riders.

"Thank you," Jari said taking off her jacket, adding the liner, and pulling her jacket over the liner again, and donning the gloves.

Outside sat the bike. Not just any bike. A Softail Fat Boy! It would growl and vibrate oh so sweetly. Jari felt very much alive, and if she was dreaming then, dream away, as long as she was on that bike!

All black, with the chrome gleaming. On the handlebars were two helmets. Thor put his on and tossed the other helmet to Jari. He assisted Jari plugging in her heated gear.

*

Asgard:

Frost crystals danced capriciously above the Bifrost. They whirled up and around the figure who stood watching. They landed in his hair and sashayed away again. They dipped into his beard and twirled back out.

The Bifrost. The Rainbow Bridge. It stretched out before the watcher flickering a myriad of colors. Chartreuse was Heimdall's favorite. He thought of little green and gold shamrocks jumping and spinning around. He wasn't Irish, but one could always appreciate a good thick stout. A stout would be good, Heimdall thought as he stood and watched. His eyes saw all worlds. He heard grass growing on Midgard, and he also had a Primus song in his head.

Heimdall watched.

Heimdall focused his senses. He paid close attention to Ljosalfheim. Nothing threatened, with no enemies near he relaxed, slightly.

Heimdall watched, ever vigilant.

RAIDHO

London, England:

It rained. Poured more like. Buckets would be a misnomer, more like torrential belting, as if each rain drop aspired to be a machinegun bullet. The rain made seeing the world like looking through a smoky green glass rippled window.

Holli dashed through the rain and down the set of steps leading underground. The Tube. People in the US would call it a subway. She looked at her surroundings. Everyone but her seemed calm, collected, like they knew what they were doing. She was sure her appearance screamed 'American Tourist' to them. Oh well that is what I am, she thought, and I don't understand a fucking thing here yet. She wished Lennie were here with her, but someone had to work and take care of the kids. She worried about Lennie home with the kids even in her present state of mind. That is what love was, worrying about the other person even more than you worried about yourself even if you yourself were in a mild state of crisis.

Everything here was confusing. The money, the language, the Tube system. But the pound coins were sort of neat, heavy, intriguing. Frustrated, Holli waited in the queue, in the US people would call it a line. She studied the posters on the walls; they depicted movies and plays. Some she recognized, most she didn't.

Rain. It was said that it always rained in London. Well, stereotypes had to come from somewhere. Holli wrung her long gorgeous red hair out, and laughed. The water made a puddle next to her. Well at least she didn't feel so heavy now, must have been a few pounds of water on the station floor. The one thing which Holli did not find frustrating or confusing was the rain. Rain was normal, just Mother Nature doing her thing. Holli was visiting London trying to locate the estate of a relative she did not know she'd had who had passed.

The letter arrived informing Holli that she would not regret the visit. It didn't directly say Holli had inherited anything, but it seemed to strongly imply that she could have. Inherited what? Money? A castle? An old shoe box filled with dust and photographs so brown with age that nothing but the brown could be discerned. An ash tray that belonged to Winston Churchill would impress Lennie. Ever since he had met a certain old man, he had taken up a liking for cigars. Cigars, and 'bloody' expensive ones at that.

"Please mind the gap," the electronic voice said. Holli minded the gap. When the doors were closing: "Stand clear the doors," even the electronic voice had a British accent. Holli smiled. She couldn't remain upset for long. If she was wet, hopelessly lost, and frustrated because she wasn't sure what Tube station she needed to get off at, these things were happening to her in London. She was in another country!

Holli took in her fellow passengers. There were businessman dressed in dark blue pinstriped suits, and there were punks with green and pink spiked Mohawks. There were nursing mothers publicly breast feeding, and there were teenagers dressed in black leather jackets. There were women students and men dressed in sweaters who looked like they must work in bookstores. All of them were going somewhere. Some of the passengers sat, but most were standing either gripping the hanging handles or the silver poles. Holli felt stifled.

Traveling. One of the things in life that could be both frightening and exciting at the same time. In that light, it could have something in common with teenage sex. There wasn't anything Holli could do about the number of passengers on the train. She might have to ask someone for directions. She hated talking to people she didn't know.

Piccadilly Circus? Hyde Park? Fuck it! Holli had time, she could get off anywhere and ask directions when she wasn't on this train. This very confined space. She got off at Piccadilly Circus.

When she was above ground again Holli knew she wasn't in the right place. That being said, she looked around. Even though it was daylight a large number of neon signs glowed through the rain turned mist.

There were a number of shops that sold pizza by the slice, and up ahead of her there was no mistaking the sign in red neon that proclaimed: Virgin. The Virgin record store. Well maybe record was an outdated term; perhaps music store would be more appropriate. Holli considered asking directions in the store and then reconsidered.

She didn't have anything against teenagers but needed someone who could give directions to actually get her where she needed to go, not someone who said something like 'bugger off' if you are not buying something, or 'I don't know'.

Holli thought about this person who was saying that he had come up with the Harry Potter ideas before J.K. Rowling did — good luck with that one buddy. It would be nice to know where she needed to go though. Well she could get back on the underground, and just try the next stop? That option didn't thrill her. She could stop into a pub; they might know directions in a pub. That seemed like a better option.

Holli stepped into a pub. And it was what one expected an English pub to be like. There were wooden tables that were old and comfortably used. The place was dimly lit, Holli saddled up.

"What can I get you, dear?" the bald bartender with owlish eyes asked.

"Fullers or Bass whatever is on tap," Holli replied trying to sound natural.

"They both are…"

"…Bass please," she sighed.

He pulled the beer and gently set it in front of her. Holli looked at herself in the mirror behind the man. Wretched came to mind. Well there was nothing for it, it wasn't like she was trying to impress.

"What is troubling the American tourist?" the bartender asked.

"Is it that obvious?" Holli looked him in the eye and picked up the pint.

"Quite," he answered staring back.

"I'm lost. I need to find 52 Baker Street."

"If you looking for Mr. Holmes my dear you need 221b Baker Street?" A smile brightened his face.

"No shit Watson," she grinned back, "I'm not looking for the astute detective, but I do need to find a 'flat' on 52 Baker Street," she said and took a pull on the beer. It was bitter as hell, how did Lennie drink this stuff?

"Get back on the Tube and take it to the Baker Station. When you get off and are above ground, walk left about four blocks. The addresses descend; you should find your place right off," he answered as he polished a glass.

"What line goes to Baker Street Station?" Holli asked taking another swallow of the bitter beer.

"Five different lines go there. You won't have a problem. Baker Street Station is a huge Underground Station," he said.

"Thank you," she said, drained her glass, and thought, you are gonna get it for telling me to have a Bass, Lennie.

"Three pound fifty," the barkeep said. Holli found a 'five pound note' and placed it the counter.

"So I need to get back on the Tube?" she asked.

"You could hail a driver, but I wouldn't walk it," the bar tender answered.

"In that case another pint please?" Holli took back the five and replaced it with a ten; the bills had different colors unlike American bills.

Holli re-boarded the underground. It was even more packed then before, but now she didn't mind as much. The second Bass was better than the first, liquid courage. Okay Lennie, I had two beers in London, there you go. She wondered about how the three kids were doing as the Tube swayed along.

She got off at the Baker Street Station and took the escalator up to the surface. Why hadn't she thought to go to Baker Street Station in the first place? Well at least her mistake had allowed her to see Piccadilly Circus and have the beer so she could tell Lennie about it.

When she breathed the open air again, she smiled. She resisted going into the Sherlock Holmes museum. The rain-mist had completely stopped; she turned left and tracked the addresses, which did indeed decrease as she walked.

The door that read 52 was a nondescript door painted brown. Holli wondered if this could be a joke or worse some terrorist group? If she was to inherit something, it was most likely that dusty box of letters or perhaps a thimble collection that wasn't worth anything. She took a breath, let it out, and knocked.

A man with a pinched birdlike face answered the door. A sharp pointed nose and small beady glassy eyes, completed his physiognomy, and he wore a black suit. Holli braced herself for fight or flight.

"We've been expecting you. Please come in," he held the door open. A slanted flight of wooden steps led up. They creaked as Holli walked wondering if the Mad Hatter held a tea party at the top? This thought was accompanied in her head by the haunting Fiona Apple song, *Pale September*.

When she reached the top, all thoughts of Hatters and terrorists left her. Sunlight brightly lit the small room from a large window that overlooked much of London. Dust showed through the rays of sunlight. It might be a small flat with a slanted staircase, but the flat was a flat with a view!

Aside from the man who greeted Holli, another man sat behind a cherry wood table with the windows to his back, his face resembled a cow. If a cow nose could be turned perpendicular instead of horizontal, and the tip of the cow's nose was this man's chin. His hair was thinning, oiled, and once might have been brown; his eyes were a muddy delta. A bird and a cow, the Mad Hatter feeling returned. Holli wanted to run. It didn't matter how much money she might get, she wanted to be done with this place.

She didn't run. She wasn't a mouse, but the tingling feeling of something being wrong here, something not right somehow, was growing in her mind and stomach. The feeling demanded that she pay attention.

Holli could feel things. Her feelings were not often wrong, but she knew that her nerves had been frayed over this trip to England. Leaving her kids and husband, flying, the Tube, and everything that went along with being in a foreign country. So she could be reading this wrong; it could be just nerves, but she doubted it.

"Gentlemen, apparently I had a relative I didn't know about that passed away; you have been waiting for me. I am Holli Odinsson, formerly Schroeder. I have identification, but could someone explain more about this relative of mine?" Holli asked.

Nothing in the room indicated violence, and Holli wondered if rooms would feel a certain way if violence took place in them on a regular basis. It wasn't a subject she wanted to explore too deeply. The two men could be just English lawyers; they were dressed respectfully and looked decent enough, but Al Capone might have presented that way too. But something about the bird and the cow still felt wrong. Holli's sixth sense kicked up another notch.

"I am William R. Tulley; we have here a copy of the will," said cow-face as he extracted some papers from an attaché case.

*

Wasilla, Alaska:

Strapping on her helmet, Jari noted that it fit just right. She wanted more than anything to ride on this bike, but she had to say something. She couldn't just leave off that she would melt if a motorcycle was involved.

"There is still snow on the ground," she stated.

"It is my day off Jari Anderson. I am not going to drive the trooper truck. Would you prefer that I call you a cab?" Thor returned.

"Reckless bastard," she climbed onto the 'bitch seat' and put her arms around Thor's waist. The Harley rumbled to life, an orgasmic feeling. The vibration oh so sweet, not to mention having her arms around this...God.

"Ready?" Thor asked.

"So much," Jari answered.

Thor exited the hospital accelerating onto Trunk Road. Wind slammed around Jari, and she clung tighter to Thor. She regretted the fact that she was pressing her breasts against his back, then she pressed them even harder. He was her ride home, and maybe he couldn't even feel her beneath their leather jackets, and if he could, all the better.

Thor twisted the throttle again. Although it couldn't have been more than twenty degrees out, Jari wasn't cold due to her gear, and the thrill of the ride kept the cold at bay. The bike continued to vibrate and heat filled her legs from the motor. Not long after that they stopped at a light. Thor flicked up his visor and looked at Jari. He grinned.

His eyes were amazing. Jari lifted her visor staring back at him.

"How is the ride? I can drop you at the station and call a cab," Thor joked.

"Save your money," she said.

"Gerard will be pleased; you will get home faster this way. Your breasts are nice," Thor said.

"Shut up and drive," Jari flicked down her visor.

Thor shut his visor and twisted throttle; the Harley rumbled. Thor took his foot from the pavement, and the bike lurched forward. The sweet vibration resumed.

Roaring over the bridge spanning Little Sue River, they continued to curve left with the road. Soon they were on West Sunrise Road. Almost home, Jari thought. She didn't want the bike ride to end, but she would be happy to see Gerard.

They reached the trailer and Gerard bounded out the door barking his greeting. Thor killed the engine and flipped the Harley's kickstand. Jari climbed off the bike, and Gerard ran circles around her. She knelt down, and he put his paws on her shoulders. Jari took off her helmet and Gerard licked her face. His breath didn't smell as rank as normal. She scratched him behind the ears.

"I missed you too," she said standing up and turned to Thor, "What have you been feeding him?"

"Nothing new, but we have been brushing and flossing every day, Mom," and he grinned one of his huge grins.

"Try to get a straight answer..." Jari noticed all the piles of wood. She couldn't have guessed how many cord Thor had cut and stacked. Not only were there five large piles, but he'd build a fence around her property complete with a gate.

"Spearmint leaves is the answer to your question. That and it never hurts to protect one's borders, Jari Anderson," he said as he climbed off the Harley. The way he said her name almost melted her heart and it pissed her off. He had done an amazing amount of work here, but that didn't mean that she had to sleep with him. That seemed to have been what her previous experiences with men had been, they do something nice for you and so you have to sleep with them. Thor wasn't hard on the eyes, anything but, however that still didn't mean she was going to open her legs.

"Spearmint leaves?" she asked.

"Gerard likes them," he said. Jari found she liked his grin more and more.

"Come on in," she wanted a cigarette. She thankfully noted that he hadn't rearranged anything inside her place. She unwrapped a new pack of smokes, took one out, and lit it. Ah, Winston.

She reached into the freezer and took out the bottle of whiskey. There was something comforting in the thin layer of frost that coated the outside of the bottle. She poured two fingers of Rich and Rare in a mason jar.

"Wanna drink?" she asked Thor.

"I would love one," he answered.

"Are you always so formal?" she asked, pouring him a drink.

"Not always. I do not take your hospitality for granted however, and it gladdens my heart that you have offered me a drink," Thor answered.

"That is the kind of shit I'm talking about: 'it gladdens my heart', people just don't talk like that normally," she explained. Thor shrugged and downed his glass.

"Another?" Thor asked. Jari poured him a new drink. She raised her drink.

"Thank you for watching my dog, building me a fence, and the ride," Jari toasted. Thor clinked her glass, and they downed the whiskey.

*

Astoria, Oregon:

Lennie sighed. A sigh of frustration and relief; the kids were finally in bed. A very strong part of him wanted to call Holli. However he also did not want to call her and make her think that he couldn't take care of the kids. There was a part of him that enjoyed being able to take care of them on his own. He missed her though.

Their move had taken them across the country to the coast of Oregon. Where the mouth of the Columbia River gushed into the Pacific Ocean in a town named Astoria, they made their new home. The family had taken the spiraling staircase 125 feet up inside the Astoria Column to look out on the 360 degree view of the area. Lennie and Holli breathed in the air, and the faint scent of the salty sea permeated their nostrils and whispered 'stay'. So they did.

Many Scandinavian (mostly Finnish) settlers founded Astoria. This suited Lennie and Holli just fine. The port had been a lumbering and fishing town when it began. Larger cities replaced it as a primary port in the modern age. Now Astoria relied on tourism and the art scene. Knowing this, Holli had always wanted to open a shop that sold 'their kind of things'. The idea scared the hell out of Lennie, but he agreed that nothing ventured, nothing gained. They took a third of their savings and bought an oceanfront store. They painted a huge earth on the building's exterior. Inside, they painted moons and stars. The shop itself wasn't large and had a rickety wooden floor.

Beyond sanding and staining the floor and building some shelves, Lennie left all other interior decorating and inventory placement to Holli. Holli took great care and enjoyed making the shop look and feel a certain way. The inventory arrived haphazardly, but Holli did not let this bother her. She worked with what she had, when it showed up, because that was the way that it was meant to be. After a month and a half the store could open.

The store didn't as yet have a name, but it opened anyway.

Lennie felt drained and ready for bed, but at the same time he felt elated. Everything had gone fine. Everybody had been fed, and taken care of, but it had been a lot of work. Normal housework aside (which was indeed work ask any mother or any direct care provider) other matters needed to be addressed. Feeding two growing boys and an infant; personal hygiene for all three, and emotional upheaval for the boys. The infant had needs too, but they were not things like school socialization issues.

He glanced at his copy of *A Dance With Dragons* sitting on the arm of their second-hand reading chair. The chair had been free as long as it was picked up. Lennie found the flower pattern hideous, but Holli loved it. Well he didn't have to look at the chair while he sat in it, and it was comfortable. He couldn't argue with the price either. It had belonged to a lady who wanted it to go to a family that would appreciate it because her own family was shipping her off to a home, and not allowing her to take her chair with her. The deal had been sealed the second Beverly set eyes on Holli.

As good as the book was, he didn't feel like reading. Lennie decided to smoke a cigar. Instead of having a drink with it, he brewed some coffee. Coffee could bring out "earthy or chocolate" notes of flavor in a stogie, or so the write-ups said. The clock read 9:42 P.M. He clipped the end of a Queen B, by A. Funte and flicked his lighter while listening to the gurgling sound of the coffee maker. He rolled the cigar around in his mouth so that the lighter's flame could properly reach the entire tip. Once a nice orange glow greeted his countenance, Lennie pulled his first real draw on the Queen B.

Ten months had passed since Lennie smoked a good cigar. They spent another third of their savings as the down payment on a house. It wasn't enough money to be a proper down payment, but not everything works out mathematically to be just ten percent, and Lennie wondered at how Holli had a way of working out deals (getting what she wanted) with people. He smiled, remembering Holli at her negotiations.

Their house was small and felt cramped some days, but they owned it. The best part of their new house was its picture window which looked out on the ocean. The house could have been four times more expensive, and it would have been worth it. The house had been a foreclosure however, and they had got it for a song.

During the time when they had been setting up their house and store, Lennie hadn't bought a good cigar. The money had to be used for more important needs. They had electricity turned on in both places. Heat, water, trash removal, and phones. Although useful, Lennie thought phones were odious things. Holli had listed the store in the phone directory and on the internet as "The Store That Doesn't Have a Name." Despite this their store was doing well. With Astoria life under way and Holli in London, he'd purchased a few good sticks, thinking of an 'old man' and their conversation about cigar write-ups.

This one is "spicy with earthy tones and finished with coffee notes coated in white chocolate." Lennie confirmed these people got paid too much for their rhetoric, but the cigar tasted good.

The old man, Odin Allfather in the flesh had visited him. Odin! God of wisdom, words, and knowledge. Hail Odin!

Lennie watched the spring rain as he smoked. Steady. Not a thunderstorm and not a light mist. Just a steady drum roll on the roof. Holli loved the rain. He wondered if it was raining in London? Lennie didn't mind rain; although, driving in downpours could be nerve wracking. Beyond the rain, the ocean looked black and angry.

Throughout this time, Lennie and Holli made a new friend. One afternoon, tired from working on the store, they'd stopped for lunch and a drink. Inside the dive by the shore under a dim light sat a six foot three man in a ball cap that could have been around since ball caps were invented, strumming a mandolin. Although the chords were simple, they carried a depth with them that seemed as deep as those places in the ocean that hadn't been explored yet.

When he sang, he sounded like Garrison Keillor with a Finnish accent. His songs were about fisherman out on the sea. Their lives, loves, catches, and woes. When he finished his set, the couple went to tell him how wonderful he sounded.

Loki's Laughter

"Name is Clayton. You could buy a thirsty musician a beer?" he asked. They got him a Henry Winehearts Special Reserve. An impressively named beer for a beer that tasted like Miller Lite.

"Are you folks just passing through?" Clayton asked. Lennie noticed that his watery pale eyes didn't look either of them directly in the eye. Was he dishonest or shy and insecure?

"We moved here about three months ago. We took two months traveling across the states looking for a place to call home and found Astoria," Holli answered.

"Pleasure to meet you," Clayton said. Lennie shook his hand.

"Do you play here a lot?" Lennie asked.

"Not a lot, but I know the owner. I am one of the artists that come here during Fisher Poets Gathering each year," he answered. Since that day Clayton and the couple had developed a friendship that likened to be considered family-ship.

Lennie looked out the window again at the rain and the sea. He took a puff on his cigar and thought about getting the boys up and off to school and taking Staley Moon to the store with him.

That is when the world began to slide off kilter. It seemed to Lennie that the rain outside the window undulated like a crazy mirror at a carnival. The window rippled and the wobbling movement increased. What the hell is this? This isn't 'normal'. Not that he ever considered his life 'normal'.

Lennie moved across the room from the window and set his cigar down. He tried to calm his mind; it didn't work. He tried to reach another world and pull a living flame to fight with; it didn't work. Why wasn't anything working?

The undulating window began to spin, a swirl of colors, clear, black, green, white. A hole opened in the middle of the window, and the glass of the pane became elastic and stretched backward outside. Lennie wondered if he'd been reading too much Dr. Seuss to Staley?

A sucking noise pounded through Lennie's head. The window turned vortex was trying to pull him in. Papers, a pen, the cigar, ashtray, empty can of Mountain Dew, and Holli's ladybug table cloth all flew into the vortex. Somehow the tablecloth would be his fault. He would hear it from Holli.

Electricity filled the air as the still brewing coffee pot's cord came out of the wall socket. The coffee pot flew into the vortex. The vacuum pulled at Lennie's clothing.

This is insane, Lennie thought. Am I having an allergic reaction to the cigar? He grabbed a chair and tried to keep himself upright. The chair flew out of his hands. The wooden table along with Lennie began sliding across the floor. The suck-hole grinned, a Cheshire Cat black-hole.

Lennie heard on the radio that two new black-holes had been discovered, but they didn't say they were on Midgard! His ass burned from sliding across the floor grasping at anything he could for an anchor and failing to grasp anything but air. This might have been funny to watch in a movie but not for real.

Shit! He'd just got the kids to bed. He screamed.

"Stan! Peter! Staley Moon!"

Peter hadn't been asleep. He heard his step-father yelling and jumped out of bed. He ran down the hallway toward the dining room. He saw Lennie being sucked into the vortex. He stopped at the edge of the dining room.

"Lennie!"

"Tell your mother that the table cloth is not my fault! Pray to Freya for help!" that was all Lennie said before he smacked off the wall and flew into the maw of the spinning vortex.

Peter stood still; he didn't know what to do. He'd just watched Lennie get sucked into a vortex. It hadn't been as cool as watching Thor fight the giant, but it was pretty frickin' cool. Once the green and black spinning tunnel swallowed Lennie, it closed. It seemed to have taken what it wanted, decided it didn't want to eat the rest of the house, and went away. What the H E double hockey sticks?

How are you going to explain this to your mom? Your brother and sister? They would ask him dumb questions like, where did he go? He didn't know. What was he wearing? He couldn't remember. What happened to the thing that took him? It disappeared. And no, he wasn't making this up.

Lennie might be dead, that thought scared him. The vortex was cool, but Lennie had been sucked into it! Mom was in London, and Lennie had been sucked away. He was gonna have to take care of his brother and sister. He loved his brother and sister, but he didn't like being the responsible one. He was too young for this.

"Stan! Stan!" he yelled as he ran back down the short hallway. When Stan didn't respond, Peter burst through his door. His brother snored.

"Stan wake up, you sack o' bones!" Peter shouted at his brother.

"I'm having a good dream about chocolate cake, go away," Stan returned.

"But Stan, Lennie just got sucked through a black tunnel," Peter said.

"Peanut butter ice cream on the cake too!" Stan rose on an elbow and glared at his older brother.

"Lennie just got sucked through the window!" Peter repeated.

"What?" Stan asked wide eyed and awake now.

"I said that Lennie just got sucked through the window," Peter reiterated.

"Like a worm-hole spinning vortex type thing that sucked him down like a monster swallowing a June-bug, and then closing as if it wasn't there at all?" Stan asked.

"Exactly. How did you know?" Peter demanded.

"Loki uses them to move sometimes," Stan replied as if this should be common knowledge.

"You know THIS how?" Peter questioned.

"Duh! Peter you really need to pay more attention. Don't you ever read?" Stan tossed a comic book in his brother's general direction.

"Stan, that is a comic book. This is real life!" Peter deflected the comic.

"Well you should still pay more attention to the things our parents are teaching instead of what bra size Sarah wears," Stan said getting out of bed.

"Leave her out of this," Peter said pissed off at his brother for knowing entirely too much about everything. Peter went to wake up his baby sister.

Peter bundled Staley up. They were going out. He didn't know where yet, but they were getting out of the house. The thing might come back and try to get them too. Once his mom made Stan and him hide in the woods at their old house. Maybe this was like that. He grabbed Lennie's cell phone, and stuffed it into his pocket. He yanked his coat off his door. Still carrying Staley, he went back into Stan's room and picked Stan's coat up off the heap of clothes on Stan's floor.

"Put this on," he thrust the coat at Stan.

"Why?" Stan needed to know.

"Duh! We are going on a bike ride," Peter answered.

"At ten at night?" Stan protested.

"Don't you pay attention, do you want those wraith things to come back and kill us?" Peter said, then continued, "When we are far enough away from the house, we will call Mom and ask her what to do," he concluded.

"Did Lennie say anything before he was sucked away?" Stan asked.

"He said the table cloth wasn't his fault and to pray to Freya for help," Peter answered as he tied his shoes.

"Not very specific. Okay Peter, bike ride it is," Stan agreed. Peter was happy that Stan agreed to go because he could be stubborn and if he didn't agree to go the night would turn into one long argument.

While Stan held Staley Peter hitched the bike buggy onto his bike. They placed Staley inside and strapped her in. The rain subsided to a drizzle. The two boys peddled away from their house into the night.

*

Traveled? Teleported? Transported. It seemed but an instant, and it seemed eons of time passed. How was time measured? Maybe time wasn't measured. Fluid or flux? The impression of deep space enveloped Lennie, black and freezing. Yet in the black and the cold he knew that he wasn't dead.

Within the black-hole, Lennie knew he was moving perhaps at speeds that wouldn't normally be possible. The speed of light? Perhaps his body changed into gaseous molecules and would reform when he reached his destination?

His brain ceased functioning.

*

Astoria:

Clayton Olson hailed from Wisconsin. A slope job moved him to Alaska where he met Jari. He had been living in Astoria ever since he'd run away from the shitty relationship with Jari a year ago. He wasn't over her, not really anyway.

Clayton sparked his lighter and pulled on his glass pipe. He inhaled, held it, and let it out. He coughed. He took a long swig from his beer. Fuckin' Jari. So beautiful, so smoking' fuckin' hot. And such a bitch. Best just to forget.

He sparked his lighter again. Weed. Nothing like it. He liked beer and whiskey too. Maybe just a little of that whiskey?

Why not. He got out the bottle and filled a glass with ice. He liked ice. He poured a little bit of amber colored heaven over the cubes and listened to the ice pop. He sipped the whiskey and took another hit from his pipe. Jari. Jari. Jari. Best just to forget.

Clayton was shacked up with a woman named Geneviva. People didn't call her that of course; they called her Jen or Jenny. Clayton called her GeGe. His little GeGe. Her teeth were a little brown and crooked. So what? She could still use her mouth just fine. But the best part about GeGe was her legs. So smooth and sexy. They were like silk blowjobs when they rubbed against him or something like that.

They weren't Jari's legs though. Fuckin' Jari. He took another hit. Coughed. Good shit. He sipped the whiskey and chased it with beer. Best just to forget.

He walked over to his prized possession. His Gibson Epiphone MM-50. A solid spruce top, a black pickguard. Nickel hardware made it look bad ass, and it had cost close to nine hundred dollars. Worth every penny. He picked it up, and put it down again. Pain. Pain. Pain. He recrossed the room retreating to the safety of the kitchen. Comfort. His pipe, beer, and whiskey, the three masters of forgetfulness.

He took another hit. Pot helped you not care about anything. Just drift, float, chill out. He had a sip of whiskey. Chill out man.

He thought about his new friends. Lennie and Holli. Holli, long red hair, and tits that wouldn't quit. Lennie was a lucky man to have her.

Maybe he had best go find GeGe? But not yet. Blissful floating. Drifting on a current, like a ship out at sea riding the waves.

Fuckin' Jari. Get out of my head. Chill out, Clayton. Chill out! He reloaded his pot pipe, flicked his lighter, touched the flame to his little green friend. So sweet when you burn for me, baby. He drained the whiskey and refilled his glass with ice and more liquid forgetfulness, and he opened a fresh beer. Best just to forget.

*

London:

    Holli stared at the papers in front of her. She wasn't reading them; instead she focused her energy on feeling the intentions of the two men in the room with her. They must have some sort of mental shields up; she wasn't picking up any of their feelings or thoughts. Miffed, she turned her attention to actually reading the papers before her. There might be a lot of legal jargon to get through, but Holli knew she could ferret out the real meaning in a will.

*

Near The Well:

    Candles guttered out and sprang back to life. In addition to the candles lighting the area were floating white globes. The globes each about a foot around, gave off only slivers of light because they were covered in dust and cobwebs.

    Verdandi cackled, as she rocked back and forth. Each of her fingers independently worked as a needle. The tapestry she sewed upon was no ordinary quilt; instead it dictated the lives of humans upon Midgard. She didn't look at her work. She didn't need to physically see it. That might have been a relief to many as Verdandi's eyes blind from cataracts, saw into the future. She cackled again.

    "Oh what a mess we have coming my sisters," she wheezed.

    Her sisters turned their heads her direction. Verdandi didn't normally speak, and if she was saying a mess was coming than things were not going to be pretty. Not at all, especially if Verdandi said a MESS was coming. It meant a nasty as hell of a SOMETHING was on the way.

    "Do tell us," Skuld wanted to know the gossip. Skuld appeared the youngest of the three sisters.

    "Use your eyes, girl," Verdandi spat.

"Don't be so hard on her all the time, Verdandi. Come on, out with it. Spill the beans," Urdr said. Urdr would be the middle sister in age between the other two. She always felt in the middle between her sisters. The bridge. The peacemaker. The center or balancing point of two weights on opposite ends of the sea-saw as it were.

All three of the sisters were sewing different parts of the same tapestry, and they continued their work as they talked. The globe lights moved around them of their own accord. The candles continued their flickering lives.

"We shall see. We shall see," Verdandi cackled.

"Keep your secrets then," Skuld pouted.

"Don't make her cry," Urdr said to her sister.

"A good cry never killed anyone," Verdandi said as a coughing fit overcame her.

Urdr put down her sewing, stood up, and stretched.

"Come sisters we have other work to do," she said and began walking. The other two sisters rose. The three moved as one connected as they were by the web Destiny.

They reached the well, and dipped their respective cups into it. The roots were hungry. It was feeding time.

BERKANO

In front of my Laptop:
Loki here. I would guess you've heard of me? Maybe you just read my name and went: 'Yes! I've been waiting for Loki to enter the story.' I am not arrogant, but I had to come into the story at some point right?

I've been doing a lot of thinking; it is something that I am good at (I do it quickly), and sometimes have to go back and put the thoughts in an order that may or may not make sense even to me. I also have a lot of time (this may or may not be a good thing; it depends on who you ask).

If you haven't heard of me, well now is the time. If you haven't met me before, well there is no better time than the present. As I have said, my name is Loki. I am one of the Gods of Asgard.

Sometimes people portray me as being evil. This doesn't hurt my feelings, but these folks are misguided, and I feel sorry for their misconception of me. They have misconstrued me if you will. I am not evil. I just like to have a little fun once in awhile; is there anything wrong with that?

Some other issues to clear up. I do not lie all the time. I prefer to say that I have been known to use prevarication to perfection now and then. If you would like you could say that I sometimes modify the truth for the purpose of mollification. I do these things with the utmost modesty.

Let me muse here on the idea of trickster or fool. I do like playing small tricks now and then; it is fun. Now the fool being a figure who does not have to adhere to societal norms, that I can get behind. Also I do have a tendency to tell Odin what I think of his ideas or plans, I mean what is he going to do, kill me?

I don't like things to go on and on as normal. How boring! We need a little chaos now and then. Otherwise nothing happens. "Same old grub again," screw that. I like to shake things up. Some call me a bastard. Oh, I am so hurt. Well at least I have a purpose; I am the one who makes things uncomfortable.

I do not have sleek black hair, well not at the moment. A few moments ago my hair was long and red which is its natural color more or less. Right now my hair is short and spiked metallic blue in color on top, and I have it hanging down over my left eye in front, that strand is pink. I like it. A few moments ago I had a finely sculpted auburn goatee, but now I am clean shaven.

I am not the God of Fire. I have no dislike for fire, and when, say, a whole building is burning the reflections of those flames in the building across the street has a certain allure to it, but I am not as they say, the God of Fire. Just saying.

Can I turn into a woman or an animal? Yes. I have taken the form of a salmon and a horse, and a beautiful Finnish goddess. Currently I am in male form. Oh and who came up with this helmet with the long horns? Please. Atrocious. No I do not go about with anything in the universe resembling THAT on my head. Might as well wear a neon sign saying I just walked out of a nerd convention, I can't get laid, please hold my hand while you escort me back to my mother's basement?

Maybe you didn't find that amusing? No. Well did I offend your sensibilities? Sensitive tonight? Are you a homophobe? Are you macho?

What else to muse about? What else? Oh, I do like chaos. Why must everything make logical sense to everyone? Is it so imperative that everything fit innocuously into illegitimate classifications? What fun is that? Why not have things that do not make sense? Should we not have anything to ponder?

So what am I wearing? Why midnight blue skinny jeans. Also a t-shirt that says "80's fashions are back", *Project Runway* please come to the rescue.

And NO I don't have a problem with eighties fashions; I'm rather fond of red leather jackets, gaudy colors, and goofy hairdos, but don't let me see that I said that on Facebook. The next thing we would see is a depiction of me in a red leather jacket and the most lovely afore mentioned long horned helmet. There would be like a gazillion shares on the thing. No doubt it would say something like: Loki, The Flaming God of Fire. Or something pathetic and pretentious that makes the poster look so clever.

To return to a previous topic, I am not evil. Truth be told, I am a positive force to have around. I bring wit, laughter, and jokes to Midgardians all the time. These are things we need to survive when things are bleak, so you see, I'm not the bad guy here.

Another matter to clear up: I did not go into the moose that hit Jari Anderson. I didn't even orchestrate it. What I did is drop all kinds of red herrings around so my brother and mother would think that I involved myself in that normal course of nature so that they wouldn't pay attention to what I'm really working on.

No I can't tell you what I am working on; that would ruin the surprise. That would be no fun at all. Nope I'll not let the proverbial cat out of the bag. Not just yet anyway. The word apex as on the apex of a precipice seems a good turn of phrase. Yes I like that phrase.

Alcohol. I don't hold much weight in it. It may seem a strange thing as many in my realm drink mead, but I do not need help being depressed, and I can make an ass out of myself and not blame liquor. I prefer to have my head clear of that substance. That is not to say that my head is not filled with other substances. I am not opposed to drugs, but if I choose to alter my state, I do not need the bottle to do so.

Cigars are another thing I detest. Why? Because my 'Father' smokes them. No I do not have an Oedipus complex; I do not want to kill my father and fuck my mother. I deeply admire my father. His mental prowess is profound and proficient. I do not desire Freya. My 'mother' is too curvaceous for me and not snippy enough. That is not to acknowledge that she is snarky, she wrote the book on that word (so says the Allfather when smoking a cigar).

Speaking of tobacco, I do not like chewing tobacco either. How uncouth, not to mention that my 'brother' Thor seems to find it somehow relaxing. All that spitting. Vulgar. I do not like pipe smoking. One might infer that with all the thinking I do, I should like to have a pipe, but alas no. They are tedious, tiresome, and very much outdated (they took away Santa Clause's). Cigarettes? The jury is still out.

What about the cats, ravens, wolves, goats, horses? Why do I not have some sort of beast or bird to aid me? I do. There is a tale about me being imprisoned with a snake dripping venom. Well the serpent and I are chums.

Weapons? A spear? A hammer? A belt buckle? See where I am going with that? I will leave you now to ponder.

*

Astoria:
"Just keep peddling," Peter told Stan.
"But where are we going?" Stan wanted to know.
"I'll know it when I feel it," Peter answered.
Stan rolled his eyes. His bother always said stuff like that when he had no clue what they were doing.
"Did we bring any food?" Stan asked.
"No," Peter answered.
"Why didn't you think of that?" Stan accused.
"I just didn't think of it!" Peter was getting pissed off.

"You don't know where you're going, and we don't have any food," Stan continued.

"I do know where I'm going, but we will not starve to death for five days. Now if you'd just shut up maybe we'd get there," Peter snapped back and peddled. Stan didn't like it, but he peddled harder to keep up. They had all better stick together, that much he knew for certain. That said, Peter was still leading them on a wild goose chase.

"Peter just stop! Just wait!" Stan yelled as he slammed on his brakes. A black skid mark stretched out behind his tire.

Peter hit his brakes and skidded to a halt. Upset he turned and faced his brother.

"Why," he demanded.

"Because just peddling because we are scared isn't going to solve the problem," Stan said.

"I'm going. Stay or come," Peter said and started peddling again. Stan had no choice; he started peddling after his brother for a second time. A little later Stan caught up with is brother, and they continued on into the night.

*

Astoria:

Clayton sat in an old red chair getting fresh ink. The tattoo artist named Cole flipped shut his cell phone muttering curses and returned to his work on Clayton's arm. The image being created was nearly finished: a kimono wearing lizard smoking a joint. The kimono was white and decorated with green pot leaves; the female lizard had beautiful human breasts.

Vintage Ozzy blasted away as Cole worked. Clayton could still hear the faint electric hum of the needle as it cut into him. He winced now and then, but the pain was part of the process. Clayton liked getting fresh ink and sort of liked the pain too. The tat looked bad ass; Cole had done an awesome job. He paid Cole with a credit card, but tipped in cash.

Clayton started his motorcycle. His bike was old but he loved it. He put on his helmet. Time to go home so he could smoke a bowl, drink, and admire his new tattoo. That is what he did, more or less, after stopping at a number of bars along the way.

He only had one beer at each bar, and there were only four of them. He had to show off his new ink. Some took an interest, but it wasn't the kind of reception that he wanted.

Once he reached home, he carefully parked his bike and entered his house. Well the place he called home, where he hung his hat. He wondered if GeGe would like the tat? He hoped so, but if she didn't, she could suck it.

"GeGe?" he called as he took off his boots and socks.

"Upstairs," she signaled her whereabouts.

Clayton nodded to himself. He looked around to see if anyone was watching, and drank a long pull from the whiskey bottle. He opened a beer and took a swig. And now feeling good, he located his marijuana, filled his pipe, and took a hit. Nice. Nice. He had a new tat. He needed to show GeGe.

"GeGe, what are you doing?" he called up the stairs.

"Waiting for my man," she replied. He couldn't tell if she was teasing or being serious. Was she horny or pissed off? Women. Why did they need to be such puzzles? He slowly navigated the stairs.

Her legs were out on the bed nice and smooth. She was reading something very intently.

"Want some?" he asked offering the pipe.

"Yes," she said putting down the book. GeGe took the pipe and lighter from him. He watched her put the pipe to her lips and the lighter flame go to the pipe. She took a good long hit. This pleased him.

"Whatever are you reading? When I came in it looked like you were trying to suck the book into your cranium like an IRS agent sucks in the discomfort of people that enter his office?"

"The Sound and the Fury," she replied.

"Are you trying to fry your brain?" he asked.

"This is a classic," she exhaled pot smoke.

"William Faulkner. Yeah I know," he said reaching for the pipe. "That doesn't make it good," he said as he lit the pipe again. GeGe had nice legs, and she gave good head, but she wasn't Jari. Jari fucking Anderson. Best just to forget. Best just to forget. He reached down and gently touched GeGe's leg. He rubbed his hand upward. He stopped and took another hit.

"GeGe, I got new ink. Check this out," he showed her the tattoo.

"I liked what you were doing to my leg," she said.

"Do you like my tattoo?" he asked.

"Yes," she lied.

"Do you love me?" she asked.

"Yes," he lied. He placed both of his hands on her legs and rubbed. They lost their clothes.

*

London:

The letters on the pages swirled like water going down a drain. Holli tried to follow it, but she was so tired. Just sleep. She would welcome sleep, nice like a warm blanket wrapped around her. Her eyes shut and her head drooped forward.

Loki materialized in the room. He clapped his hands and laughed.

"I'm back," he said doing a little dance that looked like he was starting a lawn mower.

*

Na-strond:

Lennie shivered. He couldn't stop shaking; his limbs refused to listen to his brain's commands as they convulsed. He was freezing by degrees, water dripped onto his naked stomach, a variation of Chinese water torture. The damnable water dripped and dripped, running in rivulets down his legs. Slowly it trickled leaving slick lines as it matted his leg hairs.

Drip.

Drip.

Drip.

Aside from the freezing something else, a cold clanking. Lennie felt the shackles on his arms and legs before he opened his eyes. They were hard and heavy. Lennie knew that no mortal man could possibly break the bounds. A prisoner. He might as well get a look at his cell.

Lennie opened his eyes taking in the surroundings, there wasn't much to see, but as his eyes adjusted to the dark, shapes became discernible. The vast cavern was empty but for him in the middle of it. Far above him from where the water dripped, the opening of the hole glowed with a blue light. Lennie wondered if his prison was on Niflheim. When he moved, pain shot into his back from a razor sharp rock. If he moved the rock would cut him. The shackles were becoming heavier with every passing second. He had to keep them taunt to keep his back off the razor rock, but when he slacked from their weight, the rock was there, and the water continued to drip.

Nobody said being a prisoner would be fun. Lennie groaned. He only had one enemy that he knew of; this had to be Loki's handiwork. Oh you bastard! Lennie knew Loki would find his suffering amusing.

Drip.

Drip.

Drip.

Lennie's body started shuddering. The rock cut his back; the chains grew heavier still. He strained to control his muscles and arched his back upward. His feet slipped and his body lurched backward. The rock slammed into his back. He cried out in agony, and he tried to rise. The chains rattled.

Drip.

Drip.

Drip.

"Fuck you, Loki!" Lennie screamed. He strained against the chains. He sunk back, and the shooting pain in his back brought him up onto the balls of his feet again. He stretched his mind outward to reach another realm. Some force blocked him.

"You coward cockroach Fuck-tard!"

No reply.

Lennie strained his mind trying to find some way around or through whatever force blocked him, but he couldn't locate the edges of the blocking force. Perhaps the whole of his prison had a field around it? He sank back, and regretted it as the jagged rock cut his back again.

Drip.

Drip.

Drip.

"Chalk Outline" by Three Days Grace went through Lennie's head.

*

Holli found herself in a Picasso meets H.R. Giger landscape. Gray and silver mutilated bodies hung in the air suspended before her. Visages of women's breasts with hooks sticking through them came and went as Holli walked. A place of nightmare, twisted creepy. Holli, although revolted, found herself fascinated by these grotesque vistas. She hoped she was dreaming and would wake up soon, and then again she didn't want to wake up because there was more to see.

Ahead of her there were some rock formations. They looked like huge hollow gray fossilized intestines or like elongated wasp nests frozen during winter. What would await her inside of them? She had to find out. Sickened at herself, Holli wondered how she could keep wanting to look at this stuff, but she did. Some part of her found it erotic. She needed to get inside those alien formations.

Her feet crunched along as she walked even though the metallic substance was sand like. The sound that accompanied her foot falls was the snapping of brittle bird bones. Holli didn't want to know what was below the sand she tread on. Her eyes on the formations, she kept trudging along as wind sprang up stinging her face with sand.

She shielded her eyes with her arm and staggered forward. Holli thought again that it might be time to wake up from this dream. Certainly this had to be a dream, as she had been in London looking at a will. Hadn't she? She shut her eyes and tried to wake up. When she opened her eyes, she stood in front of the formations.

Going inside them no longer seemed like a good idea. Holli didn't know what they even were. Were they living? Were living creatures inside them? She clearly wasn't on earth right now; what the hell was she thinking? And even as her brain acknowledged the doubt, she began circling the things looking for a point of egress. Holli put out a hand and felt one of the structures. It felt dead. At least in so much as it didn't throb with life.

"Shit," Holli swore as she took her hand away. Blood. Her blood seeped into the thing accompanied by a sucking noise. She studied the thing; it didn't look like a vampire coming back to life.

Then the thing moved. A door opened. Holli had paid admission in blood; she steeled her reserve and stepped in.

Before her eyes adjusted, Holli smelled the place. It smelled old, very old, and heavy of dust. The dry accumulation of eons of dust, and something else, some unidentifiable scent. A nasty nauseating fruit or floral scent. Not the smell of rotting oranges or bananas or dying plants, but disconcerting, and once detected a smell that lingered, and one that her nose did not get used too, and let her mind ignore it. A maddening perfume which never went away.

The door she'd come through whispered shut. Holli reeled around in the blackness as what little light there'd been from outside vanished. Absolute dark. Her mind screamed the phrase 'Trapped in a tomb!' at her.

Her respiration increased, and she trembled. Her nostrils flared and that damned sickening sweet smell overwhelmed her again.

"Fuck you smell!" Holli shouted and began to cry.

GEBO

Astoria:
    "Peter, just stop. We can't ride all night and not go anywhere," Stan said for the second time. They came to a halt.
    "You have a better idea, I suppose," Peter said.
    "What did Lennie say again?" Stan prompted.
    "To pray to Freya, as if that will do any good," Peter huffed.
    "It might," Stan returned.
    "Sure, right," Peter shook his head.
    Stan looked up at the night sky. It was the closest idea he had as to where Asgard might be. He thought of his mom being gone to England and Lennie being sucked away. They needed help.
    "Freya the Fair,
Please hear our prayer,
Though we are but two of our Folk,
We honor you. We need your safety cloak,
Please send us a guide,
For us on this ride.
Hail Freya!"
Nothing happened.
    "See, nothing happened," Peter snapped. Stan ignored his bother as he watched something moving in an alley between two buildings. At the mouth of the alley, it stopped, sat, and looked at the boys.
    "Then why is that cat staring at us?"
    "Because it is a cat," Peter threw his hands in the air. The cat padded out of the alley. When it cleared the buildings it grew from

house cat to panther size. And it was blue. The cat's eyes were purple and flecked with silver. It nodded at the boys, and it started running.

"That is no ordinary cat; that is one of Freya's cats sent here to guide us. Follow it!" Stan yelled. They both started pedaling after the cat.

Sometime later, the cat stopped and looked around warily. It growled low and menacing twitching a puffed up tail. From the darkness another creature attacked.

The cat evaded the snapping of needle-like green glowing teeth. The thing's shovel-shaped head resembled that of a Doberman pinscher except its slender ears stuck up like a pair of antlers, and its eyes were the same color as its teeth. The rest of the body could have been canine but for its long giraffe-like neck and the creature's lengthy whip-like tail ended in three quills. The tail snapped at the cat.

The cat evaded the tail and swung a claw at it, but missed. The paw should have connected but the beast wasn't there anymore, as if it shifted to a different location. The cat narrowed its eyes. "RRRRRAW" the cat uttered as it hunkered down readying to spring.

"Wicked," Peter exclaimed.

"Woo," Stan said.

The other beast lunged at the cat just as the cat jumped. They slammed together and hit the ground a tangled mass of teeth and paws. They slashed and bit each other. They came apart and faced off again, both of them bleeding from their wounds.

The blue cat jumped and landed hard on the ground on its front paws that should have struck its opponent. Its target had shifted again. The cat rolled and the quill tail struck just short of the cat.

"You can take him!" Stan shouted encouragement.

"Kill it!" Peter added.

The cat hissed. A metallic mist blasted from its mouth enveloping the other beast. The strange dog creature stood frozen.

"Abandon the bikes, and climb on my back," the cat spoke.

"You can talk?" Peter blurted out.

"I am one of Freya's cats," it answered.

"I knew it. What's your name?" Stan asked.

"You may call me Bygul. Get on, that abomination won't stay frozen forever," Bygul answered.

Peter gathered up Staley. Stan climbed on the cat's back. Peter handed Staley to Stan and climbed up.

"Hang onto my fur," Bygul said. Stan hugged Staley with his right arm and hung onto Peter with his left arm. Peter grabbed onto the cats soft fur.

Bygul jumped into the night sky.

Peter felt the wind in his hair. He looked down at the city below them. All the darkened buildings stood getting smaller with their lights glimmering like stars. Peter turned his head up and the real stars grew larger as they flew closer to them. He was flying on the back of a magical blue cat named Bygul. He loved it.

"Stan we are flying!" Peter shouted against the wind.

"Just hang on," Stan shouted back. He tightened his grip on his brother and Staley and shut his eyes.

"I didn't save you just to let you fall off my back, Stan." Stan heard Bygul's voice from inside his head. Telepathy.

"Okay," he mumbled aloud.

"Open your eyes. There are a few sights you will want to see," Bygul said inside his mind. Stan opened his eyes. A very large nearly full moon provided light. They were flying over the ocean. Stan dared a glance down. Below them a huge whale jumped. The top half of the whale was black, and its lower half was white. Its huge tail slapped the ocean sending up a spray of water.

"Peter look, a whale," Stan shouted.

Loki's Laughter

"I see it!" Peter yelled back. The whale shot water up out of its blow hole.

"Cool," both boys said. They passed the whale and turned to the right. They flew over a rugged wilderness filled with mountains.

"Look at the sky, Stan," Bygul's voice said inside Stan's head. They zig-zagged through green beams of dancing light. They were flying among the Northern Lights.

"This is magic!" he shouted in wonder.

"Freya's landing-strip. Hold on," Bygul said as they streaked toward the ground. Bygul's massive paws thudded on the frozen gravel and, he padded to a stop.

Alaska:

Gerard barked like the zombie apocalypse arrived as he pawed the door to go out.

"Okay, okay," Jari opened the door for him. Gerard ran forward barking and stopped. He growled preparing to lunge.

Jari blinked. Maybe she had drank too much? When she opened her eyes, the sight was still there. A gigantic blue cat with children on its back stood beside Thor's bike.

Bygul stared at Gerard. Gerard cocked his head and wagged his tail. Thor picked Jari up so he could pass through the doorway and walked forward.

"My friends! Welcome to Alaska, you must be frozen. Let's get you inside to warm up," he smiled.

"Hail Thor!" the boys shouted. They climbed off Bygul's back.

"I rather like you in my arms like this, Jari," Thor grinned.

"Don't get used to it," she shot back.

Bygul shrank to domestic cat size. Gerard barked at him. Bygul swatted the dog, and Gerard went flying.

"Inside," Thor commanded. Everyone entered the trailer. Thor put Jari down in her chair. He hugged Peter and Stan in the same embrace. Staley opened her eyes. Thor smiled at her.

"You are safe Staley Moon," he said handing her to Jari. Thor loaded more logs into the wood burning stove. They crackled as the flames licked at them with hunger. Thor turned from the stove and addressed the group.

"Bygul informs me that we need to go. I want you all to stay here. Boys, help Jari with the firewood. We will try to locate your parents. Everyone stay warm, eat, and keep your strength up. Keep an eye out for anything out of the ordinary. Jari please take care of Peter, Stan, and Staley; they are good folk, and Jari, don't worry about your bills or your job. I'll take care of those." With that said, Thor and Bygul left.

*

Astoria:
 Hung the fuck over, Clayton moved in a fog of sluggishness and pain. Truth.

*

Cyberspace:
 Loki here. Things are progressing precisely as particles or pixels are expected to propagate, and my prognosis is prominently promethean in its promiscuousness. I could have said I love it when a plan comes together, but that is trite, trivial, tedious, and tiresome.
 I got TerraFormist piped through my headphones. Beautiful modern melodies so melancholy and magnificent, masterful, the opposite of maladroitly moving music. And I wait for the drop every time.
 What to do next?

*

Asgard:
 Heimdall watched. Soon two beings would arrive; he tensed ready for action. He focused his sight tuning it like a microscope, clearer now. There they were flying at incredible speed through space. Not enemies.

Loki's Laughter

Time passed. "Sandalwood" by Lisa Loeb went through Heimdall's head. He had a lover once, so long ago. Maybe a chocolate flavored stout would be in order later? The Bifrost flared, all of its colors became brighter despite the dusting of snow covering it.

Thor and Bygul landed accompanied by the sound of thunder. Snow showered off the edges of The Rainbow Bridge. They strode forward, and stopped a few yards from Heimdall.

"I've been expecting you," he said.

"Good Gatekeeper, may we enter?" Thor asked.

"You shall not pass," he said exactly as Gandalf in the movie.

"Well played," Thor complimented.

"Unless..."

"Good Heimdall..."

"You bring me a stout later," Heimdall finished.

"Done!" Thor smiled.

Heimdall stepped aside letting them enter.

*

Astoria:

Who is this guy? Clayton wondered. Some damn Emo kid? Clayton watched him walk toward him, vanish and appear at the end of the street, only to walk forward and vanish again. Maybe Clayton hallucinated the whole thing, but he didn't think so. He was more sober this morning than he'd been in a long time. It happened again.

What the hell? Clayton watched the episode replay. It was like a time lapse, or time loop, something out of a science-fiction movie. Clayton lit a cigarette, stepped off his porch, and walked toward the guy. Maybe he could touch this dude and either help him get to his destination by bringing him into reality or make him disappear for good. Once he had done his good deed for the day, he could get to drinking; there was no other way to spend a Saturday.

The dude wore pants melded to his legs, a t-shirt, a black leather jacket, and a green Mohawk. The guy carried a bong. For some reason as Clayton approached, he became more substantial. Clayton took a drag and continued to approach. Clayton laid a hand on the guy's shoulder.

"Thanks Dog. Wanna hit?" he asked proffering the bong.

"As it is Saturday, don't mind if I do," Clayton accepted the glass water pipe. He took out his lighter and sparked it. He sucked and the water burbled. When he'd taken as much as could into his lungs, he drew out the slide. He held it in until he thought his lungs would burst and let out the green tinged smoke.

"Good shit," he said handing the pipe back to Mohawk man. The dude went through the smoking ritual and handed the bong back to Clayton. Clayton received the piece again and studied it. Milk opaque with black designs depicting some crazy dog like creature with a long neck and green eyes and teeth. Crazy cool. He took another hit, and exhaled the acrid green smoke.

"Thanks," Clayton said.

"No prob-lem-o," Mohawk said and walked away. Clayton shook his head, returned to his house, and reached into the fridge for a beer. He opened it and his body vibrated like fuzzy electrical currents, and his eyes glowed green. He shut his eyes to drift with the sensation, and when he opened them again he wasn't at home.

*

Na-strond:

In front of Lennie a life sized movie screen appeared. The blank screen stared at him. Was this a diversion from his pain? Somehow he doubted it. For some time, the screen remained dark. Lennie heard a faint electrical humming and the thing filled with snow, and loud static accompanied the millions of white and black squares. For a while Lennie attempted to see shapes in the shifting flickering snow.

Drip.

Drip.

Drip.

He slipped, and the rock ripped a new gash in his back. Lennie pulled up to the balls of his feet once again as blood ran down the back of his leg warm sticky and smelling of iron. The snow continued on the screen, and the volume increased and echoed around Lennie's prison chamber.

Drip.

Drip.

Drip.

Sometime, perhaps an hour later, the screen went black. Lennie welcomed the silence. His legs wobbled; he couldn't hold any longer. His legs slipped, and he fell sideways. Jagged razors cut into his right side but the new pain brought him up once again.

Drip.

Drip.

Drip.

Lennie shut his eyes and prayed:

"Odin Allfather I call on you,

Gray cloaked wanderer,

God of wisdom,

Though I am but one of our people,

I honor the Gods,

Grant me a bit of your knowledge,

That I may free myself.

Hail Odin!

Mighty Thor,

God of Thunder,

Grant me strength

To endure

That I may fight again.

Hail Thor!"

Lennie didn't feel any connection. Most of the time when Lennie prayed, he felt a connection to the Gods. Since that wasn't present now, he wondered again about the shielding that must be surrounding his prison. There had to be a way he could break through that shield. He would find it. Intense light glowed through Lennie's closed eyelids as the movie screen lit up.

Lennie opened his eyes. The green and silver letters on the screen read Loki Productions Presents: For Your Enjoyment. The film started and Lennie regrettably watched.

Holli fumbled through darkness. Light outlined a door, and she opened it entering a room that contained a bar, a black grand piano, a large white couch, and a king sized bed covered with a purple quilt. A stage spot light shined on the piano. Recessed lights illuminated the bar. Holli explored the room touching things, as if she were shopping. Another door opened, and the musician Clayton entered the room. He wore faded blue jeans, a sweat-shirt with a tattered collar, and the baseball cap that had seen better days.

"Holli," he greeted.

"Clayton," she returned.

"Good to see you," he said.

"Good to see you too," she said.

"You look great," he said.

"I'm glad to see someone I know," she responded. They crossed the room and hugged in greeting. They broke the embrace, and Clayton spotted the bar.

"A bar!" he exclaimed making for it. He moved behind the bar and inspected the bottles underneath it. He rummaged around and brought forth three bottles. He placed them on top of the bar. Jameson's, Crown Royal, and Glenlivet.

"Pick your poison," he said. Holli walked over and inspected the bottles. She smiled at the Jameson's bottle, glanced at the Crown, and picked up the third bottle to read it: The Glenlivet Cellar Collection.

"I've been a Jameson's girl, but why not try something new? Let's go with this one," she said.

"Scotch. Some b-a-d, b-a-d scotch," he ducked underneath the bar again searching for glasses and ice. Directly below the bar counter-top hung an assortment of glasses. He selected two, and turned his attention to the mini-fridge for ice. He opened the mini-fridge and stared at a prescription bottle. The label read: Rohypnol.

That might come in handy later? Clayton put the glasses on the bar. He found ice cubes in the freezer section of the mini-fridge. He cracked four of them out of a tray and put two in each glass. Then he opened the bottle of scotch and poured a healthy amount into each glass over the cubes. Clayton swirled his glass around and handed the other glass to Holli. They held their glasses looking at one another with the bar between them.

"Salute," he said.

"Bottoms up," Holli said.

"I'll drink to that," he said. They downed the aged sipping scotch and Clayton poured them each a second drink.

Lennie slipped. The rock cut into his back. He pulled up onto his feet again. He winced, clenched his fist, and sweat poured down his face. He didn't like where this film was heading. There was too much innuendo, even if it was innocent. Maybe he was over-reacting, but something inside him didn't think so.

Lennie screamed at the screen. His eyes remained on the screen. He didn't want to watch anymore of it, but even if he shut his eyes he could hear it.

They moved to the couch and sat down at opposite ends of it. Clayton looked Holli over. Her red hair hung just under her shoulders. He wanted to see her bare tits, suck on them, feel them; they were amazing and covered in far too much clothing. He wanted to run his hands up her smooth legs.

Holli regarded Clayton. Conventionally handsome didn't fit. He wasn't pretty, but he wasn't a total bad boy either, what he was,

was charming. Would this encounter make Lennie uncomfortable? It shouldn't. They were married; she wasn't doing anything wrong. Lennie, the kids, she didn't even know where she was; she could be dreaming.

"Tell me about yourself, Holli," Clayton prompted.

"Well okay, I have three children. Two wonderful boys Peter and Stan from my first husband Jim, a complete asshole. Peter is a lot like his father, but his heart is in the right place. Stan is a little dreamer who struggles with social anxiety like me. Lennie, who you met, and I got married a little over two years, and our daughter is Staley Moon," she said.

"Another drink?" he asked.

"Sure," she answered, and asked "What about you?"

"Not much to tell," he answered rising, taking her glass and heading for the bar. He popped two more ice cubes in each of their glasses and carefully poured more scotch over the cubes. He looked at the bottle of pills. Maybe they wouldn't even be needed? But they were there.

"What else?" he prompted handing her the glass.

"You mean about me?" Holli raised her eyebrows taking a sip.

"Yes about you," he answered.

"You want to hear something fucked up?"

"Yup," he took a drink.

"So I get this letter that says I'm getting an inheritance. I fly to London, where I meet these men resembling animals, and then I'm sucked into this alien landscape, and now I'm here," she recounted.

"I want whatever you're on," he smiled.

"I think it was that bastard Loki," she nodded and took a gulp.

"Loki, like in The Avengers?" he asked.

"That would be the one. Lennie and I keep the Old Ways," she said.

"I'm a Christian. You're not a Christian?" he asked.

"I'm an Asatru witch," Holli answered.

"Don't cast any spells on me." He took a drink.

"I won't," Holli said.

"I think your beauty has put a spell on me," he said.

He certainly was charming. Perhaps laying it on thick, and drunk, but it was still nice to hear. Holli blushed.

Lennie slipped. Thud! Slash. Pain and blood, they were the least of his concerns at the moment.

"Loki you twisted fuck!" he cried rising again to the balls of his feet. He shut his eyes. This was not entertaining. Please no more, maybe this video could just short out. He didn't want to watch any more. There were things worse than physical pain, but against his better judgment he opened his eyes again.

Clayton sat down a little closer to Holli and handed her the refreshed glass.

"Thanks," Holli said.

"Bad, bad Scotch. I need more ice though," he got up to get more ice. Holli got up to stretch her legs and look around a bit more. This seemed like a normal civilized room. Holli moved over to the piano, sat down, and began to play.

"You're really good," Clayton said.

"You play better," Holli said.

"Not," he said, downed the rest of his drink, and then added more ice and more Glenlevit. He watched her as he listened.

"You sound like the offspring of Tori Amos and Sarah McLachlan," he said.

"Stop that now," Holli said. "What is with the compliments already?"

"Just the truth," he answered. He reached into his sweatshirt pouch, found a nice green nugget, and loaded his pipe. He walked over to the piano, put his pipe to his lips, and sparked his lighter. He took a hit. Hold it in, hold it in. Listen to her play. Such music. Such a fucking beautiful woman. He could definitely tap that. Holli finished playing and stood up.

"Do you know where we are?" she asked.

"No idea. Wanna hit?" he offered the pipe.

"Yes please," she answered. She took the pipe and lighter and took a hit. They each had a few more hits. They held the weed in as long as possible and let it out coughing. The combination of alcohol and pot mixed, and put the two of them in a state of tranquil uncaring.

"Another drink?" Clayton asked.

"Might as well," Holli answered.

Clayton ducked behind the bar and filled his glass with ice. He put two ice cubes in Holli's glass. He opened the Rohypnol bottle and dropped one of the pills in the bottom of her glass. He reached up on the counter and retrieved the bottle of Glenlivet, and poured the remainder of the bottle into their glasses. He brought the glasses up swirling them and placed them on the bar. Then he shut the freezer and placed the empty bottle on the bar.

"One dead soldier," he said. They picked up their glasses, and drank. He wondered how long it would take for this drug to hit her system.

"Hey you like *American Dad*?" Holli asked.

"Don't know that one, like *Family Guy* though," he answered.

"Seth MacFarlane is a fucking genius. I'd love to have dinner with him," Holli declared.

"To Seth MacFarlane," Clayton raised his glass in a toast. They clinked glasses and drank.

"Smoke some green," Clayton cried exuberantly reloading his pipe, and they smoked.

"You married?" Holli inquired.

"Hell no. What about Lennie, tell me about him?"

"Lennie's my husband. Lennie is a hard worker, the most honest man I know, and my best friend," she answered.

"We own a store called The Store That Doesn't Have A Name..." Holli passed out. Clayton picked her up and carried her to the bed. He slowly took off her clothes getting hard as he did so. He used her well, and when he finished he redressed her.

*

Alaska:

Jari started cooking, water boiled on the stove for mac & cheese. On another burner, she flipped a grilled cheese. On a third burner, she simmered milk on low heat. She moved to her coffee pot and started it. Gerard rose, entered the kitchen, and wagged his tail. Jari filled his food and water bowls. The mundane task of cooking seemed a good distraction from having been in the presence of Thor and some huge blue flying cat named Bygul. She gave the boys plates of food, and then rinsed out her flask, which had the smallest opening, Staley could drink her milk out of it.

Jari lit a Winston, took a drag. Exhaling, she poured herself another drink and took a sip, pussy paused by a blue cat...well maybe next time, if there was a next time, she laughed. She returned from her bedroom carrying her shotgun and a box of shells. She sat down on her couch and began cleaning the weapon. Peter wolfed down his food, and held Staley, feeding her warmed milk from the flask.

"I guess you boys better tell me your story," Jari opened as she oiled.

"Cool, what kind of gun is that?" Peter asked.

"This is an old gun, but it will stop a bear," Jari answered.

Stan began recounting their story. Peter threw his two cents in.

Gerard started growling, a low threatening sound. Jari removed the cleaning cloth from the barrel, and chambered a shell.

"What is it Boy?" she asked.

Gerald stood, and his hair stood up along his back. He bared his teeth and moved to block the door. That was enough for Jari.

"Kids, get behind the counter," she commanded standing up and aiming her gun.

*

Asgard:

Odin looked at the silver and black label of the new Gurkha Ghost cigar. He peeled the label, clipped two millimeters off the end of the stick, and lit it. Spicy. Deep like his contemplation.

NAUDHIZ

Holli woke up feeling disoriented and sore. What on earth? She lay on top of a bed in her clothes. She smelled sex; her scent mingled with man scent, and she didn't remember her and Lennie getting a hotel room. Where was she and why did she feel sore?

Some of the events of the night before flooded into her memory. She and Clayton had drank some scotch, smoked some weed; she'd played the piano. That is all she remembered; Clayton wasn't in the room now.

Holli needed to use a restroom. She walked to a door and opened it. It opened into the room that Mr. Bird and Mr. Cow had been in. She found the bathroom, and relieved herself. Bruises covered her thighs. She flushed, reversed position, and puked. She threw up for twenty minutes, and painfully stood up on shaky legs. She knew sex happened, but not voluntary sex, and not sex with her husband.

Holli stumbled down the slanted staircase and started walking down Baker Street. She felt like everyone stared at her, like everyone knew; everyone must think her a whore. She hadn't wanted sex with anyone but her husband; she hadn't led him on. She threw up again. How much vomit could a body hold? It splattered onto her shoes.

"What the fuck are you all staring at? Just a fucking drunk American girl!" she screamed at the people, who averted their eyes and continued walking. Holli made it onto the Tube, sat down, and started crying. Hours passed.

"Are you lost?"

Holli didn't register that someone was speaking to her.

"Are you lost?" the question repeated.

Holli looked up at the questioner and saw a pudgy middle aged woman with a beehive of gray hair on her head, a double chin out of which twisted a few hairs, and a thin ash colored mustache above her upper lip. She wore unattractive plaid voluminous shawls, and neon green shoes.

"I don't think you can help me," Holli sniffled.

"Nonsense Deary. I have been watching you for an hour, and we have circled once, and you haven't got off. Where are you heading?" Her crooked smile and understanding eyes got through to Holli.

"I need to get to the airport," Holli managed to say.

"We will get off in three stops, get my auto, and I'll drive you," the woman said.

"Thank you," Holli choked and began crying again. The woman put her arm around Holli.

"Enough of that now. Stand up. You are still alive," the woman said. Holli did as she was told. They got out three stops later, and the lady led Holli to her modest house.

"Why don't you take a long bath, and I'll see if I can't find some clothes that might fit you," the woman said.

"I am a mess, I know. What is your name?" Holli asked.

"Yvonne," she answered.

"Yvonne, thank you, thank you, thank you," tears brimmed in Holli's eyes again.

"Gifts come in many forms," Yvonne said.

"Thank you for your gift of kindness. Didn't you have something else you needed to do today?" Holli wondered.

"Nothing more important," Yvonne answered.

Holli began the bath water. She found a towel, and stripped off her puke-stained clothes. While the bath ran, she scrubbed off her shoes in the sink. Yvonne returned with a set of clothes. They were the oddest things Holli had ever laid eyes on, and she found herself smiling. Despite what she'd just been through, she could still smile. This lady was even crazier than her.

Holli stared at the bruises. There were more than the ones on her thighs. They were on her arms, ankles, and breasts too. More than the physical damage, her insides felt worse. She sunk into the bath, the warm water couldn't wash away what had happened, but it still soothed. Holli emerged from the bathroom dressed in gray woolen leggings, an ill fitting skirt, and a top that looked like a tent. Still they were warm sturdy clothes, designed to be functional not form revealing, and right now, that couldn't have been more appropriate. She still felt hideous anyway.

Yvonne drove her to the airport. Together they made the arrangements for Holli's flight home. Holli bought a book by Yasmine Galenorn that she could read on the way home. She got Yvonne's address and boarded the flight.

The beginning of the book grabbed Holli. Despite her best efforts to stay awake, sleep won. As they were about to land Holli startled awake still feeling exhausted some twenty hours later. Time to return home and try to explain that this whole ordeal with the will had been one of Loki's jokes. Maybe she wouldn't have to tell Lennie what happened with Clayton, if he didn't know it couldn't hurt him, right? She felt ashamed.

*

Astoria:

Her fears were put aside only to be replaced by greater fears. The house was empty; people hadn't been here in a number of days. Where was her family?

"Lennie! Peter! Stan! Staley-Moon!"

No response.

They hadn't been home and where was her lady bug table cloth? The table stood before her in stark nakedness. Oh, HELL no! Someone was going to pay for this, and his name started with an L and ended with an E. It looked as if many items had slid toward the window, and yet the window sat in place prim and proper as a butler.

After an extensive search of their small house, Holli walked to their store. Holli turned the handle, and the door opened, odd. She froze in fear. Someone lay huddled in a pile of smelly blankets behind the counter. Someone's life problems made Holli put her recent rape in the back of her mind. The pile of blankets rose. Holli raised her hands, indicating that she was unarmed but ready to cast a spell if need be.

"Don't call the police. I'll leave," said the voice of a very scared homeless teenage girl.

"I am going to call the police, but not on you," Holli answered, and then continued reaching for the phone, "You may come home with me, have a bath, clean clothes, heat, and food," she finished.

"I don't want your pity," the girl said.

"Do not take my gift of hospitality for pity. You are not the only one in the world who has been wounded. Think of it as me repaying a debt," Holli said as she dialed the phone.

"Assistance. City and State please?" the voice on the other end asked.

"Non-emergency police number," Holli responded.

"Connecting you now," the operator said.

"Astoria Police," a voice answered.

"I'd like to file a missing persons report," Holli said.

As Holli gave the details, she watched the young girl. An emaciated creature, perhaps anorexic? Her hair had at some point been dyed pink, but the blonde roots were visible between crumples of leaves and grease on the top of the matted mess. Dust and tear streaks smudged the girl's cheeks. Her brown wounded eyes flitted about the store perhaps registering where she'd slept for the first time. She shook violently, and Holli wondered if it were meth withdrawal. Holli hung up when she completed the report.

"I should be going; you clearly have something to deal with…" her voice wavered like a drunk driver.

"Nonsense. We are going home, and I'm gonna crank up the heat," Holli moved toward the girl. She tried to back further into the corner.

"People who are worth anything help each other out," Holli said.

"But…" the girl's lower lip trembled and tears brimmed.

"No buts. You don't owe me anything. I was just raped; I'm not going to hurt you. Now can we go warm up?" Holli asked and put her arm around the girl. The girl allowed it, and they walked back toward Holli's house.

"My name is Arsinoe. My dad is a bit of an Egypt nut," she offered.

"Then you are stronger than you know, and you haven't been murdered by your sister, so you'll be okay. Holli," she returned.

Holli turned the heat up to eighty, put a kettle on to boil, and began preparing a homemade herb tea.

"Tea really?" Arsinoe questioned with a tone that said lady that ain't gonna help none.

"This will help," Holli said her voice sounding more assured than she felt.

"Okay, your house, I'll drink it, but a Red Bull would be better," Arsinoe said.

"Only if we had Jäger, and alas my husband is too cheap to buy it," Holli said smiling. Damn cheap Norwegian. Lennie, where in the fuck are you, she wondered.

"Here drink this; I'll start the bath water for you," she said.

"Sure," Arsinoe said sipping the herbal mixture. The tea aroma floated to her nose as she held the steaming cup, a blend of something she couldn't identify and peppermint. She took a sip finding the warm liquid soothing; she'd never admit that though.

Holli was right about the other thing too. She would be all right eventually and could make her own future.

"Bath is ready, towels next to the tub," Holli announced.

"Okay Holli," Arsinoe said heading that way. When she disappeared into the bathroom, Holli leaned against the counter with her tea mug and began crying. Where were her children? Her husband? She needed them now. Why wasn't anyone answering a fucking cell phone?

Life goes on, Holli told herself. This homeless waif needed clothes; she went to her dresser and began rummaging through it. She found some clothes that might fit the skinny girl and put them on the chair.

"Thanks I do feel better," Arsinoe said exiting the bathroom with one towel wrapped around her body and another around her hair.

"Make yourself at home. My turn," Holli said entering the steamy room. She refilled the bathtub as she pulled out two more towels. She shed her clothes, lit a few candles, and looked at herself in the mirror. How in the hell to explain this to Lennie? She hoped he understood that she hadn't wanted Clayton. That he'd forced himself on her. O, Mother Freya help me.

She poured some bubble bath in the tub and climbed in. She didn't have a book with her, but that didn't matter. As the steam rose around her, she cried again. When the water cooled off, she left the tub and toweled off. Time to make some food.

*

Na-strond:

If he couldn't reach outside of his prison, Lennie would find another way. Clayton was going to die; Loki could wait. He would kill him too, but he was going to kill Clayton first or die trying. That monster would not continue to roam Midgard. Sometimes the monsters living among us are worse than mythical ones, Lennie thought grimly. However, he needed to get free first in order to carry out revenge. Physical pain was nothing compared to mental anguish. The physical would eventually heal; the mental was another story.

If he couldn't reach out, Lennie would look inside himself. Inside himself there was an emerging God who could do anything. It felt right; this would be Odin's lesson. So he needed to break or slip these bonds somehow. How? Slipping them was the answer, which would involve altering his physical form somehow. Could he just teleport out of here?

Should he try to become a raven, a wolf, a mist? They all seemed so trite, this wasn't a vampire book. Any of them would work; anything that wasn't his normal human form would be a different shape than the metal bands that held him.

He remembered his time running with the wolf pack. Maybe a wolf? But somehow that didn't seem right. Even though wolves were associated with Odin, he also didn't want to be a lycanthrope. Something huge and powerful, or small and seemingly insignificant?

Lennie began changing before he decided what to change into, as if once he'd made the choice to change, the form knew itself. Lennie needed this, Naudhiz. His blood slowed down as did his heart, but they didn't stop. Lennie watched as his limbs grew smaller as his extremities shrunk and grew stronger at the same time. He became a beast of frost.

His ankle shackles fell to the floor as he looked at his frosted root toes. Intricate lines of white running and twisting around black root toes which ended in claws. He looked at his reflection in the now black TV screen. His knotty raw looking legs held the power of a live oak despite their thinness. His chest felt like a powerful flowing river yet appeared as white frost flakes covering the bark of a tree like leopard spots. His hair the nest of Ratatosk, a mess of leaves and acorns tipped in white caps. And his eyes, the eyes of nature saying death comes for all.

His arms were free of the shackles too, but now he felt them growing. Where his arms had ended as thin twigs the bonds had slipped off, they now grew into massive stump clubs. He jumped against the wall and began swinging. Where he smashed against the wall it weakened against his assault. Through a gaping black rift in Na-strond, the beast of frost stepped into the cosmic wind fluttering around the nine realms.

*

Alaska:

The door crashed inward showering splinters of wood throughout the trailer. At the same time, Jari's largest plastic coated window shattered inward accompanied by flying shards of glass and flapping ripped strands of plastic that resembled ribbons fluttering as they hung underneath a fan. Through the openings pounced two twisted creatures of chaos.

They mostly resembled dogs, but their necks and tails were wrong, the necks elongated and the tails ending in quills. Every since that moose hit her and Thor walked into her life, things went wonky. What the hell? Men. Jari didn't know much, but she knew that these things weren't invited. Homeland Security might sound good, but twelve-gauge security hadn't let her down yet. Gerard faced off with the thing that had come through the door. Jari drew a bead on the one that had come through the window and fired.

BOOM!

She missed. Must be getting old, she never missed. She wouldn't miss a second time, this Abyss-Dog would be returning home. Jari chambered another round, and aimed a little to the left.

"Who do you think you are, you long necked scat?" she fired.

BOOM!

She missed again. But she understood why as she watched the thing move. It seemed to shift somehow. It jumped at her, and a claw raked her cheek, knocking her backwards onto the floor. As she fell, Jari chambered a new round pointed the gun up and fired.

BOOM!

The thing thudded on top of her deader than the power in a windstorm. Green blood poured from the hole in its chest.

"Welcome to Alaska!"

Gerard and the other Abyss-Dog circled. Gerard growled; the other didn't make a sound. They lunged at each other and grappled in a hug like two wrestlers beginning a match and smashed to the floor. Claws ripped each of them as they smacked paws into each other. Gerard bit into the thing's neck when its tail quills struck him. Gerard went rigid.

"NO!" Jari screamed, chambering another round.

Peter needed to do something. Sitting and doing nothing when there was a fight going on wasn't his style. He looked around for a weapon. He could see the rack of knives, but he'd heard that in order to win with a knife you needed to bleed and that didn't seem like a good way to win. He glimpsed the frying pan.

Peter grabbed the dirty pan off the stove, climbed onto the counter, and attacked. He flew through the air; the pan raised high, and thwacked the chaos spawn in the skull. Peter continued his assault long after the creature's life force splattered the walls of the trailer. Jari put her gun down and put her arms around Peter restraining him from further battery.

"It's dead," she assured him. He came out of his frenzy, shaking and abashed.

"Uh, okay," Peter said.

"You totally smashed its brains out! Hail Thor!" Stan said emerging from behind the counter holding Staley.

"Hail Thor!" Peter said looking at the pan.

"Thor..." Jari let her breath out, and fished a Winston out of her pack surveying the carnage inside her home. Well, messes could be cleaned up, but first she needed to tend to Gerard. Jari pulled Gerard closer to the wood stove and pulled the quills out of his side.

"Don't be dead, or I'll kill you," Jari said wiping a tear away along with blood from her cheek. Gerard moved and gave a little woof.

"Thank you Gods," Jari said. She got out a first aid kit, rubbed some antiseptic ointment onto Gerard's wound, and put a bandage on it. Once she had done what she could for him, it was time to patch the house up.

"Boys, now I really do need your help. We need to get another door on there and board up that window so we don't freeze to death. First door on the left, there is a pallet on the floor. Move Gerard's blankets and pull that in here. Pull it apart, and nail the boards over the window. Put your sister on the couch, she'll be fine. Stan, drag these carcasses outside," she crushed out her cigarette and opened her closet to get her tools. She handed Peter the hammer and a box of nails. She took another hammer and screwdriver to her bedroom door, popped the pins out, and hoped that this door was the same size as her old front door.

The door fit. Peter pounded the boards up. Stan struggled with the dead dog things, but he got them outside. Jari pounded a blanket over the boarded up window and loaded more wood into the stove. Jari pulled every blanket and pillow she had in the house into the living room. Everyone, including Gerard, huddled near the wood burning stove. Jari checked her gun and placed it in reaching distance. She poured a shot of whiskey, downed it, and lit another Winston.

"What do you boys know about Thor?" Jari asked.

"Thor kicked the snot out of this giant bug outside our house once," Peter said.

"Thor is the God of Thunder and also the working man's God. One of his jobs is to protect the people of Midgard, or earth. His hammer is Mjolnir, and he has two goats," Stan explained.

"Someone has been studying mythology, I see," Jari noted.

Loki's Laughter

"I have to because my brother is busy studying bra sizes," Stan blurted.

"Shut up! Do you need to keep bringing this up!" Peter said mortified.

"Stan, does Thor have a girlfriend?" Jari asked.

"I don't know that answer," Stan admitted.

*

The Roots by the Well:

"Time to feed the babies," Skuld said.

"About that time, they are hungry," Urdr agreed.

Verdandi nodded.

The three moved as one in their strange dance like step. They filled their cups from the well and moved connected as they were by the web Destiny over to the thrashing roots.

Three humongous rainbow colored roots writhed about crying out in hunger. Skuld jumped in the air, landed on her tip toes, spiraled in a circle, and trickled the water over one of the roots. She rubbed the water on the slick root as if giving it a hand job.

"There you go baby," she said.

Urdr walked over to the second root and looked at it as it squirmed. Such life, such beauty, strength, growth, her love, and also a pain in her behind. She splashed the water from her cup onto the root as if throwing a glass of water in some one's face. The root shook.

"I love you, Brat," she said.

Verdandi stepped over to the third root. Her cup trembled from her shaking hand. She tipped it upside down and the water plummeted onto the root.

"Down the hatch," she whispered.

*

Sessrumnir:

Thor and Bygul entered Freya's hall. The glorious hall looked festive decorated in deep reds, dark greens, curtained with golden ropes. Wearing an amber necklace, Freya sat among many folk feasting. When she saw the newcomers, she beckoned them to her. They made their way through the tables.

When they reached Freya's seat, they stopped and bowed in respect. Thofnir, who looked the same as Bygul, stretched as he rose and padded over to Bygul. He sniffed Bygul's fur and began grooming Bygul behind his ears.

Thor looked up into Freya's eyes.

"Mother, Loki's pets may return to Alaska in greater numbers," he said.

"Go my son, take Bygul and Thofnir with you and give those who need it the gift of protection," she answered.

"I will. Thank you Lady of Life," he said. He turned to the cats, "Come dear friends, time to battle your age old enemies." The three of them left Sessrumnir.

*

Astoria:

Clayton admired GeGe's shaved pussy thinking 'nice, she trimmed the trim'. Her womanhood glistened before him warm, pink, and waiting. Such beauty. He wasn't hard, whiskey dick. He just stood there staring at GeGe when a vision of Jari Anderson popped into his head. She stood in front of her wood stove in nothing but her bunny boots smoking a Winston. Jari never shaved her stuff. His member stiffened. Fuckin' Jari. Best just to forget. He sparked his lighter and held it to his pipe. He inhaled and held it. When he felt like his lungs were gonna, explode he let it out and coughed. He handed his piece to GeGe. She took a hit.

"Are you gonna satisfy me or what?" she asked.

"Yup," he answered.

*

Between the Realms:

The Beast of Frost that was Lennie flew toward Midgard. Interstellar dust and ice particles, the fragments of pumice and frozen obsidian shards, all thudded into him. He circled the Horse Head Nebula.

"Nidoliah!" the Beast of Frost intoned, turned, and saw the nine realms spread out before him. He beheld the Rainbow Bridge magnificently glittering. Another time, he had other work to do. Impervious to the cold and galactic shrapnel, he continued on toward the living blue and green planet light years below him.

A crystalline claw raked his head. Sap like blood flowed slowly into one of his eyes as he buffeted off course. Fangs sank into one of his feet. An appendage from another thing bore into his stomach. Lennie didn't see them coming, three of them were on him and six more ringed him. Nine against one! He looked forward to it.

Whitish in color, they vaguely resembled ghosts of jellyfish with crystal claws and bone teeth and bat like membranous wings. Luminescent silver eyes could see in the blackness of the cosmos, and they had thin whip-like tails.

Lennie twisted and slammed his fist into the one on his foot. It exploded in ectoplasm globules. He sunk his jaws into the tentacle-like appendage which continued to work its way into him. His teeth severed it from its owner, but part of the thing wormed further inside of Lennie heading for some vital organ. The creature attacked with claws. Lennie dodged and kicked it, when his toes struck it, it froze and shattered like a light bulb struck by a baseball bat. The one that had initially stuck Lennie's head with claws sunk its claws in his back. Lennie swung his club like fists together behind him smashing the thing between them into goo.

Six remained, hovering, waiting.

*

Bifrost:

Heimdall watched. Pink's Floyd's "One of These Days" played in his head as he watched the battle. Heimdall telepathically sent the song into The Beast of Frost's mind.

*

Between the Realms:

"Seceipelttilotniuoypirannogm'i," the Beast of Frost said and began slashing his opponents. He ripped them apart. Shreds of their ghostly essence floated away like a feather-down pillow blasted with buck shot.

Pain wracked Lennie, and at the same time his limbs were paralyzed. The parasitic worm had burrowed to his heart and started feasting. Like a meteor, Lennie fell through space.

*

Loki, at my computer:
LOL

LAGUZ

Alaska:

    TooLu watched as the sun rose, a pink miasma behind the ring of mountains around her. She loved watching at this time of year because all the peaks looked like pink hats on the giants, and she found it funny. A magpie flew by with its black and white wings. Many people didn't care for magpies, but TooLu liked their coloring and long tail feathers, beautiful magpie I see you.

    A tug at her line brought TooLu's focus back to her fishing rod. One more bite now…wait for it. Tug. There it was! She pulled up on her rod, hooking the fish. The fish ran, she reeled, it ran, and she reeled. Must be a big one, fighting, even under the thick layer of ice she stood on. When you are tired, I will pull you up through my ice hole. TooLu smiled, ice fishing was so much better than school.

    She might get in trouble for skipping school. She didn't care; school was stupid. No use for the drone, drone, boring babbling of the teachers. At least you could eat a fish when you caught it. The fish must be tired. TooLu reeled it up through the hole in the ice. A beautiful rainbow trout, thank you lake.

    TooLu deftly filleted the trout, stoked up her little fire, and placed the trout on to cook. TooLu baited her hook and threw her line back in. She felt a strange uncomfortable feeling, but ignored it, she was fishing. She liked fishing on Finger Lake because she could see that ring of mountains any direction she turned, and it was good fishing.

    It was cold, but not too cold because the wind wasn't angry today. TooLu dressed for the weather; she wasn't stupid even if the kids at school called her names. What did they know? Fishing beat school any day. The boys had been looking at her too; she knew she could out-fish any one of them. Why were they looking at her? There another tug…she hooked the fish, and reeled. Crazy boys, I can out-fish you.

With care she unhooked the little fish. Too small, she let the fish go. Live, get bigger, I'll catch you again another day. TooLu sat down on her fishing bucket, time to eat. While eating some of the fish the discomforting pain twisted inside her middle again. Could this be from something she ate? She'd cooked the fish right, and last night her Grandma made a moose stew, and TooLu knew that wasn't undercooked as it had been in the pot all day.

She pulled her line up, and scooped ice out of the hole. She changed her bait, and put the new one down. Boys kept looking at her chest in school, and it made her uncomfortable. No boys out here fishing.

The pain got worse, it went away, and then it came again. TooLu stood up and looked at the hole in the ice. There were little beads of ice on her fishing line where the water froze in the air. Under that dark green water more fish swam; she would catch more and bring a bunch home for dinner perhaps that would lessen her punishment for not being in school.

TooLu doubled over; it felt like knives stabbed into her. She felt something wet on her leg and knew it wasn't pee. Transferring her pole to her left hand, she pressed her right mitten against her legging. She waited and then removed her hand; a dark red splotch stained her thigh.

She started crying. Angry she wiped the tears away. Blood could be washed out of her leggings. Is this what the girls at school had been complaining about? She should have paid more attention to those conversations.

She would have to talk with Grandma. Grandma could explain this. Irritated, TooLu reeled her line up and changed bait.

She cleared the ice hole, and dropped her line in. There a nibble, it came again; she pulled, and hooked the fish. If anyone saw her and asked about the stain she'd say: fish blood. When the fish tired she pulled it up, this one could go home with her. Thank you Lake.

After two more hours of fishing with four more caught, TooLu decided she better go home and talk with Grandma Edna. She put the five fish in her bucket along with her pole and auger. She extinguished her fire and started back across the lake through the snow.

"Grandma, I'm home," she said softly.

"There you are!" Edna said.

"I'm sorry I skipped school, but I brought fish," she held up her bucket.

"You skipped school..."

TooLu started crying.

"Hush child. Get in the truck; we're going. Bring the fish with," Edna instructed. Confused, TooLu headed back outside. Grandma never went anywhere, how much trouble was she in? She headed down their rickety stairs to the truck. She put the fish in the truck bed, pulled open the door, and climbed in. Her grandma came to her side of the truck, handed her the keys, and pointed for her to move over.

"Drive," Edna said.

"I don't know how," TooLu whispered as she moved over to let her grandmother get in.

"You'll do better than me; you are young. Just stay on the road," her grandma said as she buckled her seatbelt. TooLu put the key in the ignition and turned it. The old mottled gray truck rumbled to life like a slumbering beast awaking after a number of years.

TooLu moved the seat up so she could reach the pedals, strapped her seat belt on, and studied the dashboard instruments. She pressed the brake and moved the gear shift. R, that had to stand for reverse. She put the shifter on the R and pressed the gas pedal. They started moving.

"Stop!" Edna said. They were still in the driveway. TooLu stamped on the brake and they lurched to a stop.

"What did I do wrong?" TooLu wondered.

"Nothing child. What is wrong with you today? Get Muka," Edna said. TooLu moved the gear shift to P and got out of the truck. She went over to Muka, their husky, and undid her chain. Muka jumped in the cab of the truck and licked Edna's chin. Edna rolled down the window so Muka could put her head out.

They made it out of the driveway, and TooLu shifted the truck into drive, and pushed the gas pedal. They jerked forward. Frightened, she took her foot off the gas and they slowed down. TooLu gripped the wheel with both hands, and with determination put her foot on the gas again, this time more gently. They moved forward at a more comfortable pace. They would have to turn one direction or the other when they reached the highway.

"Where are we going?" TooLu asked wondering which way she should turn.

"I had a vision. We need to help a friend, turn right," Edna answered. TooLu turned, and accelerated. She stopped at the red lights, and they drove out of town toward Fairbanks on the Parks.

"Turn right," Edna said. Without a blinker, and ignoring the stoplight, TooLu followed her grandma's directions. She didn't want to miss the road and have to turn around. They turned and continued. When they drove over the river, TooLu saw a bald eagle.

"Hello eagle, I see you" she said.

"Good sign, almost there," Edna nodded. They followed the winding road curving left, the sky a pale blue about the peaks in the distance.

"Here," Edna pointed over Muka's head. TooLu applied the brakes, slowed down, pulled into a driveway, and brought them to a stop in front of a wooden gate. TooLu honked the truck's horn.

Edna shook her head and got out of the truck. Muka began sniffing around. TooLu shifted the truck into P, and leaving it running, got out too. They heard the crunching of movement on snow, and the unmistakable sound a shot-gun made as it chambered a round.

"What do you want?" asked a boy's voice.

"Tell Jari, it is Edna come to heal her dog."

"I hear you, Edna," Jari responded, "Peter, open the gate."

TooLu watched as the large wooded gate slowly opened, she saw the white woman with the shotgun, and then she saw the boy who opened the gate.

*

Dimitra Giovanni studied the traffic on the Glenn below her from where she sat parked on the bridge which connected the Glenn to Old Glenn leading into Palmer. Traffic was light, and nobody was speeding. Her radio crackled to life.

"Giovanni?"

"Go ahead," she responded.

"We have a 911 call in Wasilla. Gunshots."

"Am I the closest unit?" she asked.

"Ten-Four," the radio confirmed.

"On it," she shifted into drive, and turned her headlights on. Dispatch sent her the specific address as she merged onto Parks highway heading toward Wasilla. Dimitra stepped on the gas. She flew past Fairview Loop, Seward-Merridan, and slowed as she neared the intersection with the P-W. Traffic in growing Wasilla wasn't as bad as Anchorage, but still considerable. Irritated with the slow pace, Dimitra flicked on her flashers and siren. She accelerated again as cars moved to the shoulder.

*

Peter looked at the woman, the dog, and the girl. The girl's black hair curled out of the sides of her jacket hood. Her eyes were playful, and her jacket couldn't hide the curves on her chest. She was pretty, so he said the exact opposite of how he felt to her.

"What an ugly girl."

The woman gave him a stern glance and directed her gaze to Jari.

"May we come in so I can tend to your dog, and you can help TooLu?" Edna asked.

"Yes of course," Jari answered. TooLu ran past everyone into the trailer and locked herself in the bathroom.

Peter followed the other women into the trailer while the husky sniffed the perimeter of the yard. The old woman knelt down by Gerard and whispered to the dog in a language he didn't recognize. She rose and moved into the kitchen with purpose.

Stan gently rocked Staley back and forth in her sleep when the girl bolted through the house and into the bathroom. He watched the old woman examine Gerard. Peter needed to do something so he relieved Stan of Staley.

"What can I do?" Jari asked.

"Go to TooLu. You will know how to help her," Edna answered.

"Please, do what you can for Gerard," Jari said heading to the bathroom.

Stan and Peter watched Edna produce a mortar and pestle from her odd bag. She put some seeds in it and began crushing them. She set a small pot of water on the stove to boil. When the water boiled, she added the crushed seeds from the mortar to it, and a pungent smell pervaded the place.

Edna moved to Gerard, and with a razor with a whale bone handle shaved a small patch of his fur off. She sucked at his wound and spit out whatever poison she'd drawn out of him on the floor. She took the now greenish yellow paste and applied it to the shaved area while she mumbled to the dog.

Meanwhile Jari knocked at the bathroom door.

"Go away," TooLu said from within.

"It is Jari. Besides you can't stay in there forever; other people may need to use that room. Now please let me in," she said.

TooLu unlocked the door, and Jari stepped in and relocked the door. Tears streamed down TooLu's cheeks.

"Everyone thinks I'm ugly. The boys are looking at my chest; I don't like it. Why do they say I'm ugly?" she sobbed. Jari thought for a few seconds, this wasn't about her problem with men but every young girl's problem.

"TooLu. when boys like a girl they want her to notice them and remember them, so they say mean things to her that are not true so she will think about them even if it is in the wrong way. They do not really think you are ugly, but in fact they think you are pretty but don't know how to express themselves correctly," Jari explained.

"Are you lying to me?" TooLu needed to know.

"I have no reason to lie to you. I have known your grandmother for a long long time; she is one of the few people on this earth that I respect and trust. She trusts me too, or she wouldn't have sent me in here to you," Jari said. As TooLu wiped tears off her cheeks, Jari smelled the unmistakable odor of menstrual blood.

"I know how to fix your other issue too," Jari reached under the sink and gave TooLu a pad.

"What is that?" TooLu inquired.

"This is for the blood. You are a woman now," Jari showed her how to use the sanitary napkin. Jari dumped out a makeup bag; she didn't use it anyway, and put the rest of her pads in it for TooLu.

"Now you have a make-up bag," Jari smiled.

"Thank you," TooLu said.

"You're welcome. When you are ready come out and join the rest of us, we need to eat something," Jari said.

"I brought fish," TooLu beamed.

"Best news all day," Jari declared. A few minutes later, TooLu came out of the bathroom.

"When you grow up, you won't think I'm ugly," she said to Peter while going to get the fish. She pulled the bucket out and turned when she heard a vehicle. An Alaskan state trooper truck pulled up. This day just kept getting worse, a trooper just because she skipped school? Maybe the trooper was here for Peter, that would be better. Stupid mean boy, even if he was sort of cute. The trooper had a long nose and black hair.

"Got a 911 call for this address," she stated.

"I'm just visiting; I'll get the owner," TooLu responded and opened the door. "State trooper is here," she announced.

"Moose scat," Jari cursed pulling on her bunny boots. She went outside to meet the trooper.

"I'm the homeowner. How may I help you, Officer?" Jari asked.

"We got a 911 call for this address. Caller said shots were fired. Looks like you had some trouble with your window," Dimitra said.

*

LOL

*

Thor, Bygul, and Thofnir landed. The cats dashed into the woods before they were seen. Thor walked toward the two women. His boots crunched on the snow. Jari and Dimitra stopped their conversation and appraised him. He wore black pants and a flannel jacket. He chewed a wad of tobacco and grinned like it was his birthday. His red hair shimmered in the fading sunlight and his beard glistened as snow melted off it. His blue eyes sparkled.

"I'd like to see you two in action," he said.

"Shut up!" both women said.

"You know him?" Jari asked Dimitra trying to convince herself that she wasn't jealous.

"We've worked a few cases," she answered.

"Officer Giovanni, I can handle his call," Thor said.

Loki's Laughter

"Station said I was the closest unit," Dimitra stated.

"You beat me here. I've been working undercover out here for a few weeks," Thor explained.

"If you have it, less paperwork for me," she nodded.

"Less paperwork is always a good thing," Thor said, and spit out tobacco juice.

"Good day Officer Odinsson, good day ma'am," Dimitra headed for her truck. Jari watched her get in.

"She called you Officer Odinsson," she snorted at Thor

"Yes she did," Thor laughed "Yes she did, Jari Anderson," he winked at her.

"Let's go eat some fish," Jari said rolling her eyes.

*

Astoria:

As neither one of them could sleep, they watched a few episodes of *The Biggest Loser* and *Big Bang Theory*. They watched a few episodes of *Restaurant Impossible* and a few of *House Hunters International*, and even started watching *Love It or List It*. Holli wondered where Lennie and her kids could be. She'd received zero phone calls and wondered how in this day and age of cell phones and computers they hadn't reached her. Where were they? She had been raped, and out of the kindness of her heart (which she didn't regret) had Arsinoe with her. She wasn't going to be able to deal with all this on her own; she was going to need some help from her mother Freya, but first things first.

"You want a glass of wine or soda?" Holli asked Arsinoe.

"Soda," she answered. Holli got her one of Lennie's Mountain Dews and opened a bottle of wine for herself. Holli handed the waif the cold green can and took a gulp of the wine; sipping was for sissies. Holli debated how to broach the subject of religion with Arsinoe, not that she cared if the girl left, but sometimes strange things happened around Holli, like Goddesses and Valkyries showing up, and she thought it would be nice if they did so any time now. Holli started to speak when a knock at the door saved her; she went to answer it.

"My name is Helga Brisingamen," Freya said in way of introduction with a wink at Holli.

"How may I help you, Helga?" Holli asked recognizing Freya and holding open the door.

"I am a detective. Are you harboring a fugitive named Arsinoe?" she asked, all business. Hearing her name, Arsinoe came forward, indicating Holli, she said, "This lady has showed me nothing but kindness, so whatever crimes I am wanted for, she should be exonerated," she said.

The detective wore her copper colored hair in a braid. Her blue eyes penetrated the depths of Arsinoe's soul. Her face was regal and stern yet her mouth and bosom sensuous. She wore a plain wine colored coat with white fur trim and hadn't flashed a badge. Who was she working for?

"We will see about that," Helga said. She turned to Holli, "Any of that wine left?'"

Holli poured Helga a glass. Holli downed her second glass and refilled it a third time. She got another Mountain Dew for Arsinoe.

"I think I'm going to have to take you both into custody," Helga said.

"I just told you that this woman is innocent!" Arsinoe exploded.

"My "chariot" isn't working right now; I'll have to call in my partner to transport you," she informed the ladies while sipping her wine.

"Where are you taking us?" Arsinoe asked.

"A maximum security facility," Helga answered.

*

Multiverse:

The beast that was Lennie fell through the cosmos. His eyes flickered open and shut, when open they glimpsed multiple spiral arms of many different galaxies. Then he broke the atmosphere and the ice around him burned away. He smashed into the earth like a meteor. A plume of rocks, dirt, twigs, rotting leaves, and moss flew up as they were displaced.

Gravity cascaded them back to the ground burying the thing that disturbed them. In the grave, his body shattered, Lennie closed his eyes. The parasitic worm that ate his heart vacated his body and died when it couldn't find another host. Lennie's body began to decompose.

*

LOL

*

Sessrumnir:

Sleipner landed. His eight hooves thundering through the snow drifts as if they didn't exist. He trotted through a grove of fragrant pine trees coated in snow. The lane of pines ended in a glorious sight.

The golden exterior of the hall was decked with intertwining pine boughs and thick deep red velvet. The eight legged steed slowed and stopped in front of the doors, and from out of the sleigh he pulled stepped Freya, Holli, and Arsinoe.

From his seat on Sleipner's back, Odin clipped the end of a Dirt cigar by Drew Estates. He lit it and puffed out a cloud of smoke that wreathed his head. He pulled a bottle of mead out and took a hearty swig. He took another draw on his cigar and blew out a large smoke ring through which he looked at the three women.

"A good night to all," he said and waved.

"Thanks for the lift, Sleipner. Good night, Husband," Freya smiled up at Odin on his horse. Odin winked at her.

"Sleipner M'boy, let's ride," Odin whispered to his friend, and they took off into the sky.

Alaska:

"Crowded in here," Peter remarked.

"Not really," TooLu countered.

"Yes it is," Peter said. He felt squished as he surveyed everyone. Mentally he counted Thor, Jari, TooLu, her grandmother, Staley, Stan, and himself made seven people. Then four big animals with Gerard, Muka, Bygul, and Bygul's twin, and all of them in a single wide trailer; it was cramped as H E double hockey sticks.

"This is how we always live," TooLu said.

"This close, all in one room?" Peter asked.

"Yes white boy who doesn't understand village living," she answered.

"I'm going out for some air," Peter announced heading for the door. Unfortunately for him, he was followed by Bygul, Muka, and TooLu. Once outside he turned to the others.

"What the hell? I said I wanted to be alone!"

"Actually you didn't say that," Bygul said, "What you said was that you were going outside to get some air. I am here to protect you. Muka as you can see…" Muka went to a corner of the yard and pissed.

"What about her?" Peter asked. Bygul padded a few feet forward, and turned his head back to regard Peter, "I believe she wants to continue her discourse with you," and he sat down to watch.

"Now I know how Heimdall feels," Bygul mumbled to himself.

"I heard that," came Heimdall's response in his Bygul's head.

TooLu followed the heavy snowflakes with her eyes as they drifted downward. Wind gusted making the snow swirl in one direction and then back the other way. TooLu saw this as The Snow Queen dancing at a ball and opened her mouth to explain this to Peter.

"Something comes! Peter, TooLu, alert Thor!" Bygul growled as his tail puffed out.

The enemy leapt over the fence as if it were no higher than an ant hill. They came from all sides. Black coats stark in the falling snow. These were the same as the creatures from before, yet they seemed more dangerous. Older and more deadly. Perhaps the ones from before were young and unseasoned, whereas these predators had seen combat on many a battlefield. These creatures long necks were covered with fur making them more wolf-like in appearance. Four of them came at him, two from each side. Flanking tactics, Bygul noted, they were in for a fight.

TooLu opened the door and yelled.

"Thor help!"

"We're under attack!" Peter screamed.

Peter desperately looked for a weapon; there was an axe. He sprinted for it. Granted, the axe had just been used for splitting wood, but it was better than his bare hands. The axe was heavier than Peter thought, but it would work. Four of the dog things were darting toward Muka; that just didn't seem fair. He would even the odds.

The creatures snapped their teeth at Muka; they'd formed a circle around her. Peter charged the closest one; he swung, missed, and toppled into the snow. The thing pounced on him, and would have ripped his throat out if Peter hadn't thrown his arm up at the last second. The jaws clamped onto his arm. Blood splattered Peter's face from his wounded arm, but he didn't hear any bones crack.

"You're going back to the abyss," he shouted kicking upward. His feet connected, and the thing moved enough for Peter to roll and regain his footing. Peter gripped the axe in both hands, aimed a little to the right, and swung. He missed as the creature shifted a little and swung its barbed tail at Peter. He ducked and ran a few feet to his left.

Thor came through the door with his hammer in hand, turned right, saw four of the beasts, and grinned. Battle! He ran forward, Moljnir whirling. The four formed a ring around him. He swung and his hammer cracked into one of the creature's skull. The dog flew backward and crumpled into the snow in a splatter of green blood.

"One down, three to go," Thor spun in a circle. Two of the strange dogs jumped at Thor. Thor smashed one of them with Moljnir' the creature flew back a few feet skidding through the snow and rose shaking its head a bit dazed. The other one's jaws clamped onto his left bicep. Thor didn't feel the bite itself, but he felt the stinging burning of acid as it began eating his flesh.

Jari, shotgun in hand, stepped out and chambered a round. She took aim at one of the dog things flanking Bygul. She knew how to play this game now; she aimed slightly off to the left and squeezed the trigger. The thing dropped dead from the heart shot. Jari chambered another round.

Stan exited the trailer handing a bow and arrows to TooLu, he himself armed with the same frying pan his brother had used. He wanted a baseball bat, but the pan would work.

"How did you know?" she asked.

"Your grandmother can speak English," Stan answered.

"She can?" TooLu asked astonished. She never spoke English at home.

"Maybe you should use that thing while we still have the advantage of ranged weapons," Stan said, thinking 'who says you can't learn anything from video games'.

TooLu admired the weapon for a moment. It was an old authentic long bow, the handle wrapped in beaver fur. The arrows however were new with synthetic fletching and razor sharp broad heads. She nocked an arrow, drew back, aiming at one of the creatures attacking Muka, and released. The arrow missed. It wasn't a total loss though because as the dog creature shifted to avoid the arrow Muka lunged sinking teeth into the thing's throat. The black fur and flesh ripped and green blood stained Muka's jaw as the creature died. TooLu nocked another arrow wondering how she missed, but there wasn't time to worry about that now; she would get it right.

Bygul danced back and forth avoiding snapping jaws and ducked and jumped the barbed tails. If he didn't act soon though the pack would tire him out, he breathed. Frost covered one of his assailants, and he bashed it with his paw shattering the creature into frozen fragments. Another dog jumped over Bygul heading toward the house. Bygul swung upward and his claws raked the thing's belly eviscerating it.

A remaining attacker was on top of Bygul. Jari didn't have a clear shot without risk of hitting the cat. The dog thing that jumped over Bygul, landed on her, knocking the gun out of her hands as she fell to the ground. She tried to move, but it pinned her, how much could this thing weigh? Acid dripped from its mouth, and she moved her head just in time and the acid sizzled into the snow. Her eyes widened in fear as Jari watched the tail came up, and the barbs come down toward her.

SMACK!

The dog thing fell into the snow beside Jari. Stan smiled down at her triumphantly holding the frying pan. His mom had said pans were good weapons one night when they'd camped in the woods. He would have to tell her about this.

"Thanks Stan," she said getting to her feet and retrieving her gun. She put a round in the things head, she wasn't taking any chances.

Two more creatures ran into the fray from behind the trailer.

"That's more like it," Thor said and threw Moljnir. His hammer ripped through the guts of one of the new attackers and returned to his hand. Lightning flashed.

Peter swung the axe just as an arrow flashed past him hitting the creature right between the eyes. Peter turned to look where the arrow had come from when he noticed two more dogs approaching from his left. He would kill one of these things. He charged.

"FOR ASGARD!" He screamed his battle cry, and his axe struck true. Bone shattered as the axe blade cut through the thing's rib cage and into lung. It died rasping for breath. That is when the second dog's tail barbs struck Peter in the back, and he fell paralyzed into the snow.

Muka rolled grappling with another attacker, but these things didn't fight fair; they fought to win, and another of the creatures tail barbs jabbed Muka in the back and paralyzed the husky. The three dog creatures came forward.

Bygul yowled in pain as his opponent bit into his right ear and ripped it from his head. Bygul fixed his eyes on his enemy, this dog would die.

"Freya take you!" Yellow rays shot from Bygul's eyes and engulfed the creature. It disintegrated.

The dogs ringed Thor. He swung his hammer above his head in a circle knocking tails out of the way. Two of the creatures lunged snapping at him; Thor dropped down and swung backwards, Moljnir slammed into a nose shattering the thing's cranium.

"Three down, three to go!" Thor roared.

Thofnir tried to look in every direction at once. He enhanced his vision range and clarity with magic. Sight couldn't be more acute. Of the two of them, Bygul should be on the front line since he focused on war, sound, and direction. Thofnir's strengths on the other paw lay in healing magic, sight, and speed. Edna held Staley. Thofnir couldn't see anything coming he didn't relax though, as he paced.

That is when it came in from above, a green cube-like glow. The glow formed into a small goblin. Thofnir pounced at it. The goblin snatched Staley away from Edna and disappeared in a puff of green smoke, giggling.

Thofnir landed with empty paws and let out a screech. The dog creatures outside put their heads down for a second as the volume of the screech exploded as physical pain in their minds. Thofnir slumped to the floor covering his face with his paws.

Thor took advantage of his foes' discomfort. He held his hammer high in the air.

"FOR ASGARD!"

Lightning crackled forth from Moljnir in three directions. Blue crackling bolts flared through the falling snow electrocuting Thor's enemies. Smoke curled up from their charred remains.

TooLu aimed and let fly. The arrow struck home piercing the heart of the creature. It ran a few more steps forward not realizing it was dead yet, and then slumped to the ground in a pool of green sizzling blood.

Jari aimed left and right as the thing ran. She tried to aim off target on purpose, and the thing's motion made it difficult. She swayed and tried to draw the correct off center bead, too late as the thing flew at her rendering her firearm momentarily useless and it slashed her arms. Jari tumbled backward with the force of the attack bleeding from both arms. The creature went for her jugular when Thor swung with the power of hurricane Sandy and the precision of Peter Townsend's guitar playing knocking the thing fifteen feet away from Jari and into its grave.

Stan vaulted onto Bygul's back, and they charged.

"FOR ASGARD!" Stan yelled as he swung the frying pan. With the added momentum of the mounted charge the weapon not only connected with the enemy but split its head in half.

*

My Couch:

My Goblin appeared and handed me the baby.

John Opskar

LOL

TIWAZ

Irminsul:
    Tyr closed his gray eyes.
Astoria:
    A seed grew into a sapling. The sapling grew into a tree, and the tree mutated into a beast of bark and frost. The beast remembered purpose and took flight. When the Beast reached the city however it changed again. The bark splintered away, and Lennie took human steps. His purpose hadn't changed; Clayton would die.
    Lennie didn't how he would kill him. He hadn't killed a man that wasn't an Indigo Wraith or something else. Murder. The man didn't deserve to live, so Lennie would help him out of the world. Maybe that was too nice a fate for one such as Clayton; however, since Lennie wasn't going to construct some medieval device in his basement and torture him, he would just kill him. Putting him in an oubliette and pissing on him every day was appealing though.
    Lennie needed a weapon. His sword? Maybe he could garrote Clayton with his own mandolin strings? Castrating him and feeding him his scrotum seemed fitting too. Lennie walked and walked he didn't have a destination yet.
    His family. He should get back to them. Yes he should; however, he didn't want "normal" life to complicate his thought process on this. He didn't want to be Hamlet; he just wanted to kill this guy and not dwell on if he should or shouldn't do it.

"Damn you, Loki," he swore and kept walking. He would deal with Loki too, but one thing at a time. How did one kill a God anyway? He would find the way, but first, Clayton.

Lennie realized a more immediate problem; he didn't have any clothes on. He needed clothes, couldn't traipse through the city streets buck naked. If he wasn't worried about getting some indecent exposure charge, it might have been funny. Just walking up to some stranger and saying, hey I need some clothes; do you have a spare set?

"Damn you, Loki," he cursed again. A lady walked toward him. Lennie ducked into an alley behind a trash container. Maybe there would be something in the trash receptacle he could wear. Dumpster diving for clothes, Holli would laugh at that one. Lennie opened it and regretted it as the putrid smell of curdled milk and rotting lettuce sprang forth like a jack-in-the-box. This dumpster must belong to a restaurant; Lennie recoiled to consider other options.

He took in his surroundings. A narrow alley running between two streets, clearly in a shopping district. Maybe he could make it to their store and put on a wizard robe, or something, anything was better than nothing. Lennie poked his head out into the street trying to gain his bearings, yes he knew his location, and he could make it to The Store That Doesn't Have A Name, if he ran. Only a few doors down on the other side of the alley.

"Hail Odin! Hail Freya!" he said making his way through the alley toward the other street. He didn't know the time but daylight reigned. Lennie turned right and ran.   He reached the store and found the door open. It didn't look like the store had been burglarized. Lennie turned on the lights, found a robe to put on, and checked the cash register. All the petty cash remained. Well the door being open was a mystery for another day.

*

Sessrumnir:

"A bath for each of you and new clothes, I think," Freya said leading her guests into a bathing room. The tub could hold a large number of occupants, currently two women were in it. Foam obscured the women from the neck down, and steam filled the room. Faint light glowed from an undetermined source.

"Hi Champ," Jolisa addressed Holli.

"Hi Coach," Holli returned, pulling off her clothes a bit self consciously.

"You must be Arisnoe?" The other woman addressed Arisnoe.

"Yes, and you are?" she asked, still fully dressed not wanting to disrobe.

"I am Sif. Freya asked me to help both of you, is that all right with you? Look at both of you strong, beautiful women."

"I guess, doesn't look like I have much choice, does it?" Arisnoe muttered.

"You always have a choice," Sif stated.

"Yeah right," she said and pulled off her clothes.

"Ladies I will leave you and will return with some mulled mead and robes," Freya smiled at everyone and exited the room. Holli and Arsinoe stepped into the foamy bath. The hot water felt soothing and took away the chill of their recent flight.

"You know them?" Arisnoe asked Holli.

"Jolisa is a Valkyrie. Sif is a Goddess," Holli told Arisnoe. Addressing Sif, "I'm honored to meet you, Beautiful Lady." Sif smiled a hello back.

"Sure, okay," Arsinoe said.

Arsinoe couldn't decide how old the two women were; they looked young but sounded old. Their skin was firm, yet their eyes seemed to hold knowledge far beyond twenty something years. Arsinoe broke off her contemplation when Freya returned with wine, robes, and chocolate.

*

Astoria:

Lennie didn't know where Clayton lived, but he'd find him. The idea of murdering Clayton didn't seem like enough to Lennie. The man probably longed for death. One of these guys that decided in high school they were gonna die young. For some reason got it in their head that they would not live past the age of thirty-five. Once they passed that magic number and were still alive. they were attempting to die with too much booze and other drugs. The kind of man who didn't treat women with respect because they didn't treat anything including themselves with respect. Death would just be giving them what they wanted, and that didn't seem like the kind of justice Lennie wanted to give the man. Something that took a little longer, something that taught a lesson would be better.

What though? What would teach him? Maybe nothing. Part of Lennie wanted to send him to jail to be some-body's bitch, but that seemed too kind. Castration? Well that wasn't exactly what Lennie wanted; he wanted to cut off the man's penis and force him to eat it without choking on it. After that maybe a lifetime of being some-one's bitch in jail, and after that Lennie still wanted to stab him in the heart and decapitate him. All of that still wouldn't be enough as far as Lennie was concerned; some form of lifelong mental/emotional death was also in order.

The day progressed and people were beginning to move about the streets. They were giving Lennie looks, and he realized that although he didn't care what he looked like, they thought he looked like Gandalf, and it wasn't Halloween. This amused Lennie, and he entertained the idea of going about all day long in the wizard robe just to see the various reactions. As amusing as the idea was, it wouldn't help him with his objective. Time to go home and find some clothing and maybe his family would be there too. Holli. How he missed her and needed her now. And wouldn't it be wonderful to hear just how loud the boys could be. Even a red faced, pissed off, I-need-to-be-changed Staley Moon would be a welcome sight. Lennie headed for his house.

The house was empty, but there was evidence that Holli had been home which made Lennie smile. There were two empty bottles of wine, but the question was who in the hell had been drinking all of his Mountain Dew? Lennie picked up the house phone and dialed Holli's cell. No answer. He dialed his cell phone, no answer.

Lennie considered a shower, but the thought of water on his body stopped him, that could wait. He put on clothes and deodorant and almost felt like himself again. Good enough anyway. He pulled a Mountain Dew out of the fridge and took a swig. Caffeine! Maybe Clayton was listed in the regular old phone book? People used to find addresses that way before the advent of the internet, Lennie flipped open the book.

*

At The Roots:

"It looks sick," Skuld said looking at Yggdrasil. The roots lay still gray and wilted.

"Poor thing," Urdr agreed.

"Medicine," Verdandi coughed.

The three of them moved in their odd shuffle dance connected as they were by the web Destiny into their abode. Once inside their rate of speed increased. They flew around in different directions simultaneously and the strands of the web stretching this way and that, doubling back on themselves and folding out in different directions. The three sisters moved into adjoining rooms and dropped an ingredient into their cauldron, and they zipped to another alcove for a different ingredient, and back to the boiling pot again to drop that in. Each took their turn stirring the huge black kettle, and then moved to find another item to add. The recipe progressed in hisses of steam and vapors of one hue or another puffing up from the pot in a cloud.

Now the three stood before the cauldron.

"Is it ready?" Skuld asked.

"Patience," Urdr instructed.

"Soon," Verdandi whispered.

Verdandi stirred the pot. Urdr added some wood to the fire burning beneath the cauldron. Skuld tapped her foot.

"But our Tree is sick," Skuld pouted.

"You worry too much; it is a stout old tree. It will live. We will give it some medicine, and Yggdrsil will be up and thrashing again in no time, you just watch and see," Urdr huffed as she stood up from adding logs.

"Ready," Verdandi cackled her face lit radiantly from the glowing liquid inside their pot. The three of them each ladled some of the boiling fluid into a cup, and together they moved outside. They each poured their cups.

"Is he better?" Skuld asked.

Verdandi gave her a look.

"These things don't happen instantaneously you know," Urdr headed for the well, "Some water too," she said. Skuld and Verdandi followed her to the well. The three of them gave Yggdrasil some water to wash down the medicine.

*

LOL

*

Alaska:

"I've failed us," Thofnir said hanging his head. He felt horrible. How could he have failed at such a simple task? It wasn't like he was fighting on the front lines; he was just watching a little baby. He padded for the door to leave.

"This is no time to feel sorry for yourself. Right now we need your other skills! Mope later! Now use your healing magic, or you will have a few dead humans on your conscious as well," Bygul growled.

"The goblin just appeared, grabbed the baby, and disappeared," Thofnir admitted.

"Focus on the task at paw," Bygul said.

Thofnir placed his paw on Peter. The area around his paw shimmered a silvery orange color. The cat removed his paw, and the area where it'd been glowed like an after-image, and heat flowed into the air where the paw had been. The embedded barbs came out of Peter's flesh along with a clear-yellow substance that looked like venom from a snake's fangs and hovered in the air for a second before they burned to ash.

The huge cat padded over to Jari. Jari felt his sandpaper like tongue lick her arms where she'd been raked. The wounds knitted, aided by Thofnir's saliva which looked like tree sap and worked like an industrial strength glue. Next the cat padded over to Muka. Thofnir turned his head and regarded Bygul.

"Why should I?" Thofnir asked Bygul telepathically.

"Muka fought valiantly and means something to TooLu," Bygul answered.

Thofnir placed a paw on the husky's back and repeated the magical procedure which had healed Peter. The glow came, and the quills flew out and became ash.

"I'm sorry that I wasn't fast enough to save the baby," Thofnir telepathically apologized to Bygul.

"Stop beating yourself up. Freya says everything happens for a reason. I'm sure there is a purpose that we do not know," Bygul answered.

"When did you become all wise?" Thofnir asked.

"I am older than you," Bygul responded.

"By like three seconds," Thofnir said.

*

Bifrost:

Heimdall watched. He tensed, and relaxed. He lifted his sword and swung it before him in a figure eight. He put his sword down again and rested his palms on the hilt balancing it.

Heimdall liked the smell of cinnamon. Calming, sweet, exotic like a woman, and yet comfortable like family at Yule. He wasn't smelling cinnamon now, now his nostrils detected snow, but the snow could be a rat? Like a double agent, it gave off the distinct scent of rain.

The snow turned sloppy. Rain. Well at least his nose wasn't betraying him, Heimdall thought. He wasn't senile yet, Asgard remained safe on his watch. The snow splattered on The Rainbow Bridge like slush thrown by car tires in this sort of weather.

Heimdall's nose detected another scent. The cinnamon was still there but now it had adjuncts. A hint of black licorice and pepper along with a leaf that had been cured by the sun and rolled up on the thigh of an island woman, most likely wearing only a grass skirt.

"My Lord," Heimdall turned to greet Odin.

"Praise all of your senses Honored Gatekeeper!" Odin exclaimed as he approached puffing a cigar and carrying a bottle of mead. He handed the bottle to Heimdall.

"Warm yourself," Odin commanded. Heimdall drank.

"Thank you My Lord," Heimdall returned the bottle to Odin.

"Not time for Ragnarok yet?" Odin asked after a long draw on his cigar.

"Not yet," Heimdall answered.

They stood looking out over The Rainbow Bridge. They said nothing for about a half an hour. Odin handed him back the bottle. Heimdall drank, and handed it back. Odin drank. He puffed his cigar.

"Carry on Good Gatekeeper," Odin said as he departed.

"My Lord," Heimdall answered returning to his watch.

*

Sessrumnir:

They drank wine and ate chocolate, and then Freya dismissed everyone but Holli.

"Don't move, I need to show you something," Freya said.

Holli nodded.

Freya cleared the pool of bubbles; the center of the pool formed a bowl of sorts. Freya waved her hand, and the water in the bowl swirled forming an image. There Loki held a startled Staley Moon.

"What the fuck! How did this happen? I'll kill that twisted fuck!" Holli exploded.

"Calm yourself, daughter. You will get your daughter back, but we need to do some planning. One does not simply walk into Loki's realm," Freya said.

*

Irminsul:

Tyr opened his eyes.

Astoria:

Clayton's name wasn't listed in the phone book. Lennie went to the bar where Clayton had played and the owner told Lennie where he lived. Lennie started walking. The word 'stalker' came to mind, but the images burned in his brain washed the word away and replaced it with a different word.

Justice.

Justice required more than death. Death would only satisfy Lennie's masculine need for revenge. Lennie wasn't the only one hurt; in fact, he knew that Holli was emotionally damaged. What would Holli want? How would she proceed? Lennie guessed she'd do something to torment Clayton for awhile at least; it wouldn't erase the scar to her psyche, but it would be more impacting on Clayton then just decapitating him quickly.

Instead something to make Clayton think, reflect upon the damage he'd inflicted and hopefully feel remorse. Something subtle, something more poignant. Lennie wondered what that should be, he wished Holli were with him to discuss this. He missed her. Maybe if Clayton was forced to watch abused women in transition learn to move on with their lives from the acts done to them by men that might be fitting.

Lennie reached the house and studied it. A small rectangular slanting porch with warped boards from the coastal moisture, pale blue gray color with a white railing on which sat an overflowing ashtray. Lennie shook his head, staring at the exterior peeling paint didn't accomplish anything. He walked up onto the porch and knocked at the door.

"Lennie! Come in, have a beer!" Clayton greeted him when he opened the door. The jovial greeting indicated that Clayton had no idea Lennie knew what he'd done. That was a good thing for now, Lennie needed to form a plan. He would act like he didn't know for now.

"Beer sounds good," Lennie responded. Lennie accepted the cold bottle. They drank and talked about Pink Floyd, Fleetwood Mac, and Jimi Hendrix. Clayton put on some Hendrix. One beer led to a second, but Lennie nursed the second.

"Let's stand on the porch while I have a cigarette," Clayton said. They moved outside, propping the door open with a shoe so they could still hear the screaming guitar in Voodoo Child.

"Take a walk?" Lennie asked.

"Sure. Let me just take a few hits off my pipe in the house first," Clayton answered adding his cigarette butt to the overflowing ashtray. They moved back inside. Clayton sparked his pot pipe.

"Want some?" he offered it to Lennie. Lennie declined, taking a long pull on the beer he nursed. Clayton took a few more hits, and Lennie's nose detected the distinct green unique smell of the herb as it burned. For eleven minutes the two men finished their beers listening to Bob Dylan warble out the poetic mythical lyrics to Desolation Row.

"To the shore," Lennie suggested in an exuberant voice when the song ended.

"To the shore," Clayton echoed, nodding agreement. He lit a cigarette and locked the door as they headed out.

In a few blocks they were staring at the ocean. The waves crashed against the beach as they always did. They crashed no matter what bill was in congress, what the price of gas was at the pump, what war was being waged, or what the cost on a postage stamp increased to as the calendar year turned. The waves did what they did, nature didn't change according to the dollar bill. The two men stood watching the undulating greens, blues, whites, and blacks of the sea.

Lennie loved his wife, and he wanted Clayton to realize the wrong that he'd done. He wanted Clayton to feel agony and pain for uncounted years. However something more primal took over. He smashed his left elbow into Clayton's face. Clayton's nose shattered, spraying blood. The red streams covered Lennie's arm and the beach as Clayton fell backward. When he connected with the turf sand erupted upward.

Lennie descended on his foe. His right fist connected with Clayton's jaw, breaking two of his teeth free from his gums. Blood and bone fragments expelled from the man hitting the sand with a splat of crimson and pearl. Using strength he didn't even know he possessed, fueled by rage, Lennie jammed his fingers into Clayton's chest. His fingers dug into the chest cavity and Lennie ripped outward. Flesh ripped, and blood showered outward like a brilliant red bird spreading its wings.

"This is for my wife," Lennie snarled. He jammed his hand into Clayton, grasped the man's heart, and ripped it out. The organ beat once and realized that it was no longer attached to anything living. As the body part ceased to function Lennie cast it into the sea. Lennie knelt next to Clayton.

"May the sea heal her for what you've done to her heart! This is for me, fucker!" Lennie snapped Clayton's neck as he twisted the man's head off. Clayton's headless torso smacked against the cold sand.

THURISAZ

Alaska:

Snow fell in the fourteen degree weather. Eight inches descended in two hours covering every available surface. The landscape consisted of lumps; objects that had pea-cocked sharp edges were now rendered into soft crystalline domes. Through the torrent of snow, moose moved toward their next meal, another tree with nutritious bark awaited.

Wasilla, Alaska could have been any small town in the Lower 48. It sported a Wal-Mart, Target, Home Depot, Red Robin, AutoZone, and Starbucks. On the other hand, Wasilla was still in Alaska, the landscape remained in the wilderness. There were only a few roads to carry you to Wasilla; you could come from Anchorage from the south; Fairbanks from the north, or Palmer from the east, and that was it. Wasilla was the heart of The Valley sitting literally in the center of the ring of mountains and glaciers.

In Wasilla you could walk into GameStop and buy the latest game for your system, cross the parking lot and get a Starbucks, and still have to stop for a train, a moose, a helicopter in the middle of the road (evacuating a crash), and a waddling porcupine crossing the road on your way home.

"Brother, what have these people ever done to you?" Thor shouted looking up into the falling snow. Thor didn't expect an answer. Loki's goblin had stolen Staley Moon. They were going to go after her of course, but Thor knew Loki would count on that and set a trap.

"Count me in," Thofnir said jumping on Thor, tackling him into the snow.

"And me," TooLu said firing an arrow at a wood pile. The arrow stuck the dead center of a small log.

"And me," Jari chambered a round in the shotgun.

"Me too," Peter said holding the axe up.

"And me," Stan said raising the frying pan from where he sat on Bygul's back.

"Who said we were going anywhere?" Thor asked looking around at them all. Thor admired the determination on their faces, if they were scared, they didn't look it. He laughed.

"I can't bring Jari with; she is a girl," Thor teased.

"Try me Officer Odinsson," Jari stuck her tongue out at him.

"Maybe I can make an exception," he winked at her.

"You are incorrigible," Jari said.

"That is the idea," Thor said and put a wad of chewing tobacco out in his mouth.

"But I'm a girl," TooLu pouted.

"You are coming TooLu. Today you are not a girl; today you are our archer, and you will ride Thofnir," Thor smiled at her.

"I will?" TooLu asked in wonder.

"It will be my honor to carry you," Thofnir said bowing his head in respect. TooLu climbed onto his back.

"So soft," she noted feeling his fur.

"I'm a cat not a dog. When I jump hang on tight; it won't hurt me," Thofnir said.

"We need to visit The Norns first, to learn where my brother is hiding out," Thor announced.

"The three witches?" Stan asked.

"Best address them as The Norns, or The Fates, if you do speak with them, they don't like being called witches," Bygul said. Peter climbed up behind his brother. They both grabbed Bygul's fur.

"Guess you are flying with me," Thor addressed Jari holding Mjolnir up.

"If I must," she said wrapping her arms around him.

"Your breasts feel nice," he said.

"Shut up and fly," Jari snapped.

Freya's cats with their riders and Thor with Jari shot into the snowy sky.

*

Yggdrasil's Roots:

The three that moved as one were dancing around a fire. Round and round in a circle they went. They knew that Thor and his companions would arrive. They danced anyway, sometimes the dance needed to happen. Skuld giggled, Urdr laughed, and Verdandi cackled. Flames shot up into the night air.

Two huge cats thudded to earth a little way from the fire and dancers. Thor landed a few seconds later, running a few steps before coming to a halt. Jari let him go; she could walk on her own. The group approached the dancing Norns.

"Beautiful ladies, we come in peace," Thor greeted.

"Flattery will get you nowhere Mighty Thunderer," Urdr said. The three continued dancing leaping in the air and spinning this way and twirling the other direction. The flames of the fire changed colors from normal reds and oranges to greens and purples.

"Ask your question," Skuld prompted.

"Wise Norns, I need to know where Loki is," Thor asked.

"Answers like that have a price," Verdandi whispered.

"If there is any way we can pay we will," Thor answered.

"Our tree is sick," Skuld said with teary eyes and trembling lips.

"Yggdrasil? Thofnir, will your powers work on The World Tree?" Thor asked.

"I am willing to try," the blue-gray cat answered.

"Please do," Urdr urged. Thofnir padded over to the three roots. Instead of their normal scintillating rainbow colors they were gray and lifeless like limp corpses. TooLu slid off his back to let him work. The blue cat looked at the roots and hoped there was hope and he silently prayed.

"Mother Freya, Goddess of magic and love,
Grant now your healing aid to Yggdrasil,
Give The World Tree a motherly shove,
Take away all that is ill." Thofnir placed a paw on each of the roots. Green and silver energy flowed from his paw into each of the roots. Cuts opened in the roots and a black sap oozed out of them as a slow vomiting. The roots began thrashing about.

The red squirrel Ratatosk scampered down to the tip of one of the roots and as his ale colored eyes regarded Thofnir, he sniffed, and his whiskers twitched, his tail swished.

"I can't believe I'm saying this. Thank you, Cat!"

"You are most welcome, Ratatosk," Thofnir answered. Thofnir smiled a feline smile, whiskers twitching, and returned to the others, as the squirrel ascended the tree trunk again.

"Ljosalfheim," Verdandi said to Thor!

*

Asgard:

"Go Hugin, Go Munin," Odin told his ravens. The huge midnight hued birds stared at him.

"Yes, I did promise you that, didn't I?" Odin said as he opened a bottle of blueberry flavored mead. He poured half of the bottle into his raven's quartz drinking horn. Their drinking horn was a man-sized quartz statue of a drinking horn. The statue was solid with just a few inch dish at the open end, out of which the ravens now drank. When they finished Odin spoke again, "Now go do your job faithful feathered friends."

Odin poured the other half of the bottle of mead into his drinking horn. He took a sip. His ravens had good taste. Odin clipped the end of a Fuente OpusX and lit it. He took a draw and exhaled a cloud of smoke thinking about Loki. An hour later, he rose from his seat, and went to feed his wolves.

With that accomplished, Odin entered his walk-in humidor and after some deliberation selected an Oliva series V. He clipped the end, and lit the cigar. A nice smoke with a sweet smell. Smoking the Oliva he saddled Sleipner.

"Loki you are going to drive me to spend money!" he said aloud, then to his horse, "To Midgard M'Boy, we need to buy a car!" The eight legged steed flew between the worlds.

Odin struck a deal. He now owned a 1949 Hudson Commodore. The boat of a car was cream colored. The bench like quilted seats could fit four people in both the front and rear. Odin admired the automobile. The whitewalls with a red pinstripe impressed him, and he thought the exterior sun visor a wonderful touch of class.

*

Ljosalfheim:

Layers of cloud cloaked the land like a golden fog with the sun behind them. In the distance castles rose like mountain peaks, snow covering their highest towers. Where the sun touched their ramparts they glittered silver like falling stars in the night sky.

The castles we'd viewed from the air before we crashed into the side of a mountain. There was a pass of sorts and up we went. I put a wad of chewing tobacco in, and broke the trail for our group through the snow. A few thousand feet later, we reached the peak of the mountain.

We looked into the valley below us on the opposite side. Smack dab in the middle of it sat a fortress. Loki's place. There was no mistaking his aesthetic. A neon purple and indigo glowing castle that appeared to be constructed of Legos. We could hear the hum of electricity it gave off from this distance away.

"Why don't we fly down," Bygul asked.

"I thought you a better tactician, he'd see us coming that way," I answered.

"Thor, you honestly think he doesn't already know that we are here?" Bygul said.

"Good point," I admitted cursing my brother in my head.

"Flying sounds good," Stan said.

"I'm gonna kill him," Peter said.

"Peter this is a rescue mission not a seek and destroy mission. We need to get our sister back safely. Besides, you know Lennie is gonna kill Loki," Stan argued.

"I don't care about that," Peter seethed.

"What is our plan?" Jari asked me.

"Why, we storm the castle, save the girl, and all is well," I answered.

"Somehow I don't think it will be that easy Officer Odinsson," Jari grinned at me. So I pulled her in and kissed her.

"Why did you do that?" she asked.

"Just in case we die," I answered.

"I think I will keep living if it is all the same with you," Jari said.

"Works for me Jari Anderson," I said. "Any other ideas Thofnir? TooLu?" I asked. After some time they shook their heads no.

*

I knew my brother and his band of freedom fighters were coming. The second they entered Ljosalfheim I knew their exact location. Time to have some fun. Thor has courage and strength but he's not bright, he would storm my castle.

"Do your worst brother," I laughed.

*

Asgard:

Heimdall narrowed his vision to just Ljosalfheim and Asgard's borders. This little sibling rivalry would be a time Loki might use as a diversion, for something else. The Watcher had a horn section of a Modest Mouse song stuck in his head. It wasn't driving him bat shit crazy, but it annoyed like the sound of a buzzing fly trapped inside a windowsill.

*

Ljosalfheim:

    We landed about a hundred yards from the fortress, and charged. Out of the snow, around us erupted monsters. Twelve giants ringed us. They might have been Loki's Displacers but they were bipedal. Still black in color with abnormally long snake-like necks, and they still had tails. Their facial features were still Doberman pinscher-like with long snouts, but their eyes burned like glowsticks smoldering with a racism for anything smaller than eighteen feet tall. In each of their human hands they wielded double bladed battle axes, the edges of which flared in Ljosalfheim's golden light.

    Bygul spun to the left as Thofnir turned right. I left Jari to concentrate on the foes in front of us. A blast of noise came from Loki's stronghold, causing the cats to drop and cover their ears with their front paws. Peter jumped off and ran forward with his axe raised. TooLu dismounted, nocked an arrow, and fired. I spun to our rear. Battle!

    I swung at the giant on my right. My blow connected with Displacer-giant. The thing's knee should have shattered, instead the giant just jittered. The Displacer-giant swung his axe. I jumped away just in time, for as insubstantial as the creature may have been I guessed that if the axe struck the result wouldn't be binary.

    I ducked a blow from the center creature, and jumped another attack from the left hand most Displacer-giant. I lost my footing and the right hand beast's axe came toward me. At the last second I rolled out of the path of the weapon and jumped to my feet.

    Whirling axes came at me from all directions. If they wanted to play the game this way, so be it, I knew how to play. I began twirling Mjolnir in circles and then slammed him into the centermost Displacer-giant. The blow landed with cacophony of sound on the giant's chest armor but again with little effect.

I felt a sting in my neck as one of the creatures tail barbs struck me. I felt the poison beginning to run through my veins. I knew the barbs would paralyze me, but I had one more attack in me.

I jumped as high as I could and swung Mjolnir above my head with the might of Thor at the giant that had started out on my left. Mjolnir smashed into my opponent's nose crushing his skull. I heard an electrical hum and felt the crackling of lighting, and then the poisonous paralyzing barb overcame me. I knew nothing more.

Jari aimed her shotgun at the center most of the three beings in front of her. She inhaled and held her breath. She braced herself for the recoil and squeezed the trigger. Boom! She exhaled and chambered another round at the same time. Her blast stuck home. The creature faded out of existence.

Jari aimed at the right most Displacer-giant and fired. Her shot struck true, and the being collapsed. Jari chambered another round and aimed at the remaining giant.

Before she could pull the trigger the Displacer-giant ran forward covering the ground between them in a few leaps and both of its axes cleaved Jari into pieces. In a splatter of blood and gore her body fell to the ground in three parts. Her head, her torso, and her legs.

'Freya be with me,' was her last thought.

*

LOL
How do you like dem apples, Brother?
*

Peter attacked with the axe. His blow sliced into the Displacer-giant's foot. Bones splintered like dry twigs. The creature howled in pain and dropped its axes. It attacked by wrapping its neck around Peter's neck and constricting. Peter couldn't breathe. He turned the color of a canned beet.

"Get up Bygul!" Stan shouted. Bygul rose, ran, and jumped at their foe. Flying through the air, Stan swung his frying pan with all his might.

"FOR ASGARD!" he screamed. His weapon bludgeoned the Displacer-giant breaking its jaw with a sickening thud. Teeth fragments plummeted to the ground along with Peter as the creature's neck stopped constricting when its jaw broke. Peter breathed and regained his feet.

While jumping Bygul inhaled, and as Stan attacked the giant holding Peter, Bygul turned his head left and breathed at that giant. His breath blasted the thing full in the face and when the thing's head was covered in frost Bygul kicked with his hind leg shattering the creatures skull into crystal shards.

The third Displacer-giant swung his axes. One of them sliced Bygul's tail off. A spray of crimson and the long puffed blue-gray tail landed in the snow. Losing his equilibrium Bygul smashed into the earth, and Stan was thrown from his back. They both rose to face the battle axes.

Bygul growled and rays shot from his eyes turning the Displacer-giant into a fine ash as it disintegrated.

"I believe the modern expression is FUCK YOU!" Bygul yowled lamenting the fact that he was now a bobcat.

Peter ducked an axe from another giant. He dodged another axe swing, looking for an opening. When he saw his opportunity he ran between the giant's legs swinging with all his rage.

"Die Ass-Clown!" he screamed. His axe cleaved the thing's calf. The giant wobbled. Peter swung doing similar damage to the thing's other leg. As the giant fell there was an electrical humming noise and Peter watched as green lines enveloped Bygul, Stan, and himself.

Thofnir thundered forward claws extended, he crashed into the groin of the giant. Howling both of them thudded to the ground. Thofnir spun and placed his paw on the Displacer-giant's chest. A sizzling sound accompanied the smell of burning flesh. Thofnir lifted his paw up, leaving a blackened brand behind. The paw shaped mark sunk into the giant, burning the thing's vile heart, but before it died its tail struck Thofnir in the side and he felt himself unable to move again.

TooLu's first arrow missed. She shook her head, nocked another, pulled back, and released. This arrow lodged right between the thing's eyes. TooLu sensed something behind her. She spun as she drew another arrow. She nocked it, aimed, and let fly. The arrow found its mark. Right through the neck of the giant that killed Jari. The creature gurgled as blood showered from the hole in its throat as it died.

As the Displacer-giant tumbled backward from a plate on its armor green lines sprang into existence in a hum of electricity and TooLu and Thofnir were in cages.

*

LOL

*

I opened my eyes and looked around. We were all imprisoned in clear cubicle cells. TooLu and Peter were in one together; they stared at anything but each other. In separate cells Bygul and Thofnir paced. Stan occupied another cell. Jari was missing!

"Where is Jari?" I shouted.

"To the victor go the spoils," Loki's voice answered as he opened a door at the end of the cell block.

"Brother!" I shouted in fury and slammed my fist into the cell wall.

"Temper, temper," Loki said walking down the corridor between the cells inspecting his prisoners. He stopped in front of TooLu and Peter.

"Thought it fitting to put you two together," he clapped his hands and laughed.

"Don't you lay a hand on Jari, Loki," I addressed him.

"Thor, I plan to have my hands all over her luscious body," Loki said and walked out.

I screamed.

"Thor!" Bygul attempted to get my attention.

"Thor!" he repeated.

"What?" I demanded.

"It is not what you think. A sick joke of Loki's. I am sorry…"

"What, Bygul?" I asked.

"I'm sorry. Jari is dead," he answered.

I slumped to the floor of my cell.

ANSUZ

Ljosalfheim:
Thick heavy snowflakes floated down to earth in Ljosalfheim's golden light. Across the valley floor toward Loki's fortress a lone hooded figure walked. The cloak and hood were crimson trimmed with white fur. Before reaching the building the figure stopped and looked down.

Freya knelt in the blood splattered snow next to the remains of Jari Anderson. Tendrils of wine colored smoke tinged with silver flecks flowed from Freya's fingers. The magic smoke entered the three parts of the corpse. Freya spoke ancient words as the irises in her eyes turned gold. Her voice rose in volume and she gestured with her hands.

The three parts of Jari's corpse reconnected themselves.

Freya moved closer to the body. Golden smoke flowed from Freya's fingers and seeped into the corpse where it had been cut. Tears rolled down Freya's cheeks and landed on Jari's eyes. Freya kissed Jari with her red lips and breathed into her body.

The Goddess stood up.

"Jari Anderson I call you!" she called.

"Freya," Jari mumbled.

"I am here," Freya answered.

"I called to you as I died," Jari said.

"I heard, and now I'm answering. Jari Anderson I call You!" Freya repeated.

The deceased stood up.

"Jari Anderson, slain in battle, I claim you as one of my half of the chosen dead," Freya claimed.

"Now I'm dead?" Jari asked.

"Yes and no," Freya replied.

"What does that mean?" Jari asked.

"Jari Anderson, Valiant Warrior, I Freya, now name you Valkyrie." The Fair One spoke.

"Me, a Valkyrie, you must be joking?" Jari asked.

"Not joking, Warrior Maiden," Freya answered.

"So I am dead?" Jari asked again.

"You are one of the valiant dead. I have called you. I have chosen you. I have named you. You Jari Anderson are now a Valkyrie," Freya said.

"So now can I date Thor?" Jari asked.

"Maybe later, now you have some training to do," Freya put her arm around Jari.

"Training?" Jari asked.

"Yes, and to answer the question you are going to ask me for third time, you are both dead and alive. I'm taking you to Valhalla."

*

Loki here. My plan worked beautifully, and so I am smoking a substance that is a gift from the earth. "'If you don't like my fire than don't come around, cause I'm gonna burn one down. Yes I'm gonna burn one down,'" I sang, "Thank you, Ben Harper."

I'm not sure what Old One Eye would think, and I don't give a fuck. Not a fuck was given by me. Odin. I do respect him, and yet he is the most monumental of all pains in my ass, ever. Do you see the problem? I respect him for his intelligence and wisdom and yet, he doesn't get it. He just doesn't get it. Fuckin' old dudes. Still he tries. Ah, fuck it; I'm gonna burn another one down. I have a bunch of high 'dollar' prisoners in my cells, and I don't know what to do with them. They can wait, "'cause I'm gonna burn one down," I sang Ben Harper again.

Thor. My brother, and I have him in a prison cell. When we were younger we would wrestle as wiggling weasels. Thor would beat me most of the time if I didn't use magic, but now, now look at the mighty Thor, slumped down mourning the death of some mortal chick. Bitches. I win.

Love. Love is an emotional weakness I don't have time for. Why would one let oneself be put in a position where they need to capitulate to the copious wishes of another? Do this for me, do that for me, can you…no I can't, fucking deal with it yourself.

Now that you are in your proper place Thor, you pompous, promiscuous prig, I will deal with the numbskull of a needling Norwegian. I put a call into the police station.

*

Asgard:
Odin stood at Heimdall's post on the edge of the Bifrost. What sort of leader would he be if he couldn't do the job he expected his followers to do? He watched. It was time he gave Heimdall a reprieve. Heimdall was the best of watchers, the guardian of their realm.

Odin watched. Nothing threatened their borders at the moment. Ragnarok would not happen any time soon. At the edge of The Rainbow Bridge, a little squirrel slipped toward him.

"Ratatosk, what is the news?" Odin inquired.

"Allfather, Thofnir healed an illness in Yggdrasil, and Thor and the offspring of Lennie and Holli have been taken prisoner by Loki," the rodent informed.

"Good Informant, I thank you," Odin said.

Ratatosk bowed and scampered away.

Allfather pulled out a cigar known as Seduction made by Gurkha and with his gold and silver clipper sliced two millimeters off the end. From his pocket he took out a butane lighter and charred the end of the cigar.

Odin studied his cigar. He could see the bumps and stems in the leaf. He took a puff and thought of his magazine write up, "a beautiful medium colored brown wrapper. The cigar is a little hard to draw on. A spicy beginning, and slight grassy tones as smoked with hints of chocolate on the palate," Odin chuckled to himself.

Hints of chocolate indeed, Freya was gonna get it good when he visited her next. She may be the Goddess of Love, but he was the one knockin' boots with her. She never complained, and he knew that if she wasn't happy she wouldn't hold her tongue.

*

Astoria:

Lennie retched. The taste of his vomit hung in his mouth as he tried to stand up and failed to do so as more puke spewed out. He stumbled and fell onto the beach. A few yards away lay Clayton's corpse, the sand stained black with blood drops.

Lennie tried to rise again, and his legs betrayed him a second time. His stomach heaved and brought forth bile. The green acidic substance landed on the sand in front of him. He'd killed a man with his bare hands; the fucker deserved his fate! Lennie heard the unmistakable wail of sirens. He looked up and sure enough an Astoria cruiser came to a stop with its lights flashing red and blue.

Not good. Gore stained Lennie's hands and arms up to his elbows. Splatters of blood covered his clothing, and he clearly wasn't in any shape to run away. Justice, ha! The irony didn't make the situation any more bearable.

Two officers approached their hands resting on their side arms. Guns that would fire rounds as fast as they touched the trigger, either Glocks or Sig Sauer 9mm. Lennie raised his hands, waiting for the policeman. They cuffed him and shoved him in the back of their car.

At the station they fingerprinted him, booked him, and put him in a holding cell. Lennie went along like a zombie. Now as he stared at the concrete walls and very real bars, his mind started working again. Could he explain any of this? Holli, the kids, he needed to get out of this jail and fast.

*

LOL

*

Ljosalfheim:
Certain that she didn't notice him, Peter looked at TooLu. Her straight black hair hung to her shoulders. Her native coloring, with her small nose, and thin lips made her attractive, but how could he tell her that now and have her believe him? Not wanting TooLu to notice he'd been looking at her Peter started a conversation with Stan.

"Stan, I wonder what happened to Lennie?" he called across to his brother's cell.

"Good question. I hope he is okay," Stan returned across the corridor.

"Lennie is not that smart you know," Peter said.

"Dude, you see how much he reads," Stan fired back.

"That doesn't make him smart. That means his head is in the clouds reading science fiction," Peter countered.

"You might have a point there. Still, he loves Mom and treats her right," Stan said.

"You do have a point there," Peter conceded glancing again at TooLu.

"What are you looking at White Boy?" TooLu asked.

"My brother Stan across the hall," Peter answered.

"I may be ugly, but I'm not blind," TooLu said.

He'd been caught, now what? He could continue to lie or tell the truth. Neither of them seemed like good options at the moment. Girls were so confusing; he could try changing the subject.

"Did you see how huge those giants were?" he asked.

"I just told you I'm not blind. Are you deaf, or do you just not listen to me because I'm a girl?" TooLu asked.

That backfired, now Peter truly was at a loss.

"Do you know what the Alaskan state bird is?" TooLu asked.

"No. Why should I know that?" Peter shot back.

"It is the Ptarmigan," TooLu said. "They are beautiful white birds. You never know, that might be something you should know," she said.

"I used to live in Michigan. Do you know what the Michigan state bird is?" Peter asked.

"No," TooLu said.

"Robin red breast," Peter said.

"Do you know what the Alaskan state flower is?" TooLu asked.

"I didn't know we were playing twenty questions. But how should I know that?" Peter said.

"I guessed as much. It is the forget-me-not. Little beautiful blue flowers. Any boy who thinks I'm ugly most likely is not that smart," TooLu said. Peter got the message loud and clear. But he couldn't let her win.

"Do you know what the Michigan state flower is," he asked.

"No," TooLu answered.

"The apple blossom, but I didn't think you would know anything that didn't involve fish guts," Peter said.

"Nothing wrong with fish guts. That means you caught them," TooLu smiled.

*

Astoria:

Lennie needed to get out of jail. Lennie wanted to see his wife and kids again. One thing at a time, getting out being the first. He thought about turning into the beast and smashing out, but that wouldn't allow him to escape unseen. He silently prayed.

Odin Allfather, God of wisdom

I need your guidance.

Help me find a way out of here.

Hail Odin!

This wasn't Loki's prison, so Lennie could reach out to one of the realms. Or maybe he could turn into something inconspicuous? Which presented the best option? If he turned into something else, a bird for example, there was the chance of immediate recapture or getting shot. On the other hand if he could teleport to another realm he'd be out without the chance of getting caught again. That seemed like the way to go. Odin told him he could visit the other realms anytime. Could he teleport?

Teleportation. Physically move from this jail cell to another location. Lennie needed to believe in himself, that was Odin's message. He could do this. He had courage, and this would exemplify industriousness. He could do this he told himself again and believed it. Odinsson would visit Allfather by teleporting onto the Bifrost, The Rainbow Bridge. There Heimdall could permit him entrance into The Shining Realm.

Lennie closed his eyes and put his power of mind into moving himself out of the cell, through space to another place. He thought about the shimmering colors of The Bifrost. Pictured himself standing on it, the gateway to the realm of the Gods.

He opened his eyes. It worked! He'd teleported.

"Yes!" he shouted with joy.

"Welcome to Asgard Lennie Odinsson," Heimdall said from where he stood in front of Lennie.

"Heimdall," he said with awe.

"You may enter," The Watcher said and gestured for Lennie to pass.

"Thank you," Lennie said as he passed Heimdall and stepped into Asgard. The room Lennie entered had a white stone floor with a blue star in the middle of it, and silver tapestries hung on the walls. Lennie crossed through the room and found himself on a long golden bridge. The other end of the bridge led into a golden domed building. The city stretched back as far as Lennie could see with silver and golden domes shining in the sunlight. He traversed the bridge admiring the beauty of Asgard.

He entered a feast hall, rows of long tables sat ready for occupants. Lennie smiled and walked through the hall. Lennie remembered some distant past, and he knew Odin's throne room would be two rooms away. He passed through the other rooms and found Odin's audience chamber. The floor of the room was white with a red triple triangle in the center of it.

"Welcome," Odin said rising from his throne. He wore his azure traveling cloak and his hat.

"Loki imprisoned me, I've killed a man, and I have no idea where my family is," Lennie spilled out.

"I know. Holli is safe with Freya. Loki has your children and Thor in a different prison, but Freya and the Valkyries are going to rescue them," Odin said.

"May I go see Holli?" Lennie asked.

"That is why I have my traveling clothes on," Odin said, "but we may want to get you some different attire," he continued, a hint of a smile appeared on his face. Lennie looked at himself in prison orange and nodded understanding.

A door opened and a beautiful blonde woman entered bearing clothing.

"Some of Balder's, as you requested Allfather," she handed them to Odin.

"Thank you Fair Sif," he answered.

"Orange is not your color Leonard, they should fit," she said and turned to leave.

"Thank you Beautiful Sif," Lennie stammered.

"Your wife is beautiful, I've met her. She will be very happy to see you," she said and pulled the door shut behind her.

Lennie discarded the prison garb and dressed in Balder's clothes. The deep green pants and tunic fit well, though Lennie couldn't identify the fabric. The clothes smelled of the woods and the air during spring.

"Now we need a drink and a cigar," Odin said. Lennie thought of protesting as he wanted to see Holli, but he didn't think rushing Allfather the best idea, so he held his tongue. Odin ushered him into a humidor and handed him a Seduction by Gurkha. Odin himself selected an Oliva V.

"That one I've even written a blurb about," he laughed handing Lennie the clipper.

"Is that so," Lennie raised an eyebrow. Odin chuckled. He uncorked two bottles of mead and handed one to Lennie and whistled. Sleipner trotted into the room as a section of the wall slid open. Odin climbed on his horse and reached down to help Lennie up.

Sleipner jumped out the now open wall and they were flying above the city. They landed a short distance away on the edge of a forest. Sleipner thundered through the rows of trees, and they came out at Sessrumnir. The door opened and Freya and Holli stepped out. Odin and Lennie dismounted. Lennie and Holli ran toward each other and hugged. Tears ran down Holli's cheeks.

"Husband," she murmured.

"My beautiful wife," Lennie said wiping her tears away.

"My trip to London was a trap of Loki's, but I had an awful beer for you. How can you drink that crap? Where is my ladybug tablecloth? Loki has the kids, but we are going to get them back,"

Holli told him. Lennie didn't want to let her go, but he released her from the hug.

"The tablecloth wasn't my fault," he said.

"I don't believe you," she said, smiling.

"Everyone come in; let's eat," Freya said.

The feast hall was filled with light. Red, green, and white tapestries filled, the room, and a fire roared in the hearth providing warmth. Lennie and Holli couldn't keep from looking at each other through the meal, as they each recounted what happened to them since they parted. Holli omitted the rape, and Lennie didn't mention killing Clayton. They would tell each other those things later in private.

Odin didn't eat but drank mead from a golden goblet. He raised his goblet now and said, "Dear friends I need to return to my hall. Lennie, I know you wanted some of my wisdom and this I will tell you. Other than myself, Freya and her Valkyries are the best warriors in all of the nine realms. I have no doubt that the strategies she comes up with will work. My blessing on all of you." He stood, kissed Freya, and exited.

KENAZ

Ljosalfheim:
Bygul paced in his cell. He guessed that Loki magically shielded the cell so that he couldn't blast his way out, but he could still try. He breathed frost at the glass. Then he shot a disintegration ray from his eye at the frosted area. His ray dissipated the second it touched the wall, and his frost melted off the glass. Well, he tried. He went back to pacing.
LOL
"Bugger off," he told the air swishing his stub of a tail. He wanted to sink his claws in Loki. He hated being confined, and he returned to pacing.

*

Staley Moon tracked the goblin with her eyes. It flitted about directionless; it tinkered with something, moved onto something else and tinkered with that. She didn't like the goblin, not just because it guarded her, but because it was much too chaotic for her taste. She would escape from the chaotic goblin somehow.

*

Sessrumnir:
Holli and Freya stood outside the doors of the hall watching as the sun shined through the scintillating snow. Freya led Holli around the building into the trees. They walked through the pines and came to a small building.

"Hail good Magadi," Freya greeted.

"Hail my liege," Magadi answered.

"Border quiet?" Freya inquired.

"Did you hear an alarm bell?" Magadi answered.

"Very good. We need some snowshoes," Freya said. The guard produced two pairs. Holli strapped them on without being told. Freya tightened hers and the two set off. They climbed steadily through the trees into the mountains. About an hour later, they stopped to take a breather.

"Daughter, you and Lennie must return to Midgard and sell your house and store to Arisnoe. That is how she will find her calling," she instructed.

"How can you ask me to do this? How can you ask me to do anything when my children are prisoners?" Tears brimmed in Holli's eyes, her cheeks were red, and her voice broke as her chest heaved with emotion. "How? How am I to concentrate on mundane stupid ass things when my children are in danger?"

"Daughter, the teams are not ready yet. Loki will be expecting us to act quickly, rashly," Freya continued.

"But we need to do something fast," Holli pleaded.

"Loki will not harm your children. That would give him no joy. I am sure he has some more twisted scheme in that mind of his," she said. Holli processed Freya's words.

"What are these teams you're talking about?" Holli asked.

"Let me show you," she answered and set off again. Holli followed, and they snow-shoed up a mountain pass. Without the snowshoes on they would have sunk to their waists. The snow-laden pines were fragrant. As Holli gasped for breath the scent gave her half-crazed mind a moment of respite. The two women crested the mountain peak and Holli looked down on a sea of glittering silver. As they descended toward the large plateau Holli discerned three distinct groupings of brown and silver shapes on three different sections of the flat land formation.

They reached the plain and snowshoed up to the first group. The brown and silver things were groupings of massive animals wearing armor. Holli guessed they stood about eight feet tall with racks of antlers. Armored moose.

This team consisted of twelve of the huge beautiful animals. Their hides a deep brown they stood proudly on their legs that didn't look like they should support the thousand pounds above them. Their armor a plate mail designed to give protection while allowing maximum maneuverability was intricately engraved with runes. Holli moved down the line admiring the team. She'd never been close to moose before. They had large eyes, and tan, ridged ears, and some of them sported beards.

The team was a variation of a dog sled team, but these dozen didn't pull a sled, but a massive battering ram. Jolisa finished tightening a saddle-strap on a moose and turned toward Holli and Freya. She rubbed the moose's nose affectionately.

"This is my lead moose, Jack," she introduced. Jack's rack of antlers spanned eighty eight inches. Those antlers could do some damage. He stood with a brown hide with red highlights about eight feet tall, and weighed 1500 pounds without the armor.

"Hello Jack. Thank you for being part of the effort to rescue my children," Holli said. The moose nodded.

"Would you like to see a demonstration, my liege?" Jolisa asked.

"A very impressive team, Shield Maiden. Let's see what they can do," Freya answered.

Jolisa jumped and pulled herself up into the saddle. She bent down and whispered in Jack's ear. The team took off kicking up snow. Jolisa shouted commands, and the team ran one direction, and then veered another direction. The battering ram behind them whipped in an arc on pulley lines and slammed into a wall with a deafening boom. As the wall broke apart, the blast echoed off the distant mountain peaks.

"That's what I'm talking about, boys!" Jolisa shouted. Her team all nodded their huge antlered heads in agreement accompanied by the jangling of their armor. The team ran again turned, and thundered past the two watching women.

"Let us see the second team," Freya said. They crossed a section of the plateau and arrived at the second team. This team had ten animals in it and pulled a sled. Not a sled that only carried a musher, but one that held eight Valkyries, rows of two foot round stones, blocks of salt and copious amounts of bark for the moose to eat. Holli and Freya watched as the commanding Valkyrie named Hild, yelled commands. All the moose dropped as a unit, the sled stopped, and the Valkyries jumped out as a unit, moved something, and jumped back into their sled. The team rose and ran forward again. Holli noticed their obstacle course as the team began weaving around boulders and tree trunks. They moved on to observe the third team.

This team only had eight enormous animals. Every other moose carried a catapult on its back. The other four carried a basket containing a Shield Maiden and more catapult stones.

"Morning Jari, how goes the training?" Freya asked. The newest Valkyrie turned to the Goddess.

"How do the other teams look my liege?" she asked.

"I am very pleased with your work," Freya began, "Jari this is Holli, Holli this is Jari Anderson who was with your children and Thor when she fell in battle. She fought the day Loki took your kids."

"How were they when you saw them last?" Holli asked.

"They were fighting huge Displacer-giants; you should be proud of them. I am sorry that I failed them," Jari said.

"Thank you for all you did. You must have fought valiantly or else you wouldn't have been chosen by Freya," Holli said.

"I'll get them back," Jari said. She shouted to her team, "Hi-ya!" The team ran about two hundred yards forward and the four moose carrying catapults moved to one position. The other four positioned behind them. The arms of the catapults were pulled back and fired. The four Shield Maidens reloaded them and fired them again and again in rapid succession at another wall. All the stones struck true caving the wall in half.

*

Fires burned brightly in the feast hall. The human members of the three teams discussed their progress and strategies. The smell of slow roasted pork and strong beer dominated the hall.

"A toast to operation Hail-Smash!" someone called and tankards slammed together.

Feeling like a minority, Lennie slipped out of the hall into the cool night air. Holli followed him and wrapped her arms around him from behind. He felt her warm body press against him. He held her hands.

"You look very handsome in those clothes," she said in his ear.

"Thanks, Love," he responded. Together they stood looking out into the night.

"I hope they are all right," Lennie said.

"Freya assures me that Loki wouldn't kill them, that he has some other plan," Holli said. As if summoned Freya exited her hall and stood looking out with the couple.

"Beautiful Freya, what part are we to play in this mission?" Lennie asked.

"Son, when you are done helping Holli settle your properties you must go and find the Aurochs. You will ride the Aurochs and lead our attack. Holli will be with me to identify we have your true children and not some decoys that Loki created. We will get them back. That bastard has my cats too," she answered.

*

Astoria:
Loki here. I'm sitting across the street from Lennie and Holli's house. People put far too much value on material items. Now if I just push this key on my computer it will execute the

program. Push. And now the gas valve busts, now there is a spark. Whoosh. How beautiful, yes, see the flames shoot out of the windows like twin bursts of napalm out of a flame thrower. Thick black billows of smoke curling skyward. All of the baby pictures crumble to ash, irreplaceable moments in time, lost.

I have to laugh. Time to get home before the fire department shows up.

Ljosalfheim:

Back home on my couch eating Hot Cheetos, and drinking a Code Red. Code Red like the flames from the burning house. Let me check the security. Nothing threatening my borders. I think I'll cut my hair.

Asgard:

Sif escorted Lennie, Holli, and Arsinoe to Heimdall. Heimdall only had one ear as he sacrificed the other at the well of Mimir in order to gain the hearing he currently had. He didn't mind when others gave him friendly jabs about being Van Gogh. He hated Loki ever since the battle over Freya's necklace and wished he could go throttle the bugger right now, but that wasn't his duty. He knew his duty. He patted his horn, which hung in its customary place on his left hip. His sword hung on his back. He had a Dropkick Murphy's song going through his head, and he thought about her again. The Watcher kept still his eyes fixed on something distant. He heard the group approach, but didn't turn to greet them yet. Ljoslheim remained unmoving and he pondered what Loki might be plotting? Nothing threatened Asgard's borders.

"I've been expecting you for some time," he said turning at last.

"Heimdall our friends need to return to Midgard," Sif said.

"If the three of you walk down the Bifrost you will reach your destination," he said and winked at Arsinoe. She blushed.

"Goodbye Sif," Arsinoe said turning around to look at Heimdall again.

"Thank you Good Watcher," Lennie took Holli's hand. Holli took Arsinoe's hand, and the three of them began walking down The Rainbow Bridge. Wind buffeted them, and eddies of snow swirled in front of their vision. A half inch of fresh snow covered the Bifrost so each impression of their footprints glowed rainbow colors. From where Sif and Heimdall watched the white narrow expanse was dotted with rainbow spots.

A flash of light as if the sun at noon and the full moon collided, danced, into the punch bowl, and stumbled out under the mirror ball blinded their eyes. When the three could see again they were in Astoria standing in front of The Store That Doesn't Have a Name.

The door opened at Holli's touch, and they entered. All of them were amazed that the store still hadn't been pilfered. Lennie looked on as Holli turned to Arsinoe. They looked at each other, and some womanly understanding passed between them.

"Arsinoe, how would you like to own a your own store?" Holli asked. Lennie opened his mouth to object and shut it again. There went their livelihood. Arguing with Holli at this time however would be pointless. She wouldn't change her mind, and most likely she would be upset with him for interfering in some cosmic doing. They would find another way to make money.

"I think my path has been set before me," Arsinoe answered.

"It's yours. We will do that paperwork at the same time we do the house paperwork," Holli said. The women embraced. Lennie thought he could use one of Odin's cigars.

"What are you going to name your store?" He asked.

"Sif's Hearth," Arsinoe answered.

"Very good," Holli nodded.

"A fine name. Well I hate to be all male-thinking," Lennie grinned, "but does anyone even know what day it is?"

"Come you two, let's go home and get cleaned up and eat something. We can work on all the real world stuff after that," Holli said. They headed toward their house when they heard the wail of sirens. A second later fire trucks squealed past them. They began running, and Lennie wondered if his old dog Greedy would have enjoyed chasing the fire trucks?

"My baby pictures!" Holli screamed sinking to her knees. Silent sobs shook her frame. Lennie knelt and put his arm around Holli's shoulders.

"You have the memories in your head," he tried to comfort.

"That's not the fucking point!" Holli yelled at him. Lennie backed away raising his hands.

"Don't fucking do that!" Holli said.

"I love you, wife. I would bet anything that our house burning is no coincidence, no mere accident of faulty wiring," Lennie said. Loki was behind this, Lennie clenched his fists in fury.

LOL

Over the next few days while staying at a hotel, they took care of the paperwork. Homeowners insurance covered the house. Holli signed the deed over to Arsinoe so when a new house was built it would be hers. They also sold the business to her for a song, the amount of which could be paid at a later date when the business actually turned a profit.

*

Sessrumnir:

Jari walked her line and touched each of her moose, her team training for a rescue mission with catapults on their backs. She loved them. It wasn't running the Iditarod but doing something even grander. They all stood over seven feet, and their racks spanned eighty some inches. They varied in color slightly, and she named them all. She whispered into their ridged ears as she went down the line. Thor to her lead moose after a man she could love. Steepter, a combination name for the two boys she would rescue. Seward after the man who bought Alaska. Lance after Mackey, the true Iditarod champion. Denali because he had to be a few inches over eight feet. Winston after her fathers' cigarettes. And her last two after whiskey: Rich and Rare.

She walked back up the line, and climbed onto Thor's back. Never in her life had she imagined mushing a team of moose. She was happy; her father would have been proud of her. Now she'd taught Jolisa and Hild her techniques and all three of them had strong teams. She looked up the mountain to where Jolisa trained and smiled.

*

"I'm damn tired Boys, so let's do it again," Jolisa called. Her team took off down the mountainside as fast as they could. When they reached the bottom they thundered across it and pivoted in their run. The battering ram smashed into the wall blasting concrete every which way.

"Hel yeah!" Jolisa yelled. They'd done the drill so many times she'd lost count. Up the mountain, down it, across, turn, smash. She loved her team. Mushing moose was her new passion, and Jari Anderson had taught her everything she knew. She needed to thank the new Shield-Maiden. Tonight she'd share her special Moonlight Mead with Jari. Odin crafted it five years ago. It tasted like sex felt and intoxicated like the poetry of Shakespeare and Bukowski an eloquent punch to the brain.

"Jack, Allen, Rudy, Sam, Simon, Brandon, Terry, Gus, Mike, Chris, Craig, Zirkle, bring Momma home," Jolisa called. The team ran back up the mountain pass. Jolisa kept thinking of the Moonlight Mead. The thought didn't bring any warmth to her frozen limbs, but she knew the honey wine would.

*

Hild swore as a strip of skin pulled away from her hand like lint removed from a dryer trap as she removed her hand from the steel. She stood up and clenched her hand. They'd hit a tree trunk and their runner snapped, their sled overturned spilling people, stones, salt blocks and copious amounts of bark. Her team thankfully licked the salt blocks and munched on bark. A moose could eat fifty pounds of bark a day and she'd been working them hard. Well at least this wasn't a total loss, the guys had to eat.

Her lead moose was Owl. In general moose couldn't see well and like their smaller cousins, they relied on their sense of smell and their hearing. Of all the moose on her team he could see the best; that is why she named him Owl. The next three she named after some of the food the moose ate: Cedar, Pine, and Spruce. Then she named the middle of her team Winter, Snow, Frost, and Ice. Her ninth moose was Elliot because she liked the name. And the tenth "wheel" moose and favorite member of her team was Joey, his beard was white and he had a quirky sense of humor.

"A little help here," she called to the other Valkyries, looking at her bloody hand.

*

In her room inside her hall, Freya took off her top freeing her breasts. She felt her breasts, and rubbed her nipples between her thumb and index finger. Her nipples responded as she hoped, she felt them harden and felt her womanhood began to pulsate with desire. She was the Goddess of beauty, sexual pleasure, eroticism and desire. Also she was strong in magic and other than Odin she had no equal on the battlefield.

Freya undid her belt. Her belt buckle, not a necklace, was Brisingamen. The translation of "fiery belt" worked on numerous levels.

*

Ljosalfheim:

"Mjolnir!" Thor called. Tired of sitting, he couldn't mope around forever. He needed to do something. He outstretched his fingers to accept his weapon. He didn't know where his magic hammer was, but he knew he was the only one who could wield it.

"Mjolnir!" He repeated.

"Sucks Broski," came Loki's disembodied voice.

"Brother, you will pay this time!" Thor shouted.

*

On the couch:

Does my computer miss me? Is it forlorn because my fingers are not touching it? Maybe I need a new set of headphones? It could be, it just might be, one never knows. Over here I have a jack-in-the-box. Turn the handle click click click click click Pop! A Street Named Mystery, sounds like a good title for something…

I am thinking that I need to build a snowman, or rather an army or them, or maybe zombies, but both of them seem so trite, but then again they would be very frightening. Creatures of discord resemblances of life, filled with disharmony and detrimental to the order of the multiverse. Disheveled deranged drunks in diapers in the desert are desiccating.

Snow Zombies? Owly Owl was an odd ornithologist. Yup I went there. Owly Owl, the voyeur! Owls…huge blue owls like on the Rush album cover. Rush, Canadian rubbish. Rubbish I say, Old Chap. On the contrary Sir, you are but a Cyclostome. Are you calling me a jawless fish Old Chap? Maybe I am, maybe I am, Sir Hagfish. LOL Sir Hagfish.

Sordid sultry seductress…

The life of a cheese ball? There will be no rap music played up in here tonight.

Voluminous volleying voluptuous vixens the Norns are. Owly Owl ogled the vultures. Sir Hagfish contemplated the palpitating pompous puff-ball of orange goodness that placated itself before him. Life of a cheese ball, still better than life in a dice bag. Who would name a book of poetry that?

*

Yggdrasil's Roots:

How could he?

You already knew he would.

He what?

"Loki called you a vixen and Verdandi a vulture," Urdr explained to Skuld.

"What did he call you?" she wanted to know.

"Voluptuous," Urdr answered.

"Nothing wrong with a vulture ripping strips of flesh off dead things," Verdandi cackled.

"I am not a vixen; I don't prance around like a slut," Skuld protested.

"No?" Urdr laughed and she raised an eyebrow.

"Feed them," Verdandi said.

"Yes Sister, now dip your cup in the water," Urdr instructed Verdandi.

"I know that," Verdandi hissed. Skuld danced up and dipped her cup.

"No definitely not a vixen," Urdr said with mirth in her eyes.

"Shut it, Miss Cleavage," Skuld replied. The three that were one dipped their cups and moved to the roots of The World Tree.

"Always hungry, aren't you Children?" Urdr said and she doled out the liquid in her cup over each of the three roots in close to equal portions.

"Can't you ever be satisfied?" Skuld asked as she gave each root a hand job with her liquid.

"Can't get no satisfaction," Verdandi whispered as she made little holes in the dirt and poured a little bit from her cup in each of the small graves.

URUZ

Just breathe, Lennie told himself. They had just sold their house and business. Only the things in life that were stable and normal. A home in which to raise the children. A place to return to when the work day finished, and lay down to sleep with the woman he loved knowing that he'd done something useful. A job to do that gave a man purpose. All have been whisked away in the blink of an eye and to top it off apparently they were going to move to Alaska.

Alaska. The end of the United States, The Last Frontier. Maybe it wouldn't be so bad, everything Lennie knew about Alaska made it seem like Norway. He'd lived there for eighteen years. Lots of snow, cold temperatures, rugged mountain beauty, and it didn't matter to him where he lived as long as he was with the ones he loved. His family.

Family. Inhale, Exhale. Keep living, everything would work out. Wouldn't it? He needed to help rescue their children from the fucking bastard who made him watch and listen to his wife being raped over and over again. Lennie took care of Clayton, and wished he knew how to kill a God. Not funny Mr. Trickster, not funny at all. Stay on task Lennie, the kids, he reminded himself. Loki is an agent of chaos, so keep order, keep organized, follow instructions. Freya told him to find the Aurochs so that is exactly what he would do.

How to find the old beast? A dream state, perhaps? The last time he'd encountered the ancient creature, he'd been dreaming. Was that the only way? Aurochs. Aurochs, at least now he knew the name of the beast he'd faced, and chopped its legs off with a living flame. That thing nearly killed him and Freya wanted him to ride it into battle. Anything is possible, he told himself.

Lennie didn't like the idea of going into a dream state, Loki wounded him there before. He steeled his nerve, courage. Nothing wrong with dying in battle, this was a battle. No time like the present, Lennie laid down on the bed and tried to relax. Slow your breathing, calm your mind. Not as easy as it sounds.

Think ancient beast, think Aurochs. A wild ox, with long fur and fire in its eyes, horns that are long, black and white, and beautiful even though they spell death. Sleep evaded Lennie. He got up and paced. Damn sleep anyway, when he wanted to stay awake it claimed him, and now that he tried to let it take him it refused.

Try again. Lennie undressed, and got under the covers. Maybe that would help; he shut his eyes and thought about the warmth of the covers. Carry me into the realm of sleep he thought and tried not to think about anything but drifting. Drifting away on a current of warmth into the land of dreams. Leave this world behind and go somewhere else where anything could happen. Where he could ride an old ox and kill a God.

Too much heat, the covers were stifling him, but he refused to get up again. He might sweat a little, so what he'd smelled far worse when he lived in a cave for five years. A little sweat could be washed off. Old One I'm looking for you he kept repeating to himself. Drifting, blackness, don't open your eyes, let the dream realm claim you. This shouldn't be this hard; all he wanted to do was take a nap. Just a little nap. Old One I'm looking for you. Old One I'm looking for you. Old One I'm looking for you.

Rolling fields of grass stretched before Lennie as far as he could see a vast prairie. Here at last. All right you ancient ox, show yourself. I've traveled to find you and I've got to be in the right spot.

The Aurochs stood before Lennie. Lennie blinked, it was still there. None of his senses detected The Ancient One's advent as they had in his dream before. This time the Aurochs just appeared without warning.

Lennie registered the Aurochs' presence now as its breath washed over him, a mixture of ruminated grasses. His ears picked up the swish of its tail, and he looked into those eyes that knew billions of years.

"You wish for me to charge into battle?" the Aurochs spoke.

"I'm glad I didn't have to explain that. Yes that is my wish," Lennie replied.

"What are you going to do for me in return?" it asked.

"What do you require?" Lennie asked.

"You must bring me The Ring of Taurus," the Ancient One answered.

"I don't have time right now. I need to rescue my children but you have my word on my life that I will bring you the ring once my children are safe," Lennie vowed.

"I will hold you to your oath," the Aurochs said.

"You may."

"Climb on mortal," the Ancient One said. Lennie jumped as high as he could and pulled himself onto the ox's back. The hide smelled of wildflowers and spider webs. Lennie hung on as the beast galloped, when the air felt colder and smelled of snow Lennie looked up to see Sessrumnir gleaming golden before them.

The sentries spotted them and were poised for action, but they lowered their spears when they recognized Lennie. One of them opened the door and disappeared inside the hall. The other called out a greeting.

"Hail travelers welcome to our hall!"

Lennie climbed down off the Aurochs' back.

"Is your liege within?" he asked.

"My partner went to notify her of your arrival," she answered.

"Many thanks," Lennie said. The Aurochs snorted and steam streamed forth from his nostrils. "Could you please bring my traveling companion something to drink?" Lennie asked.

"I can, but you must wait outside," she answered.

"I will obey," Lennie agreed and he watched the woods surrounding the hall. Sometime later, she returned with a large pot filled with some liquid. She placed it in front of the Aurochs.

"I am grateful Daughter of Sessrumnir," he told her in his deep, smooth voice, and began to drink.

"You are very welcome Ancient One," she said resuming her post.

EIHWAZ

The Roots near The Well:
　　Ratatosk listened to the sibilant speech of the snake. The message made little sense. The squirrel asked the snake to repeat it. The snake narrowed its eyes.
　　"Hey, I'm not your lunch. If you eat me you are gonna have to answer to the Eagle. Is that what you want?" Ratatosk asked. Ratatosk started thinking about lunch; some spicy Sriracha peas would be just the crunchy hotness to make his palate happy.
　　The snake repeated his message. The three sisters wished a conference with Odin. Now Ratatosk understood. After he delivered this message maybe he could eat lunch.
　　"Okay Boss, I got it," he said and began scampering on his upward climb. Although The World tree was ancient, Yggdrasil's bark had different textures and temperatures. Most wouldn't know this, but most (unlike himself) didn't make multiple journeys up and down its length Ratatosk thought. Ratatosk knew that the realm Hel existed but as its location was in fact below the roots he didn't venture through it.
　　The squirrel knew he ventured through Svartalheim now because his paw pads felt oily. The climb itself became precarious as he fought to gain purchase with his claws. He also coughed as the smell of sulfur stuck in his sensitive nose. The smell did funny things to his mind too, he felt all mellow and just wanted to take a nap. He fought the urge to rest. He had a message to deliver, he had a job to do. Even more important would be eating a yummy lunch. The one nice thing about the realm of the dark elves was the taste on

his tongue. The realm tasted like extra stout Guinness, as if the malt clung to his taste buds like a candy bar. Good old St. James's gate in Dublin, Ireland on Midgard.

He made it through that realm. The bark returned to normal, Ratatosk called this stretch 'the straight-a-way' because it ran for miles without passing through one of the realms. Just normal bark. He kicked up his speed to full blast and ran for the fun of it. The cosmic wind whipped his whiskers back and the air smelled clean. A happy stretch of Yggdrasil, this.

The bark began to burn his paws. He leapt as far as he could before touching lightly down, and leapt again. This realm he disliked even more than the last. He tried to stay airborne as long as he could. During this part of his journey he always wished he were one of those squirrels that could glide, so that he wouldn't have to have as much contact with the scorching bark. Muspelheim, the realm of fire. His paw pads were in agony. Every time he touched he winced as his feet were further singed. Here he didn't smell sulfur, rather the collection of smells that clogged his nose currently most knew as natural gas. Ratatosk twitched his tail angrily and leapt again straining his legs to jump as far as he could. He landed and felt relief as the bark felt cooler; he'd passed through the furnace realm.

He called this portion of Yggdrasil The Second Stretch. He didn't run fast though, instead he took his time letting his paw pads recover. Here The World Tree's bark again felt good. In The Second Stretch the tree was white and green in color and felt just right. He felt comfortable knowing that he wouldn't slip off or burn to death. He scampered this way and that as if he were doing a drunken dance. Soon he could have some of the chili garlic coated peas. Soon.

He reached Midgard. This was the fifty-fifty realm. It would either smell wonderful or awful. Fifty percent of the time the realm smelled like ozone. Clean, pure, the fragrance of growing, he could almost eat the smell. The other fifty percent of the time the realm smelled of pollution. It made him nauseated, and he felt sick. His stomach would cramp and his limbs shake as if he'd ingested a disease. And for some reason when this was the case the words of some wise woman filled his mind and said, "Ah the humanity, too much humanity."

Today at this hour the air smelled clean. The squirrel smiled and ran on. He called this next area 'Tertiary' not only because it was the third stretch between realms but because the word had something to do with bird feathers which reminded him of his task, reach the eagle and deliver the message. Somewhere off to his left the realm of Vanaheim rested amongst the trees branches.

Once when he'd gotten lost in a rain storm when he couldn't see, and kept running thinking that he was on the main trunk when he was on a thinner branch he'd ended up in Vanaheim. He wouldn't make that mistake again! It made him feel bloated as if he were pregnant.

Ratatosk slowed as visibility diminished. Dense fog surrounded the timeless tree in this region. Niflheim, the mist home. Many sources stated that this realm's location was underneath Midgard. Those sources were incorrect. They should have asked Ratatosk, he would have set them straight.

The rodent also knew that Jotunheim existed many branches away to his right. The realm of the giants. Once so long ago that he forgot it and then remembered it, forgot it again, and re-remembered it, Odin had asked him to deliver a special message to Laufey. Ratatosk ventured to see the Goddess of Trees where she resided. The mission took a long time as crossing the mountain ranges of the vast realm of Jotunheim proved arduous. He'd done his job though, carried it out. When he returned, Odin let him have a sip of mead. One sip of that stuff and he had stayed drunk for a few days, and he was warm the whole time. If Odin let him have any more mead he might have to call the honey wine a job benefit.

With that happy memory Ratatosk entered Ljosalfheim. The realm of light, he squinted upon entering. The light here the color of Bushmills whiskey watered down and filtered through a prism. He twitched his nose as the air smelled of honey and walnuts. Despite the beautiful senses assailing him the messenger doubled his speed. He knew that this realm could sometimes be deceptive as Loki currently resided here.

Scrumptious Sriracha Peas. Very soon now. He dodged to the right, and circled the trunk of his beautiful tree. This was his tree. Think anyone might know it better and he'd chitter in your general direction. He ran in circles spiraling ever upward. This section of Yggdrasil he affectionately named Wunjo after the rune meaning joy according to Odin.

"Almost to The Watcher. Almost to The Watcher," he repeated to himself as he ran and ran. The temperature continued to drop as he ascended. Icicles formed around his whiskers.

Asgard. The realm of the Gods. Ratatosk jumped onto the edge of the Bifrost and slid into Heimdall's boot. Heimdall knelt down and held out one glorious Sriracha Pea. The rodent took it and tucked it in his cheek.

"Thank you, Good Watcher," he said as the taste began warming his body. Heimdall gently scraped the ice off his whiskers.

"Warmth to you up above, Good Messenger," Heimdall answered watching as Ratatosk jumped back onto Yggdrasil continuing upward. Ratatosk liked Heimdall, they both had jobs to do, but The Watcher extended kindness to him, and for that he thought him a jolly good dude.

The bark froze his paw pads and he started leaping again as the bark of Yggdrail glittered with millions of icicles. Ratatosk skittered here and hung on for dear life by one claw before he made another jump. He had a job to do. He would deliver his message, though this part of the journey always made him nervous as he never knew if the eagle might be hungry?

Even though the eagle itself had a job to do, he never knew what went through the mind of the predator? Once it had tried to eat him; Ratatosk still wore the scar of the bird's talon. The eagle still had a hole in its left foot from the rodent's front teeth. Since that time they'd reached an understanding.

He couldn't smell anything up here. However, the nebulae were amazingly spectacular from this height and so clear it made up for the lack of scent. He marveled at them every time.

What was the message again? Ratatosk couldn't remember. His brain along with the rest of him felt frozen. Frost hung heavy from his whiskers and ear tips. He could no longer feel or move his tail. Navigation became difficult and he slowed his pace. He'd make it to that blasted bowl of sticks where the eagle nested if it killed him. Odin depended on him, that old codger should give him another sip of mead for this one. That reminded him. The sisters wanted a meeting with One Eye. That was the oral missive! Yay! Almost there! He climbed into the bowl of sticks. If the bird wanted a snack it would have to break the ice armor surrounding this messenger, resulting in a broken beak, no doubt.

"Tell AllFather that The Three Sisters want to see him," he stuttered. The Eagle let out a terrifying screech.

"Glad you got that," Ratatosk mumbled and began down The World Tree again. Yummy Sriracha Peas awaited.

*

The Top of Yggdrasil:

Hugin landed on the Eagle's nest.

"Tell Odin that the Norns want to see him," Eagle said.

"And if I don't?" Hugin's raven face had a smirk on it.

"I told you. I've done my job. If you choose not to do yours it is no feather off my back," the Eagle said.

"Bad Eagle, real bad," Hugin took flight.

*

Bifrost:

Loki's Laughter

Heimdall listened. He heard the icicles breaking as Ratatosk skidded down. The Watcher smiled picturing the rodent surfing along the frozen bark of Yggdrasil. Maybe Heimdall could convince Sif to make The Messenger a scarf?

The Watcher had a Journey song in his head, and longed for a good stout. Thick black beer, the kind you could chew on, the kind that coated your throat and warmed your soul. Damn all the poets too. Who were these guys wooing women with their words, calling themselves Bards and such?

There he was, Heimdall smiled as Ratatosk skidded into his boot.

"I heard you icicle surfing up there," he said.

"Who me?" Ratatosk feigned shock.

"Take your lunch at Himinbjorg. I left a bowl of those peas you like out and I'm pretty sure that I accidentally forgot to drink a beer. I left it sitting next to that bowl of god-awful chili garlic coated peas," Heimdall said grinning.

"I can't thank you enough," Ratatosk said.

"You just did, my friend. Now go eat," he said. The rodent scampered away. Now he had Black Sabbath going through his head, much better. The sun rose, and on Midgard a musher won the Iditarod. Odin and Freya were getting it on, sometimes having excellent hearing sucked, he tuned that out.

ELHAZ

Sessrumnir:
Freya walked among the three teams. She knew that Elhaz had multiple meanings. The European elk, later in the new world known as America, the animal called Moose. Marsh plants, which they ate, harmful or protective? Both, depending on the circumstances. They were beautiful animals she thought as she ran her hand over their coats feeling them as she walked among them. Protective of their young, and dangerous in battle. She smiled; they were her Elhaz. Goddess of Magic indeed, the Elhaz were magic. She touched each of them telling them how much she loved them, and about the importance of their mission.

"Jolisa, take Jack and fetch Holli," Freya commanded.

"Yes my liege," she answered.

Ljosalfheim:
Bygul turned and turned but couldn't see his stub of a tail. Dismayed he sat down, and stared out of the cell at his sibling. Thofnir chased his tail; at least he still had one. He looked like an idiot, albeit he was self entertained. Bygul missed his tail.

At the Roots:
"You received our message?" Urdr asked.

"That is why I am here Sisters," Odin answered the Norns.

"You are aware of the battle coming?" Urdr asked.

"Yes the Valkyries are training to take on Loki," he answered.

"That is not why we called you here One Eye," Skuld said.

"Somehow I figured that," Odin said.
"Ice. Death," Verdandi whispered.

At My Laptop:

Loki here. Noisome has nothing to do with sound, but rather it is to annoy, offensive. Just thought I'd let you all know that. The French are flatulent flagrant foppish fools. Just saying.

Nothing on my defense monitors. I'm gonna listen to An Endless Sporadic: Impulse.

Astoria:

"Ready Champ?" Jolisa asked Holli.

"Sure am Coach," she answered as she climbed onto the moose's back and put her arms around Jolisa.

"Jack, Mush," Jolisa said.

Sessrumnir:

"Come my daughter, let's have a glass of wine," Freya took Holli by the arm and led her to two chairs in front of a hearth. A fire burned sending heat and light into the chamber. One of Freya's handmaidens brought them glasses of white wine. Chilled just right, it refreshed Holli.

"Lennie and the Aurochs will charge first, the three teams will attack second, both are diversions. We are going in through a secret passage that starts in Vanaheim. Loki modernized and computerized, but he built on the ruins of an ancient stronghold, and he may not even know about this secret escape route," Freya took a swallow of wine.

"Mother, why are you and I doing the sneaking?" Holli asked and took another gulp of the wine.

"Because my dear, we are the ones that actually need to get inside. We can't be killed on the battlefield and still accomplish our goal," Freya responded.

"I trust your battle strategy," Holli took another gulp.

"That is what I'm saying." They both laughed.

"What about Lennie?" Holli fretted.

"You know he would gladly lay down his life for your children," Freya said as she sipped her wine.

"Doesn't mean I have to like it," Holli said.

"Trust in the Aurochs, he is a sagacious old ox."

"Yes, Mother," she finished her drink. Freya did likewise.

"Let's go see the teams," Freya suggested.

"Can I see Lennie?" Holli asked.

"Not at the moment, he is in Niflheim," Freya rose and extended her hand. Holli placed her hand in Freya's.

HAGALAZ

Ljosalfheim:
    The Aurochs and the Beast of Frost materialized one hundred yards from Loki's fortress. They knew that he would know they were coming, and they also knew they were but a diversion, battle tactics 101. The air crackled and sizzled around them as the portal they came through closed.

    Emaciated snowmen moved with unnatural celerity toward the intruders. They were things of nightmare, rotting carrots for noses, sunken holes for eyes, like tunnels to the abyss. Their leprous moss covered branch arms wielded scythes. Each of the mowing weapons was black with a magical purple energy flickering along their slicing blades.

    "EGRAHC!" The Beast of Frost gave a battle cry. The Ancient One snorted and ran forward toward the fortress with Lennie in beast form on his back into the ranks of snow-zombies. The Aurochs' horns had been outfitted with spikes. He'd refused armor but had allowed his hooves to be covered with spiked metal razors. The Beast of Frost was armored in layers and layers of primordial ice from the realm of Niflheim. Below that he'd petrified the bark around his vitals including his brain. He carried massive swords in each of his primary arms. His eyes glowed with primal emerald rage.

*

    "Oh this will be fun," Loki grinned punching keys on his computer as he watched the screen.

*

The Aurochs collided with the first of the snow-zombies smashing it to pieces. Another of the things swung a scythe at the ox, but he leapt into the air and the attack missed. He kicked a second and third to smithereens as he landed, and gored another with his horns.

The Beast of Frost decapitated his first enemy, and slashed another in half. A third's scythe cut into his side, but all the purple energy did to the ice of Niflheim was chip it.

The two beasts charged further into the fray. Behind them the snow-zombies they'd decimated reformed and attacked them from behind. They were surrounded by the undead snow beings. They fought on.

"IKOLTIGNIRB!" The Beast of Frost cried and slashed to either side, two more opponents fells in chunks. The Aurochs gored two more out of his way and plowed onward. The Aurochs and The Beast of Frost continued forward slashing and goring toward the main entrance of the stronghold.

*

"Gee" Hild called and the team pulled to the right around a tight group of pines. They trotted easily, "We are doing fine Joey," she told him. Up ahead they were going to have to veer to the left to start their decent.

"On Owl! Haw!" she called. They turned left and started down the mountainside.

*

Jari's team with their catapults ran ahead of Hild's. The moose mushed through the snow like champs. Her mind wandered to thoughts of Thor, not her leader, but the man/God/whatever. Maybe when they completed this mission she could see him? Now that she was "half dead" some of her worldly insecurities had disappeared. Thor with his muscular arms, she intended to have him put them to use.

"Whoa!" she yelled. Theoretically the team should stop, but they kept pulling in their harnesses.

"I said Whoa! Did you think I was blowing smoke? Whoa!" she screamed. At last her team stopped just in time before they went over a cliff. She watched the avalanche below. Hopefully that didn't blow the element of surprise.

"Gee," she called. They went right.

*

Jolisa's twelve moose team approached from a different direction. They would attack the left side of the fortress with the battering ram. The other two teams converged on the rear of the stronghold.

"Whoa!" She called. Her team kept moving.

"I fucking said stop, Jack!" she yelled. A hundred yards later they stopped. Jack looked back at her with embarrassed eyes.

"You guys better get your act together. We are attacking a fucking castle. This is no time to be daydreaming about munching on marsh plants. Now, no showing off. We are going to do this in military fashion. We are going to do what we need to do, get the job done, and go home. Everyone understand? Good. Haw!" The team took off to the left. They ran down the mountainside at about ten miles an hour, Operation Hail-Smash was underway.

Asgard:

Odin stood riveted to his viewing pool. He smoked a Partagas Black Label Maximo. Lennie and The Aurochs were almost at Loki's gate. They'd both sustained wounds, but they weren't slowing. Ruthless, relentless, he loved it.

The Eagle landed on the edge of his viewing pool.

"What?" he asked with a puff of smoke.

"The Norns wish to see you," the Eagle said in eagle language.

"Again?" he asked engrossed in what he watched.

"I have delivered my message. If you choose to ignore it you may not kill the messenger, unless you want to gut the squirrel," The Eagle said and flapped away.

Odin puffed the Partagas. One didn't simply ignore The Norns, not even him. The thought of seeing them again this soon almost made him want to buy another car. He took another draw on the Black Label, and exhaled with a sigh.

Vanaheim:

The narrow tunnel was well lit. Oil lamps burned making Holli think of the late eighteen hundreds. She felt like a cross between Sherlock Holmes and one of The Charmed Ones. Most likely Piper. Her Leo, in other words Lennie, battled on the front line, and she would go in for the rescue. Lennie you better come through this alive or so help me I will kill you myself and haunt the shit out of you. You do your part out there Lennie, and I will do mine, rescuing the babies.

Freya stopped, and Holli halted behind her. The Goddess grasped her belt and uttered some words Holli couldn't understand. Light flashed and over Ljosalfheim the Northern Lights danced in green lines. The signal sent the teams of Operation Hail-Smash could attack.

The two women kept moving twisting and turning as the secret passageway crafted by master dwarves, led them under the mountain toward their destination. They were almost there. They reached an old door covered in black mold with rusty hinges. This door led into Loki's stronghold. They held their breath, waited, and listened.

Ljosalfheim:

The zombie snowmen kept falling to pieces and rising again. The Displacer-giants waited on the outskirts of the flurry of flying snow and blood. They would finish the job if the snowmen couldn't.

When The Northern Lights danced in the sky, the teams of moose and valkyries hit the plateau and raced toward Loki's fortress. Jolisa's team came on with the battering ram ready to do some damage. Jari and Hild's teams were ready to send hail stones into that castle like it had never seen.

*

The Aurochs slammed his leg into another Zombie-snowman. The thing's middle section obliterated and it stopped moving, momentarily. With his other leg he repeated the procedure, and then ducked his head and raised it up with one of the things on each horn. He threw them over his shoulder without a second thought moving forward.

His mind dwelled in the realm of physics most of the time, what would happen if he could get motion to harness power? Currently his mind was not theoretical science, but biology. Trajectory pointed him at the main gate, he needed to get this task over with, he had other things to do. Defecating being of the foremost importance followed by eating some nice grasses and chewing his cud. With those thoughts in mind, he wished to get this triviality out of the way. He bucked a few more of his pesky opponents out of the way, the doorway loomed before him.

If two stars collided? Smashed together and we could actually physically see the event, that would be fireworks! That was gonna happen now when he smacked into that gate. If Loki, God of whatever, had computerized the thing to have whatever electrical effect, the Aurochs might feel a tingle as he laughed it off. Did Loki have any clue how old he was?

When the Aurochs hit the door, The Beast of Frost plummeted backward and slammed onto the ground. His fingers sprang open, and he lost his grip on his huge bladed weapons that sort of resembled swords. He didn't feel the impact of the fall but knew that layers of ice armor shattered away from his trunk. Just part of the deal, not consequential, nothing to be upset over. Time to get up with a vengeance though. Numerous Zombie-snowmen loomed over his prostrate form, ready to deliver death blows; three of them raised their scythes and brought them down. The blades flashed, flickering silver streaming downward.

The weapons slammed down on virgin earth because Lennie moved, he knew that this story didn't have that kind of ending. With both of his legs he kicked while arching himself upward off the ground. His feet connected with his enemies, and his root like toes borrowed through the snow fiends midsections, it looked like confetti blasted forth from their backs.

On his feet again, The Beast of Frost grabbed two fallen scythes to use as his new weapons. He adeptly swung them, and on both sides of him opponents found themselves headless. They had a horde of Zombie-snowmen behind them, the Beast of Frost turned to face their foes as The Aurochs smacked his head into the door a second time.

"DRAGSAROF!" The battle cry deafened the land from The Beast of Frost, and he and The Aurochs charged back the way they'd just come, piling up bodies in their wake.

*

From my Control Room:
WTF. WTF! I calmed myself. NP, I got this dawg! I directed my snow minions at the attackers with the catapults. I directed the Displacers at the battering ram. I reinforced the front door with another dose of voltage.

I wondered what Old One Eye was thinking about at this moment? The old bastard. I respected him, even if he happened to be out of touch with modern technology, so I put on a Black Sabbath song in his honor. So old school, old, old, old.

Once upon a time there was a phantom heater that attacked a crazy cat lady, do we need a punch line? She might have been under the influence of certain substances at the time? Maybe? IDK, but I was under attack. Need to focus. I got this. Where is my energy drink?

I needed some good music, I put on some TerraFormist. Much better. Wait for the drop. There it is! Power up! A new shield formed around my front door, and my army's weapons increased to grenade power on impact. Fuck yeah dude. Where is that energy drink?

You want to know about the crazy cat lady? So this phantom heater, she thought that it was a living animal. There is my energy drink.

I knew that my mother wouldn't let her precious cats be held captive forever. Why now? Damn and I was looking at anime porn and eating Funions. Freya knew battle tactics; it reasoned that the two at the front gate were merely a diversion for the others? What else though? She should be bringing more, this all seemed a feign; what was I missing? Nothing more entered my realm, so clearly not more cannon fodder but what?

*

Jari's team raced across the open ground, followed by Hild's. Four twelve foot tall creatures holding massive battle axes came forward to meet them. Thor crashed into the first one with his rack. Nearly jolted off, Jari grabbed on to her lines tighter and clamped her knees inward. The giant flew backwards from the collision. Jari smiled, she'd named her moose well.

Steepter deadlocked with another giant as they clashed together and the creature grabbed his rack. They pushed against each other, neither gaining the advantage. A third Giant slashed at Rich before he could react and moose blood sprayed a bright crimson mist into the air. The Giant slashed again and again. Rich's body hung as dead weight in his harness, and his catapult smashed into pieces as it hit the ground.

"You cock sucking scat head!" Jari yelled at the giant. She knew firsthand what these things were capable of though, and her team knew the risks of the mission. Unfortunately that meant they were down one catapult. She would mourn Rich later; now she needed to stay focused.

Rare attacked before the Giant could react; his antlers impaled the creature all along its middle piercing vitals and blood splattered the area. Rare tossed the thing's corpse away as if it weighed no more than a bale of hay. The dead giant hit the ground twenty yards away with a thud.

Winston bit down on a third giant's arm, and the appendage snapped off like a stubborn branch in his teeth. Blood droplets coated Winston as they gushed from the hole where the giant's arm had been. Winston tossed his huge rack into the giant's head. The thing's skull exploded like a melon hit by a sludge hammer. Winston snorted, I told you.

Silver flashed, and a spear punched through the head of the giant locked with Steepter. The Valkyries were not going to allow any more of their catapults to be destroyed. Two more spears pierced the giant that Thor had knocked down, ending its life.

The sky rained spears. The fourth giant assailing Jari's team and the four closing on Hild's team perished by steel. The two teams set up at the perfect distance for the most effective catapult range.

"FOR ASGARD!" Their war cry rang out along with the thrumming of their first volley of hailstones. The hail smashed into Loki's stronghold. BOOM! BOOM! BOOM! BOOM! BOOM!

*

Four huge Giants ran toward the team. Jolisa didn't flinch; she'd fought Giants before. Her team just needed to plow through them. Jack smacked the first one out of the way as if it were a fly. Allen, Rudy, and Sam did likewise, nothing would hinder them. Jolisa executed the exercise just at they'd practiced, the battering ram swung into the fortress. The entire team felt the reverberation as the stones shook. They turned and trotted back, to repeat their rehearsed drill a second time.

Four more giants appeared and slashed with their axes. Terry, Gus, and Chris went down fighting before Mike, Craig, Brandon, and Zirkle impaled the new foes on their antlers.

Jolisa cut the harness lines. She touched each of the fallen wishing them well in The Summerland. Her twelve moose team became a nine moose team. They could still swing the battering ram. They WERE smashing in!

"Let's do it again Boys!" She yelled.

Asgard:

Hailstones crashed into Zombie-snowmen, and they didn't rise again. Stones rained down on Loki's place sending sparks into the night air. From where he stood watching, Odin smiled. He wanted to keep watching, but knew he needed to visit the sisters three. He turned away from his viewing pool, and went to harness Sleipner.

*

Under Ljosalfheim:

The booming overhead commenced. Time to go. Freya opened the door and she and Holli entered the crypt under Loki's fortress. They moved cautiously forward every muscle taunt in anticipation of attack.

Freya's instincts hadn't failed her. If Loki knew the crypt existed he hadn't bothered to protect it, most likely dismissing its importance. They encountered no resistance, and reached a set of stairs leading upward.

At the top of the staircase they opened another door into the cell block. It wasn't a dungeon with straw and rats, the cell block floor and walls were white and flooded with light. The cells themselves were fashioned of some clear glass like substance.

"Mom!" Stan yelled. Holli put her finger to her lips and kept watch. Freya grasped her belt and chanted. Blue rays of light shot in all directions striking the cells. The clear walls evaporated hissing and bubbling.

"Mjolnir!" Thor held out his hand. The door at the other end of the cell block caved in as the hammer flew to his waiting hand.

"Now Brother, you will know pain!" Thor said running through the decimated door, back the way his hammer pounded through.

Bygul and Thornir jumped to Freya and rubbed against her legs. Freya petted each of their heads. She tensed and waited, watching for any forthcoming threat.

"Mom, Lennie got sucked into a vortex. He said to tell you that the table cloth wasn't his fault," Peter said. Yes these were her real children; she nodded to Freya.

Holli knelt down and Stan and Peter ran to her, and the three of them hugged. Holli kissed the tops of their heads, tears of joy streaming down her cheeks. TooLu watched. Holli waved her over, and she joined the embrace.

*

Control Room:

"Cunty Valkyries! Try this!" Loki frantically punched keys. Lazers blasted from his ballistae. One of them burned through Hild, killing her instantly as it carried her eighty yards back off her sled. Another killed the moose Winston when it stuck his head. Three more blasted Valkyries loading hailstones into the catapults.

The door smashed open. Loki looked up from his screen to see his brother, Thor, standing there. Game Over! He hit auto fire on his ballistae, and after that tapped the Esc key, before standing up to face Thor. The Fortress began shaking.

*

"Staley isn't here?" Holli asked.

"She never was," Peter explained.

"We need to find her," Holli said.

"Follow Thor," Stan said. Freya took the lead, followed by her cats. The others followed them through the door, down the hall, and up a long flight of stairs. The steps violently shook and the walls began collapsing.

Thofnir sprinted ahead of the group and found Staley. Thofnir roared out their location. The rest of the group caught up with the cat. Holli hugged Staley tight to her chest. They all held on to each other as Freya uttered some words of magic. In a flash of light they teleported from Ljosalfheim.

*

The teams saw the pillar of light and knew the signal to retreat, the mission completed. Jari cut the harness as tears streamed down her cheeks. They couldn't pull dead weight.

"Goodbye, Winston," she choked, and climbed onto her sled. Her team had started with eight, and now they were six. Time to go.

Jari flicked her reigns, "Mush," she commanded and her team started running back over their trail.

*

"On Jack! Take us home Boys," Jolisa shouted and they headed back up the mountainside.

Randgrid took Hild's place. There would be time to honor the dead later, but right now they needed to get out of here. The team responded following Jari's team.

*

The Beast of Frost and The Aurochs saw the pillar of light. Success. They continued to hack through the army of enemies making for a portal that opened at the far end of the plateau. The circle of swirling blues and greens, would take them out of the realm of Ljosalfheim.

Four giants stood in front of the portal. The Auroch reared and kicked the first one in the face. It went down with a thud in a shower of blood from a broken skull. The second the Ancient Ox gored and flung aside. The Beast of Frost raised the two scythes dripping with blood and slashed downward in an X motion. The two decapitated giants flopped headless to the ground.

The Beast of Frost and The Aurochs jumped into the portal. It closed behind them, and the two warriors were transported to the pine forest just outside Freya's hall.

*

Thor had no intention to kill Loki; he just wanted the trickster in pain. He threw Mjolnir. The hammer passed through Loki or rather the image of Loki. Loki appeared farther back in the room. The floor tilted as the fortress crumbled. Both of the brothers slide down along the plummeting floor. Thor let the momentum carry him forward and swung at Loki's kneecap. Loki screamed as his kneecap exploded.

"You fucktard, what did you do that for!" Loki screamed at Thor.

"That one was for Jari. The next is for me," Thor bellowed and swung again. The hammer smacked the tile floor where Loki had been, but he was gone.

"This isn't over, Loki!" Thor yelled and pointed Mjolnir skyward. Thor shot into the air, smashing through a window and flew for his mother's hall.

He landed in the pines outside and put a huge wad of Copenhagen in. He walked in thought among the evergreens spitting every few strides. At least he'd smashed one of Loki's knees; that ought to slow his brother down for some time. Too bad he hadn't gotten both of them.

*

Jari knew the hall would be crowded with bodies pressed close together in celebration. She didn't really like people all that much; especially large groups of people packed in a small space. If she needed to endure the company of another person, she preferred just one and only for a small amount of time. She knew she was stalling like a child who didn't want to go to bed, but she didn't care. She patted each member of her team as they ate.

"Nice breasts," Thor said, watching Jari.

"It suddenly smells like bacon, hello Officer Odinsson," she returned.

"Not bacon, you are smelling roast boar," Thor spit tobacco juice.

"I might kiss you if you didn't have your mouth full of shit," Jari smiled.

"Jari Anderson, let's go have a drink," Thor said.

"Trying to get me drunk and take advantage of me?" Jari raised an eyebrow.

"With breasts like that I'd be crazy not to," he said.

Chew be damned, "Fuck it," she thought and ran into his arms and kissed him. Thor carried her into the feast hall.

Sessrumnir:

Smoke carried the scent of roasting boar with it as it wafted through the feasting hall. Peter focused on not drooling in front of TooLu. It smelled delicious and he couldn't remember the last time he'd eaten. He turned his attention to the two huge fireplaces at each end of the room. They blazed brightly giving the room light and providing heat simultaneously. Fire, a beautiful thing.

Mugs were raised again and again toasting various stages of Operation Hail-Smash.

OTHALA

Alaska:

The Northern Lights danced, green undulating waves. A flash of red with purple edges appeared in the night sky. The flash only lasted three seconds then it was gone, maybe a caribou saw it? The Northern Lights bowed and they were gone from the sky too.

Holli, Lennie, Stan, Peter, Staley, TooLu, and Jari landed in the driveway to Jari's trailer. Edna, Muka, and Gerard opened the door to great them. Muka jumped on TooLu licking her face, tail wagging. Gerard wagged his tail too as he sat in front of Jari.

"I missed you, you sexy beast," she told him.

Edna motioned for everyone to come in the house. They all entered to the smell of simmering stew, fresh baked bread, and smoke from the wood stove. Despite the negative twenty degrees outside, they were all warm in the house. TooLu helped Edna serve everyone food. She didn't have to be asked three hundred times or even once to help, that is just what you did. Around a mouthful of stew, Jari explained that in the morning she would go get the homestead deed transferred to Lennie and Holli. She'd tell a tale of leaving for the lower forty-eight.

Jari asked Edna if she could use her truck in the morning. She nodded, and Jari went to plug it in. When temperatures were below zero sometimes car batteries would freeze, plugging them in heated them so they would crank over.

In the morning, Jari, Lennie, and Holli brushed the snow and ice off Edna's old truck. It started right up after being plugged in all night. They drove into town to transfer the deed. Lennie and Holli acquired their third home since they got together.

Holli, Jari, and Gerard stood in the driveway.

"Strange how things work out," Jari commented to Holli.

"Yes," Holli agreed, "I can't thank you enough…"

"Freya told me what you did for Arsinoe. What comes around goes around. Watch Gerard for me won't you?" Jari said.

"Absolutely," Holli said.

"I'll miss you Sexy Beast," she told Gerard as she petted him. He licked her hand. In a flash of light she disappeared to resume her place with the Valkyries.

*

That night Edna slept on the couch. TooLu slept with the two dogs near the wood stove. The boys shared the small room that Jari had used as a catch-all room. And Staley slept peacefully in the room that Lennie and Holli shared. Everyone fit in the small trailer. They had piled extra wood in the stove before bed.

Holli and Lennie huddled together under the covers wearing night clothes even under the blankets. They warmed up, and Lennie inhaled the smell of his wife's hair and body. His member rose with desire, and he tried to caress Holli's breasts.

"No, I can't," she said pulling away from him.

"Why not? We haven't since you left for London," Lennie said.

"I can't, not since…" Holli began crying. Lennie threw off the covers and sat up in frustration.

"Loki, if you've ruined my sex life, I will kill you!" Lennie ground his teeth.

"I'm sorry. I love you. I, I, was…" Holli sobbed.

"I know what happened. When Loki held me prisoner I had to watch," Lennie said. He walked around the bed and kissed Holli's forehead.

"Not your fault. I love you too," he said.

LOL

Lennie walked out of the bedroom, and near the stove pulled on his boots, coat, gloves, and hat. He opened the door and the dogs bolted outside in front of him. He watched them do their business and began sniffing around the yard. Too bad Greedy couldn't join them.

The Norwegian followed Muka and Gerard along the edge of the property wondering what they smelled. This land he walked was theirs now; Jari gave it to them. The wood piles astounded Lennie, Thor hadn't half-assed it. The Working Man's God, Lennie almost smiled thinking of Thor, but his thoughts returned to Loki.

"Fuck you Loki!" He said into the still night. He heard snow crunching behind him; Holli put her arms around his waist.

"Don't be mad because I can't put out right now. I still love you. You have no idea how much," she said.

"I understand; I'm still pissed and frustrated though," he answered.

"I could give you a hand job," she offered.

"Could you make coffee instead?" he asked.

"Yes," she answered. He turned her offer down, that wasn't a good sign. Edna slept in the living room, but if what her husband really wanted was coffee she would make it for him, since she couldn't do the other.

"Good. I'm gonna split some of this wood into smaller pieces for the stove," Lennie said picking up Jari's old splitting maul.

Each time a log splintered into smaller pieces it made Lennie feel a little better. There was some satisfaction in the doing of the task. Hail Thor! Crack, split, a few more pieces for the stove. Odin grant me guidance in this new home. Crack, split. It began snowing. Crack, split.

"Coffee is ready, Husband," Holli called walking toward him.

"You're awesome," Lennie said setting down the maul and accepting a steaming cup.

"It is beautiful here," she said.

"A bit like Norway," he answered sipping the coffee.

"Feels like home to me," Holli said.

"Where you are is my home," Lennie smiled at his beautiful wife. Holli hugged him again.

"Don't leave me because I'm damaged," Holli pleaded.

"You will heal. Afraid you are stuck with me," Lennie responded. The dogs rushed the door and looked at it. Time to go in.

JERA

Alaska:

Staley Moon turned four. Holli guessed she'd baked a wonderful cake as she watched everyone devouring it. She didn't feel cramped in the little trailer with everyone and the dogs, and she knew that Lennie would expand their home. When Staley finished smearing frosting over her face Holli picked her up and hugged and kissed her.

Lennie chopped down trees. Thor had ensured that Jari had enough firewood to keep her little trailer toasty for a few winters, but Lennie intended to make some additions to the place to accommodate everyone with a little more space for comfort. As he swung the axe, he remembered working on Irvin's lake cabin. The sun rose as Holli came and gave him a kiss.

"Going for a walk, Handsome," she said.

"Looks like you are protected," Lennie said indicating the dogs as he leaned on the axe.

"Best guards ever," she smiled at him and walked toward the river. Lennie smiled at her backside, nice ass. His wife was so beautiful, getting hand fasted to her was the best thing he'd ever done.

*

Holli listened to the river for awhile and turned to walk with the smell of the birch trees in her nose. The dogs ran ahead sniffing the woods, alert for any danger that might present itself to one of their new feeders. Holli reflected that the boys and TooLu were doing well with the home schooling and that was worth the fact that

Loki's Laughter

Lennie and her were still wondering how they were going to pay off the computers the three of them used.

"Hiya neighbor," a voice called. At first Holli couldn't see the owner of the voice, but as Holli rounded three birch trees that grew out of one large trunk she discerned the caller.

"Hello neighbor," Holli returned, approaching.

"I have been watching you all the way," the woman in her forties said from where she stood on her second story porch.

"I couldn't see you till now," Holli said, creeped out at having been watched. Gerard sat at Holli's heels while Muka continued to sniff around. Holli shielded her eyes from the sun as she looked up at the woman.

"My name is Holli; this one is Gerard, and that one is Muka," she introduced.

"My name is Onnalee, come on up so you can see the view. Just go around, through the front and up the stairs. There is coffee on the counter if you want some," she said. Onnalee clearly wasn't leaving her porch, so Holli walked around the house. This woman wasn't the oddest person Holli ever met but bordered on very close.

Holli opened the front door, telling her faithful four legged friends to remain outside, and went up the teal carpeted stairs. She moved through the living area not taking it in, as her goal lay through it, bathed in golden light. Holli wasn't a coffee person, but her Lennie drank the bitter stuff by the gallon. What was with his taste buds anyway? He liked that awful Bass beer she'd drank for him in London, and bitter ass coffee. Something must be off with his bitter meter?

"Hello neighbor," Holli extended her hand.

"Don't be silly," the woman hugged Holli, "You moved in Jari Anderson's place. I recognize Gerard," Onnalee opened the conversation. Holli looked at her. Who was this woman that told her to walk through her house, hugged her, and wanted to know about the late owner of their place? She didn't feel comfortable telling this woman anything, she didn't think she trusted her.

"My husband's name is Lennie," she said.

"I think I've seen him chopping trees; now tell me what happened to Jari?" Onnalee persisted. The purple dye in Onnalee's hair didn't mask her gray, and lines were visible in her face in the sun's truthful blaze. Holli noticed that she didn't hold a coffee cup, but a glass that evidently held something else. Onnalee's breath confirmed that she'd been drinking before nine in the morning; she didn't deign it or make an excuse for it.

"Want a Jäger-Bomb?" Onnalee asked.

"Sounds better than coffee," Holli answered deciding she could trust the woman.

"I'll make you one, look at the view," Onnalee went inside her house. Holli took in the view. She could see their trailer to the left, in front of her the river glistened in the sun, and to her right mountains rose. The view indeed stunned her with nature's beauty in this harsh land.

Onnalee returned handing Holli a drink which smelled vile yet smiled at her at the same time through energy drink tingle.

"To friends. Call me Onna, not many folks in Alaska," Onnalee raised her glass.

"To friends," Holli returned the toast. They clinked glasses and downed the shots.

"Now tell me what happened to Jari?" Onnalee asked again.

"I'm not sure if you will believe the story," Holli said.

"Honey, I live in Alaska. You really think you can surprise me?" Onnalee raised an eyebrow.

"You better pour me another one of these things," Holli said, "Jari was sliced into three pieces fighting giants. Having died valiantly in battle, the Goddess Freya claimed Jari to become one of her Valkyries," Holli said.

"I'll get us each another one," Onnalee said.

*

It was Evenight so they woke the children at four in the morning. They started their festivities at five. Prior to their rite, Lennie and Holli set up an extremely hard Ostara egg hunt, knowing that five would participate. Peter, Stan, TooLu, Haley, and Amanda, the last two being the Onnalee's daughters aged twelve and seventeen. Lennie harbored mixed feelings toward the lady. On one hand he couldn't be happier; Holli acquired a friend. On the other hand, the woman drank excessively.

Lennie knew about drinking; he'd left a car, stumbled along with Greedy, and given away a wedding ring to a girl by a church. For five years he'd lived alone in a "cabin" in the Minnesota Boundary Waters, and most of the time he'd been drunk. He wasn't a stranger to the bottle; however, that didn't mean that he wanted his vibrant wife to follow that dark depressing road. He did want Holli to have a good friend though, not that Edna wasn't, she was, Lennie liked the Native woman.

Ice and snow still covered the ground, with more snow predicted, yet the birds sang songs of spring. Temperatures fluctuated between negative five and thirty five above. Soon what they called Breakup would happen in Alaska, and the world would become a mass of mud. Spring in Alaska, a short season, lasted about a month and a half from approximately late mid April till the beginning of June.

Summer for that matter lasted from about June to mid August. From mid August to the end of October was autumn, and then winter reigned. In Alaska winter lasted most of the year, approximately eight months, because "fall' might be as soon as the leaves fell to the ground.

Now spring filled the land even if latent under the thin layer of snow and ice that covered the earth. The land radiated warmth and birth. When the day reached its warmest temperatures ice turned into water and animals were became frisky.

A fire burned in the pit, and banners were hung to Odin, Freya, Thor, and Ostara roughly to the north of their area close to where the river burbled. Holli's homemade cookies covered a platter on one of the benches. Gathered around the fire were Lennie, Holli, their children, Edna, TooLu, Onnalee and her two daughters, and Gerard and Muka. Lennie raised his hands, looked all the guests human and canine and began.

"I bid thee to join in a celebration
Of the season of spring, and of new beginnings.
This is the time for all things new,
We Hail you Ostara, the awakening of the land."

Holli held up a bowl of seeds, presented it to the river, and passed it around the circle of humans. Everyone took one and ate it. She held out a handful to the two dogs who slobbered them off her palm. They spoke of family and hearth, health, and home, and ended the rite at which point the children took off in search of Ostara eggs.

At eight A.M., when the sun rose above the peaks of the The Valley, they put out the fire. The children had dropped into sleep about four thirty and Lennie carried them into the house. Muka stationed herself in front of the children's door while Gerard stayed next to the adults. Thus the Spring Equinox finished with the world was bathed in light from eight to eight, while darkness threw a cloak over the other twelve hours of a day. They thoroughly cleaned the house for the season.

Later that day it snowed, but it was a light spring snow, just pretending.

*

Lennie hoisted another of the logs he'd cut in the spring into place, his muscles straining, as sweat dripped off his hair onto his nose. In spite of the sweat he smiled to himself, thankful that this addition onto their trailer home was almost complete. Jari now ranked among Freya's Shield-Maidens; he knew she missed Gerard, but they would take good care of him. The smell of Onnalee's Marlboro Red gave her away.

"Onna, those things will kill you," Lennie said as he tucked homemade insulation between the log wall.

"I like the taste of death. I don't like it sugar coated; I prefer it raw," she exhaled.

"Let's go find Holli and have a drink," Lennie said wiping the sweat from his brow onto his jeans. Having a drink seemed like the thing to do in Alaska's summer heat.

Holli poured a double shot of Jack and diet Coke into glasses for the ladies and handed Lennie an Alaskan I.P.A. They toasted the land becoming green overnight.

*

Summer Sunstead, the Summer Solstice, Litha. June in Alaska, the temperature soared to seventy seven above. The family celebrated with a bonfire and gave thanks to the Gods.

It was light about twenty three hours of the day, the other hour merely an attempt at dusky gray. Now even at eleven P.M., the sun shinned as if it were noon. Ignoring this fact Holli lit candles and handed them to the children including TooLu and Onnalee's girls.

"Place these candles
About the edge of our ritual area,
So that the Great Ones
May be with us," Lennie said. When all the candles were stuck in the earth in a semi circle because they couldn't complete it due to the cliff and the river, Lennie continued.

"Friends, I now bid thee
To join in a celebration
Of the season of Midsummer…"

…Holli was about to say, "Let us now remember the Earth, Mother of All," when Onna collapsed. They got her into Edna's old mottled rusty truck and brought her to Mat-Su Regional. Four days later she was released after having been diagnosed with COPD and having a hysterectomy performed. Despite her age and lack of a male participant, the Alaskan woman grieved the fact that she could no longer bear children or smoke. Nothing like a fucking double whammy.

"Told you to give up them death sticks," Lennie said holding Holli's hand as they walked along the wheelchair as the nurse wheeled Onnalee out to their waiting truck.

"Fuck you, Sweat-Monger," Onna told Lennie as she held Holli's other hand. A few days of bed rest later, Onna felt better as she stood on her porch and watched the golden leaves fall onto the river. Soon it would be August, which meant the State Fair in Palmer. As wonderful as the fair was for the economy unfortunately it announced the end of Alaska's brief summer and the advent of its even briefer autumn.

"Here's to ya," she said lifting her glass of Jack and diet Coke. She downed it feeling the burn as she lamented the fact that she could no longer enjoy a cigarette along with her drink or have more children. She could however have another drink. If Holli stopped by later she'd offer her one, and if she didn't stop by that meant all the more Jack for her.

Holli stopped by, and that was even better as she needed the company. Onna watched the young woman's body as Holli poured drinks for them. Onna wished she could be the bottle and feel Holli's hands on her body.

*

By the end of August, Lennie's additions were finished. Three extra rooms, one for the boys, one for Edna and TooLu, and one to serve as a "study room" for the children. In his spare time, Lennie fished and hunted for the family's food. TooLu and he exchanged fishing techniques and learned from each other. Edna and Holli prepared meals and learned cooking secrets from each other. The boys found living in Alaska boring.

The family celebrated the Autumnal Equinox, Haligmonath. It was a thanksgiving and they made offerings to the Gods for luck and health. They talked about the cycle of life. When their feast finished Holli and Lennie kissed while listening to the river.

Lennie found work at a local gas station. Holli continued drinking, not a social drink here and there, but three quarters of a fifth of Jack Daniels blackout pass out kind of drinking. Lennie stood behind the counter at the cash register when his cell phone rang.

"Hello Love," he answered.

"Hi, Hi," Holli slurred.

"What's going on," he asked.

"I'm, I'm drunk," she announced.

"Sounds like it," he returned.

"You're mad at me!" Holli said.

"No Dear, I'm just at work," he said quietly.

"So, so some guys stopped by on a four wheeler. They said they are having a Decanter, can I go?" she asked,

"No," he answered.

"You are mad at me. Mad at me for drinking," her voice declared that he was at fault even though he wasn't the one drunk and asking to go to a college fraternity party.

"Holli, you know what a Decanter is, right?" Lennie asked.

"Sure, sure, just a place to have a drink or two," she answered.

"No it is the kind of party where everyone drinks till they sleep with someone," he explained.

"Can I go?" she asked oblivious to or ignoring his explanation.

"I said no," he repeated.

"You are mad at me 'cause I'm drinking!" she screamed.

"I'm not mad because you are drinking. What I'm not doing is giving you permission to go fuck around on me with some drunk ass frat boy!" Lennie yelled.

"Fuck you!" Holli hung up on him.

That night his boss fired him. He walked in the house prepared to scream at Holli. She was passed out on the couch. Lennie picked her up and carried her to their bedroom, and tucked her in instead. In the morning, he told her he'd been fired.

LOL

The leaves fell, and the snow line moved down the mountainsides. Gone were fifty degree days replaced with twenty degree days. The Week of the Spirits passed in two feet or more of snow. Winter arrived heralded by howling winds, more snow, and negative twenty-two degree days.

Lennie visited the library and found something that looked interesting so he checked it out. He brought home the hardcover of *Mistborn* by Brandon Sanderson and started reading. The pages flew by as he experienced the amazing characters and world that Sanderson created. He needed to get the second book, the character Vin was a bad-ass.

Holli couldn't get Tab in Alaska so she switched to Dr. Pepper Ten and read everything by Yasmine Galenorn.

*

Somewhere in the wild:

Bob Muldoon watched the idiot walking. The man wasn't dressed properly, and he carried a spear. A spear! Maybe the elements would kill this joker? Alaskan winter didn't allow stupidity. Bob hoped like hell the man was stoned; it would give him an inch of an excuse.

Bob continued to watch the man with the spear. He tracked something, the idiot thought he was hunting with a spear, and he was the furthest thing from a Native, whiter than white this one with long blond hair and flashing blue eyes. Who did he think he was, hunting with a spear? A spear, Bob found it amusing…really stoned.

The man slowed, and stood silent. Bob cursed himself as he held his breath, unfortunately he wished all hunters luck, even this one. Quick, effortless, fluid, motion as the hunter tensed, ran three steps, and threw the spear. The weapon flashed in the pale sunlight and killed its quarry, a large beaver that Bob failed to see earlier. I'll be, Bob thought, one lucky stoner. Bob hated talking; most people were complete idiots, this one being no exception even if he was lucky. However Bob couldn't forgive himself if the man froze to death in his lack of protective clothing.

Lennie grinned as he cleaned the blood off his spear, now the family could eat. Lennie heard a twig snap and turned his attention that direction. A man gave an "I mean no harm" wave as he approached. The man wore huge white boots and carried a rifle which he clearly knew how to use. He looked about forty, although his full bushy white beard might throw that number off. He reached Lennie, and took off his hat revealing a bald head, and he pulled off one of his gloves extending his hand.

Lennie rose from his crouch and shook his hand. The man's hand knew labor, huge and calloused, his grip strong and firm. The handshake expressed to Lennie that the man was honest. Lennie trusted him even though they hadn't said a word, and it seemed that Lennie would have to break the ice as the man hadn't introduced himself.

"Name's Lennie Odinsson," he said.

"Not dressed right," Bob nodded at Lennie's clothing.

"I'll have to get a pair of boots like yours." Lennie agreed "Say, do you know how to gut this thing?" Lennie asked indicating his beaver.

"Let me show you the joys of skinning a beaver. Fatty little bastards," Bob said as he took out his knife.

*

Wasilla:

The first thing shut off were their cell phones. They used every cent they had to purchase baking staples, and keep the electric on for the children's schooling, other than that the household became subsistence based for the winter. Activities centered around heat and food. They heated with the wood stove. The family brought the wood into the house by way of a human assembly line. Lennie and TooLu hunted and fished. As the winter progressed, they taught Peter how to do both, Stan had no interest in learning either activity.

The women of the house had spent a few months mastering the art of candle making. So when they celebrated Yule and The Festival of Lights in honor of Freya the homemade candles flickered throughout the house.

January brought more wind and even colder temperatures. Now daylight lasted about five hours a day from ten in the morning to three in the afternoon, otherwise the land remained in darkness but for the pale moonlight.

The winter stretched on. Holli read the same three books over and over as she sobered up without the means to buy alcohol. Lennie worked at reading a book, and it took him all winter as he'd fall asleep after making it only partway through the same paragraph most nights.

Everyone had eaten enough wild game and fish to last them centuries.

"Mom, is there anything good to eat?" Stan complained.

"Hold on let me just…no dear there isn't any GOOD food. But what we have will keep us alive," she said.

"Sure could go for a nice greasy pizza right about now. Gooey cheese and spicy pepperoni on some nice tomato sauce with a crust coated in butter and garlic," Peter expounded.

"Oh will you shut up," TooLu rounded on him.

"No fighting in the house. If you too want to scrap, take it outside," Holli said.

"I'm gonna have to get a job. I miss my beer and Mountain Dew," Lennie put in his two cents.

"Edna, may we use your truck to go to the food bank?" Holli asked.

Edna nodded yes.

*

Still the cold and snow lingered. Yet spring filled the air. The bird song changed and the weather warmed. It still snowed, but during the day temperatures rose into the forties. The trees seemed to be ready to burst into bloom. The air felt lighter, daylight stayed longer and longer each day.

Staley Moon turned five. The Spring Equinox came again. They'd survived their first year in Alaska.

ISA

Alaska:

Lennie carefully walked across the ice on the river. He looked for weak spots knowing that if he fell through he could freeze to death. Once he reached the middle where the ice was the thickest he drilled a hole with his auger.

The world was silent other than the sound of the river running beneath the ice. Lennie baited his hook and dropped a line in. He felt bottom and the tug of the current. He slowly reeled.

By the light of the moon as he fished Lennie beheld the beauty of the landscape around him. Pine and birch trees coated with a thick layer of snow. The green of the pines showed where the wind had cleared snow and the contrasting white and black bark of the birch. He loved Alaska, the sky had layers of color at sunrise there were variations of grays, blues and whites. At sunset there were lines of light blue, pink and fire lit amber descending into the horizon behind the stark naked black trees.

An hour later Lennie pulled up his hook again. The fish weren't biting here, time to try another spot. Lennie began walking on the frozen river; maybe around the bend he would find a better hole.

He heard something. It sounded like a cry for help? Lennie strained his eyes and quickened his pace to a jog. No sign of his quarry yet, but the cry came again a little louder he must be getting closer.

"Help! Help!"

Lennie heard the distress call clearly now. He increased his pace again running through the six inches of fresh snow covering the layer of ice on the river. At last he saw the little girl hanging from a tree trunk partially submerged in the river. She must have walked out on it and slipped. Lennie put down his auger and pole and ran forward.

"I'll help you," Lennie called out. Focused on reaching the girl, Lennie didn't hear the ice cracking. Underneath the trunk, Lennie looked up at the little girl, and knew he could catch her.

"Let go, and I'll catch you," he told her as the ice gave way underneath him.

The river sucked Lennie under before he could react. He tried frantically to gain some hand hold but there was nothing solid, nothing stationary all turbulent and tumbling. He shut his mouth and held his breath as he battered against rocks with the current. Above him the white of the frozen river was visible, but he couldn't reach it.

The water varied in color from green to brown, and Lennie knew he would freeze to death if he couldn't surface. He tried to swim to punch the ice above him, but the current was too strong and carried him along. He tried to grab a root, a rock, anything, but his fingers slipped off them.

Lennie couldn't hold his breath any longer he expelled air and water rushed in filling his lungs. His brain registered that he was freezing to death, yet he didn't feel cold; he must be past that point. Lennie's two last thoughts were that he had failed to save the little girl and failed to bring food home to Holli and the kids.

At My Computer:

LOL

Some people just never learn. Lennie didn't remember his father's message, did he? Know thy enemy. The girl, merely an illusion of mine. I placed the illusion where I knew the ice would break. That is what he gets. He should have been paying attention, but his human need to help brought about his demise. It almost makes me cry, no not really. Stupid fool that one. That is what you get. I have the last laugh.

LOL

Huston, Alaska:

Bob Muldoon saw the body washed up on the bank. Bob would have to tell someone, and have them call the troopers. He didn't consider himself smart; he liked living simply by trapping and living off the land by himself in his cabin. He debated dragging the body further up the bank, but didn't want to touch it in case he muddled up some investigation the Troopers would need to do.

Well it looked like the body would stay put. He walked back to his snow machine and drove it to Millers. He went in and asked for Ruth; she came to the counter.

"Ruth, you better call the troopers. I found a body on the bank of the Little Sue," he explained.

"Will do, Bob. Can I get you anything while you wait for them?" she asked.

"Burger and coffee," he answered taking a seat. Ruth placed the call, and went to make him a burger.

Dimitra Giovanni walked into Millers. Bob rose to meet her, nodding his hello.

"Morning Ruth, Bob," she greeted.

"Morning D," Ruth answered.

"Jump in the cab, Bob, and you can lead me to the site," Dimitra said. Bob headed for her truck.

Bob led her to the body. She pulled on gloves and pulled the body up onto the bank. They looked at the body. He hadn't been old. Bob recognized that blond hair, and was fairly certain he'd watched this idiot kill a beaver with a spear. Bob wished he were wrong.

"Any clue who he was, Trooper?" the grizzled trapper asked. Dimitra looked at Bob. Strange. She'd never heard him speak before. Unfortunately, she thought she knew the answer to his question; some days she hated her job.

"Kinda looks like the new fella moved into Jari Anderson's old place. Thanks for notifying us. I'll bring you back to Millers," Giovanni said. After dropping Bob off she drove back toward Wasilla.

The sun painted the clouds periwinkle as it rose behind the mountains bringing a new day to The Valley. Above Pioneer Peak the clouds were veined with orange dragon fire and the songs of mining dwarves floated on the wind with whips of snow spraying off the peak. What was she doing thinking about dragons and dwarves, it was gonna be a long day.

*

Holli answered the knock on the door. An Alaskan state trooper stood outside. Holli wondered why in the world an officer was calling.

"You and your husband move in about a year ago?" The trooper asked.

"Yes. Are we already in some trouble?" Holli asked.

"No."

"May I help you?"

"Unfortunately I hope so. Can you come with me?" Dimitra asked. Gods what now, Holli wondered pulling on her coat. She grabbed her hat and gloves and sat down in the trooper truck. Lennie hadn't returned from fishing; she hoped he hadn't gotten into some sort of trouble. Dimitra reversed out of their driveway, put the truck in drive and they were on their way to Huston.

"Are you going to tell me what this is all about Officer?" Holli asked.

"Need to see if you can make a positive I.D. on a body," Giovanni answered all business.

No mistaking her husband, Holli just nodded as her tears flowed. Dimitra couldn't let Holli take the body home, as there were regulations against public burial. Holli explained that they had no money, and the authorities should do what needed to be done with the body. Officer Giovanni drove Holli home. As if in a dream state Holli closed the trailer door.

"Lennie is dead; he drowned," she told everyone. They spent days cutting pine boughs and gathering rocks for their service. They placed the rocks in the shape of a ship on the cliff by the riverside. Holli memorized her words and with the bonfire the boys built blazing, she said them.

> We call upon Allfather Odin,
> Mighty Thor, and Mother Freya,
> To receive Lennie Odinsson,
> One we have loved.
> Welcome him in the emerald gardens and golden halls,
> Of high Valhalla.

She paused and felt snow land on her nose. Lennie would have laughed at her. She continued:

> Friends, let us now fashion,
> In the ancient way
> Of our ancestors,
> The ship that shall travel
> Between the worlds,
> With the soul of our loved one.
> His time with us was too short,
> Receive him with our loving payers,
> That when we may meet him again,
> In your presence with joy and laughter,
> In the shining lands.
> Shall our beloved be one with Mother Freya,

With Hearty Thor,
With Allfather Odin.
Farewell, good friend
We will meet again,
Until then, may the Gods be with thee.

They all took up pine boughs and brought them to the fire. Holli choked back tears and finished.

"As the tree is green forever,
So may thy soul live to eternity."

Stan elbowed Peter and pointed as two ravens took flight.

INGWAZ

At The Roots:
    "Where is that little rascal Ratatosk?" Urdr wondered.
    "Hear he likes Sriracha peas," Skuld put in..
    "He will come," Verdandi coughed.
    "Well we don't have all day," Urdr said.
    "Really?" Skuld said.
    "No?" Verdandi raised an eyebrow.
    "You want to feed him that bad?" Skuld asked her sister.
    "If it is all the same with you," Urdr said.
    "Knock yourself out," Skuld said and did a few dance steps.
    "Choices, choices, choices," Verdandi croaked.
    "Strands of the Web," Skuld said.
    "Feeding time," Urdr announced, and they headed outside.

Bifrost:
    Heimdall looked into each of the nine realms. He pulled his vision back to almost human range as his ears picked up skittering. Ratatosk would land and slide into his boot soon. A few heartbeats later the rodent jumped down and slid through the half inch of snow and thumped against his boot.
    "Hail Good Messenger!" Heimdall greeted.
    "Hail Good Watcher!" Ratatosk returned.

Cyberspace:
    Thor messed up my knee pretty damn good. I've fixed it now; I am a God you know. And the real shitty thing about the whole deal was the number of my Displacer-giants that they took

out. Displacer-giants come from the regular Displacers, and it takes them years to mature and evolve into giant form.

Now I'm listening to "Finding Beauty" by Craig Armstrong. It is about time for some Hot Cheetos and a Monster. Enough Craig, just enough. I'm gonna put on some Dubstep. Let me just hit this...

Sessrumnir:

Jolisa patrolled, riding on Jack's back as he stepped through the snow. Jack stopped to bust off a twig. Jolisa scanned the distance; she didn't perceive any threats. The sun shone and she removed her hat shaking out her hair, the day had warmed since she began patrolling.

Astoria:

Arsinoe ordered more supplies for Sif's Hearth. The store increasingly continued to grow. A few more patrons came each month; the business began to show a profit. Arsinoe put on a CD and lit incense. Maybe next month she would run a special on incense? Maybe even set up a website, the information highway?

Alaska:

As the fire crackled Peter stared into the flames. The two dogs sniffed in opposite directions along the cliff. Snow still covered the land, but Peter decided to build a fire anyway. He knew that he wasn't Lennie, and he didn't want the responsibility of being 'the man of the house', on the other hand he didn't want his mother finding some other man. She said she wouldn't, but Mom sometimes changed her mind.

Peter added more logs to his fire. He dusted snow off a few logs that had been set up as chairs even though he didn't want company. Shortly after he brushed the logs off, TooLu took a seat on one of them. Damn, shouldn't have done that.

Just what he didn't need. Peter found it hard to think when TooLu was in close proximity. Short and thin, she couldn't have weighed much, and her straight black hair hung just below her shoulders framing her eyes which always mocked him and her smile which didn't. Her teeth were very white in contrast to her hair, and her lips were a light pink.

    He inhaled the smell of burning birch and didn't speak on purpose. Restraint, not his forte, he forced himself to remain silent. If TooLu wished to talk she could initiate the conversation. He added another couple of logs to the fire and returned to his seat staring into the flames; he had a good hot coal bed.

    Peter never thought he'd miss Lennie so much. The man had been in constant motion. At one point Peter told him that he was a busy-body. Peter missed that now; Lennie constantly did mundane things for the household. He'd walked the dogs, split the wood into stove sized pieces, hunted, fished, shoveled, took out their garbage, burned anything that could be burned.

    The man had still found time to talk to the boys, and tell them how much they meant to him, and encouraged them to be who they were. Rarely did he demand anything of them, and when he did it was because he was stretched thin, and needed their help. He didn't overly criticize them, even when they may have deserved it, and he didn't discipline them like a 'normal' father would have. And he had loved their mother with all his heart. Peter never doubted his loyalty to the family, not even for a second, not ever. Lennie loved Staley, but never once had he loved her any more than Stan or him, and he knew they weren't even his biological sons.

    Damn you Lennie, how could you go and die! Shit man, I could have done more. Peter was getting choked up, but he tried to stifle his tears; he couldn't cry in front of TooLu. It was too much, enough was enough, what did he care what TooLu thought? He could no longer hold back the tears, or his thoughts.

    "Why? Why TooLu! What does anything matter? Fuckin' Lennie! Just go and die on us? Who has the right to take him away? The Gods, Fuck them! This isn't right," Peter ranted.

TooLu sat in silence for awhile looking at the tears streaming down Peter's face. Now wasn't the time to rip into him for calling her ugly, his pain trumped her trampled on feelings. He truly missed his step-father, and struggled with loss. She needed to keep him talking, and she wasn't a girl of a lot of words. Before Lennie died, TooLu had listened to Peter talk about all kinds of subjects. He talked about musical theory, the history of World War II, current events, physics, politics, and many other subjects that she didn't know anything about, it all flew over her head. She knew she wasn't stupid because she could teach him things he knew nothing about, like fishing, hunting, cooking, and, making dyes for wool. All that in mind, what could she say to offer comfort? That might come to her, for now, she would try to keep him talking, even if she didn't understand his answers.

"What is your best memory of Lennie?" she asked him.

"We were driving across the country and Mom, Staley, and Stan were sleeping. Lennie takes a drink of his Mountain Dew and says 'you know you are a musical genius, you should pursue that.' He puts down his can, smiles at me, and turns his eyes back to the road," Peter answered and continued, "Like an idiot I told him that I wanted to be a salesman and make tons of money. Lennie nodded, took another swig of his soda, and said 'Whatever you decide to do you will be good at,'" Peter finished and stared at his hands.

"So he believed that you would be good at whatever you set your heart on," TooLu extrapolated.

"Yes damn it. Yes! Damn! But he saw in me what I really want to do, and told me to do it, and now he isn't here and we need to pay the bills, heat the place, eat, and I don't want to be a salesman, all I want to do is play music, I don't care about money and maybe someday have a girlfriend who loves me for who I am," Peter spouted.

Nothing like thought overload, Peter was much deeper than TooLu gave him credit for. How could she respond to all this? She would respond in the only way she knew. She would be herself and try to console, and if it didn't work for Peter maybe at least sometime down the road he would know that she was as genuine as Lennie had been.

"Do you see the fire?" she began.

"Well of course I see the thing; I built it!" Peter answered.

"And do you hear the river?" TooLu continued ignoring his anger.

"Are you stupid? Yes I hear it," Peter threw his hands in the air. That was enough; TooLu only had so much patience. She was gonna lay it out there for his sake despite the fact that he'd called her stupid. This was his therapy session not hers. He needed to make music, and if that helped him grieve, heal, and move on, that is what he needed to do.

"Do you hear the creaking of the trees? You need to take the sound of the trees and the river and write your first song in honor of Lennie. After that you need to keep playing and making music for your own happiness, and then you might become the man that you think you so desperately need to be. Until you know who you are, you will never be able to be anything but a little boy. I shouldn't have been the one to tell you this, but there it is. After that, you need to know that I can hunt and fish so everyone will have food and someday even stupid Native TooLu could be a girlfriend who understands you," she rose and went to find Muka.

Holli and Stan stood in the kitchen. The sunlight came through the kitchen window and outside the temperature sat at about forty degrees. Holli cried, big tears dribbled down her cheeks. Stan hugged his mom.

"You're my best friend, Stan," Holli sobbed.

"You're mine too, Mom," Stan said.

"I don't even know what to do now?" Holli admitted to her son.

"Same thing you would do if Lennie were here, Mom. He wouldn't want you crying," Stan said.

"Right you are. The sun is shining; let's go outside," Holli said.

"Okay," Stan agreed. They went out into the sunlight and discovered TooLu transfixed watching Muka and Gerard engaging in some strange behavior. TooLu just pointed at the dogs.

"It is spring TooLu, Stan, guess we will see if we have puppies soon," Holli smiled thinking of the forthcoming fur-balls, picturing their coloring.

Cyberspace:

I put on some TerraFormist. Amazing shit. Not like crooning Bob Dylan old people stuff called poetry shit that so many so called hippies liked. Instead of all of those mumbled muscovite bits of rock, TerraFormist flowed fluently like flirtatious flittermice.

What next? I'm sitting here typing on my new laptop. My last one went down with the ship so to speak, like that 'unsinkable' ship which smashed into an iceberg. Something like that. I have a new computer, and I am checking on everyone, see if the violin player is still at it or what?

WUNJO

Cyberspace:
Ohlongjohnsonohlongjohnsonohlongjohnsonohlongjohnsonohlongjohnsonohlongjohnsonohlongjohnsonohlongjohnson.

Bifrost:
    Ratatosk slid on his belly through the water on The Rainbow Bridge and thumped into Heimdall's boot. The Watcher handed him a Sriracha pea. He popped it in his mouth, and shook off the water.
    "Why thank you Good Watcher," he said munching happily.
    "Most welcome Good Messenger," Heimdall answered.
    "That hit the spot," Ratatosk said rubbing his belly.
    "And how are you this fine day?" Heimdall asked.
    "Fine, thanks for asking. And you?" asked the rodent.
    "Good. Warming up," Heimdall replied.

Alaska:
    Holli bought Mumford and Sons. She wasn't a hundred percent sure if Lennie would have liked them or not, but she guessed he would have. She thought of them as a strange cross between Dave Matthews and Coldplay. She loved them, and she turned up the volume. Music made house cleaning almost tolerable. It remained daylight now for over seventeen hours. Holli found it hard to sleep, but it wasn't insomnia any longer, but natural energy from the sun keeping her in go mode.

EHWAZ

Holli chopped logs into quarters. It gave her something to focus on, and she knew it must be improving her upper body strength. She heard the thundering of a galloping horse and turned to see Odin and his eight legged steed land on the driveway kicking up gravel as they approached.

"Allfather, to what do I owe this visit?" Holli asked.

"Not the welcome I expected, Daughter," Odin said dismounting.

"Why would I want anything to do with a God who lets my husband die?" Holli clenched the splitting maul.

"Because Daughter, I'm here to help you. Lennie owes the Aurochs a debt. We are going to pay it off," Odin answered.

"Lennie's debt should have been settled upon his death. You may go without me," Holli said.

"Doesn't work that way. I will go away, but I'm leaving Sleipner here for you," Allfather answered giving the horse a pat, and wandering off into the birch trees.

Sleipner whinnied.

"What do you want?" Holli asked.

The horse flicked his mane and scattered flecks of silver dust into the air. The motion clearly meant, I'm ready climb on let's go.

"Go on after your master," Holli told him. He stood resolutely. Holli resumed her splitting. The horse watched her with a bored expression.

"Stubborn. I'm going in for the night, see you," Holli told the powerful eight legged creature.

A few hours later Holli grudgingly put her book down and tried to sleep. She couldn't, this didn't surprise her. Insomnia wasn't a stranger. She got out of bed, and threw a few more wood chunks onto the fire. She padded to the fridge, retrieved a can of soda, opened it, and took a swig. The state of the mess in the house reached atrocity level, but Holli didn't care at the moment.

She opened the door to see if the damn horse was still there. He was.

"What are you still doing here?" she asked walking out to him. Sleipner looked at her with his mercury colored eyes that glinted with intelligence.

"Go on, get out of here. I'm female; I will win the stubborn contest," Holli told him and went back inside.

In the morning he was still there. Damn. Holli took a shower. She made coffee for Lennie. She should have had sex with him that night, but anyone touching her felt like the oily phantom touch of Clayton, even though she hadn't been conscience to feel him. Lennie asked for coffee instead of a hand job... she shook her head and looked out the window. Sleipner remained. Damn, damn, damn.

She absently took a sip of the cup of coffee she'd poured for Lennie. She knew he wasn't there to drink it but just the smell of it reminded her of him. He'd always drank it black. The bitterness overcame her.

"Ugh! How the hell did you drink this crap? Even beer is better, at least that will get you drunk!" She put his cup down and shut off the pot. Tea beat coffee too.

Think Holli, think. Lennie told her he needed to get something for The Ox. What? She hadn't been listening to him; she'd been looking at his kind beautiful eyes, and not listening to his words. Although she nodded to look like she followed him. Remember now what did the ancient beast want?

Ring? Ring of something...The Ring of Taurus. Taurus, as in the astrological bull? She needed to do some research, and as much as there was on the internet Holli didn't know if she could find what she needed there. She needed a library that had texts in it like the Library of Alexandria. She put on her wool coat, the same one she wore the night she and Lennie discovered Widdershins. She pulled on her boots, hat, and gloves, and went out to the horse.

"You win," she sighed, "Let's do this!" She said climbing onto Sleipner's back. She didn't know the extent of the horse's knowledge. Clearly he had above normal horse intelligence as he was Odin's steed. She guessed she'd find out if he knew Spanish?

"La Biblioteca!" she cried and grabbed onto his mane as he started running. Holli's breath ripped away from her as they jumped into the air. Odin's steed galloped among the Northern Lights. The Aurora whirled around them green and purple.

Up, up, up they went, leaving Earth behind them and continued to run into space. Holli closed her eyes against the silvery dust that coated them; so this is the stuff that the horse had shook out of his mane. Holli needed to open her eyes again though, she needed to see where they were, and not everyday did one get to ride an eight legged steed among the stars. She opened them and beheld stars as she'd never witnessed them winking at her in all their glory. Amazing!

Sleipner landed. The building in front of them didn't look like a library to Holli. Rather it looked like an observatory as it was tower shaped with an opening which looked like the ones on earth where the telescope magnified the celestial night. Holli dismounted, and petted the horse. She walked through the open door and began up the spiral staircase.

She arrived at the top in the viewing chamber which contained a blue leather armchair. On the wall above the chair engraved words read: Library of Constellations. Holli sat down in the recliner and gazed at the stars.

The constellations came to life before Holli's eyes as the chair or the floor moved and brought each constellation into view. They were no longer mere groupings of stars, but they flowed with substance, life. First, Leo the Lion blazed before her.

His golden and orange being with his purple and silver mane came into focus. His emerald eyes blazed with a haughty aloofness that said, "I'm first even if that doesn't make chronological sense." Holli noticed that about his neck hung a gold medallion lined with tanzanite and ruby stones in the shape of the sun. His attitude confirmed the stereotype: "I'm good and I know it." The smell of frankincense incense and palm trees filled Holli's nostrils.

The twins known as Gemini came into view. Genitalia proclaimed them male; however, their age proved more difficult to discern. Their cheeks were rosy as if from drink, laughter, and merriment indicating they were a jovial pair. They wore yellow vests and wooden shoes. A smell of wormwood and nut trees played about Holli's nose. Holli thought about TooLu telling her about a magpie when she beheld Gemini.

Holli's chair or the floor moved again, and she wondered how she might acquire one of those wooden shoes if that were her task? What if the Ancient Ox wanted one of those Dutch relics? Wooden shoes reminded Holli of the Tulip Time Festival in Holland Michigan where she used to live. After she met Lennie, they moved to Fennville, Astoria, and now she lived in Alaska of all places. Somehow it was the right place to be; Mother Freya hadn't ever steered her wrong.

The chair stopped and Holli squinted into the outer darkness. Had the chair made an error? A constellation wasn't visible. She blinked and looked out again. Nothing. Wait, did something move?

The scent of opoponax incense and blackthorn trees flitted about Holli's nose. Dark red nearly black stars, the stinger swung and Holli jumped back against her chair. Another name for Scorpio was death.

In contrast to the shadowy blood coloration of Scorpio, Cancer blasted into view a brilliant green along with the overpowering smell of onycha and maple trees oozing sap. Cancer most resembled a crab but the being had a pearl shell veined with silver. Cancer wore a pirate captain's hat, and in one claw held a bottle of rum and in the other it held an amethyst pipe. Holli wondered if the Ancient Ox would have wanted the hat, rum, or pipe?

As Holli continued to gaze at the night sky a bizarre creature materialized before her accompanied by the scent of galbanum incense and ash trees. The thing had pale blue breasts but a long pink elephant trunk. It has a copper shell encrusted with sapphires. What in the hell was this? It dawned on Holli when she beheld the item the creature held. Scales! This was Libra. It made Holli think that beer wasn't so bad when she compared it to coffee. Oh hell Lennie, can't I just like my Jack?

Next into focus flared Sagittarius. Fire sign didn't even come close to the detail Holli witnessed. The centaur glowed purple and dark blue flames of passion. His bow gleamed tin and topaz, and around his bicep glowed a tribal tattoo. When he came into sight the chamber filled with the smell of an oak tree. The centaur fired a flaming arrow.

The arrow landed next to a goat with a fish tail. The brown goat head of Capricorn sported a forked braided beard like that of dwarves, and each of its ends were held together with turquoise rings. The black tail of the fish smelled of willow trees.

The constellations were unique and beautiful, but Holli squirmed in her chair with impatience. Where was Taurus? Come on already, library. The chair or floor moved again, and she found herself gaping up at Virgo.

Holli gasped. Virgin? My ass, Holli thought looking at the woman before her. The diaphanous shift that she wore emanated nut trees and narcissus. Her skin was navy blue, but her nipples, lips, and eyes were dark gray. Her sardonyx belly button ring couldn't be missed.

Holli tried to figure out the next constellation. What in the world? If a peacock, an eagle, and a man mated this might be the result. The thing glowed with an electric blue light, smelled of galbanum and moss, and wore a garnet necklace. Holli nodded, none other than Aquarius. And in her head she heard *The Turning* by Robin Trower. How many times had Lennie made her listen to that song? "To show the world reborn…the turning shall begin"…the age of Aquarius. Oh, Lennie, I miss you so much, she thought as the tears rolled down her cheeks.

Pisces swam into the picture a soft sea green in color. A tin fishing lure decorated with moon and stones hung from the fish's lip. As Pisces swam, the smell of ambergris overwhelmed Holli, there was no mistaking the whale smell that went into many perfumes. Somehow Holli found herself thinking about fig trees and dolphins. What a fucked up trip!

Dragon Blood incense filled Holli's olfactory. One of Lennie's favorites, this star ride of memories might kill her.

"What the fuck, Odin!" She shut her eyes to bite back more tears. When she regained her equilibrium, she opened them again. A red and copper ram with diamond tipped horns stood before her.

"Hello Aries. Tell me Taurus is next?" Holli asked the constellation. Aries nodded.

Last Taurus sauntered into view. Regal, proud, the bull snorted, and the odor of ruminated cypress and storax oppressed Holli. Pale blue in color he shimmered with confidence or stubbornness, or a combination of the two traits. His horns were copper, and his eyes where sapphires. He had a nose ring. At last, The Ring of Taurus! How in all the realms could she obtain that?

The chair came to a stop, and Holli stood up her mind reeling, but she knew what she sought. She exited the Library of

Constellations and found Sleipner waiting. She climbed on his back and gave him a scratch behind his ears.

"Thanks for waiting for me. We are off to Taurus," she said.

Sleipner ran in a straight line, but it felt like flying to Holli. No visible road existed in space yet the horse's hooves hit some invisible substance. Or perhaps they traveled through more than one dimension at the same time? They traveled so fast Holli didn't know if she would be able to perceive the road he used, what an amazing horse. A thick layer of the metallic dust coated them as they moved onward.

Taurus stood huge before them though still miles and miles away. Holli studied the bull as they approached. How to get a nose ring off a constellation and give it to an ancient ox?

Darker black shadows appeared and disappeared in the distance. Holli watched, and blinked and blinked guessing that her eyes were playing tricks on her. Maybe space consisted of pockets of blackness?

The Displacers popped into existence, bit Sleipner's legs, and they blinked out, their damage done that quickly. Their acidic saliva sizzled into the horse's flesh. He plummeted.

LOL

Sleipner threw Holli, so he wouldn't crush one of her legs. Holli smacked her head into a rock. Sleipner crashed to the ground beside her and didn't move. Holli realized he threw her on purpose so as not to crush her beneath him.

Her nose, gashed forehead, and lips bled. She'd have one or two black eyes, but her appearance was the least of her worries; she needed to help Sleipner. She crawled over to him and appraised the damage. She needed to stop the spread of the acid before it reached his heart. Holli cleared her mind and asked Freya for assistance.

Holli placed her hands on Sleipner's neck, sending the will to heal into him. Yellow and pink energy flowed from Holli's fingers into the horse. She watched as her magic streamed through the insides of the eight legged steed. Her magic devoured the acid and the bite wounds on Sleipner's legs closed. He stood up and whinnied.

"Thank you, Daughter of Freya," Sleipner said. Holli heard it telepathically.

"You're welcome," she answered aloud.

"I'm ready when you are," Sleipner said. Holli climbed up, and they took off again. Holli watched for Displacers as they galloped.

Taurus loomed closer, they were making progress. The Displacers reappeared, Holli saw them, and she'd been waiting. They were not going to interfere with her quest again, attacking her mount and running like cowards. Guerilla warfare in space, well Holli knew how to fight. Holli channeled her anger into energy.

"FOR LENNIE!" she screamed and sent her magic out. Dark green lightning blasted out from Holli's chest in all directions. Each bolt struck and disintegrated one of her enemies. Exhausted from her effort Holli slumped down and put her arms around Sleipner's neck.

"Let me know if more of the bastards show up," she said.

"I will," Sleipner answered in Holli's mind. He galloped even faster, how fast could he gallop anyway? Holli clung tighter, and gritted her teeth. Sometime later, she fell asleep.

*

"We're here," Sleipner said.

Holli opened her eyes and beheld Taurus. The colossal astral bull's pale blue skin flickered and rippled like wind blowing wild grasses in a field. His sapphire eyes twinkled, and starlight reflected off his copper horns. His nose ring looked to be made of titanium.

"I see Odin's horse without One Eye," Taurus boomed.

"My name is Holli. I need your nose ring," she said.

"And why would I give away my only possession to a girl I don't know?" Taurus asked.

"Here is the story," Holli told Taurus the story of Lennie needing the Aurochs' aid so they could rescue their children. When she finished her story, Taurus didn't say anything. Holli looked up at him waiting, hoping her story would sway him enough to part with his ring. She was about to plead, when Taurus laughed so hard his whole being shook.

"You tell my cousin he wins this round, but he had best know that the game is still on," Taurus said and he winked at Holli. His nose ring vanished and appeared in Holli's hand sized so she could carry it.

"Thank you Taurus," Holli said.

"Make sure you deliver my message to my cousin. The game is still on," he repeated.

"I will, and thank you again," Holli said. Taurus snorted.

"Sleipner let's ride," Holli said. She didn't need to tell him twice; Odin's steed shot forward, and they were on their way to the Aurochs.

*

"Your cousin says you win this round, but the game is still on," Holli said as she placed Taurus' nose ring on a black and white horn of the Aurochs.

"Your debt is settled," the Ox said.

*

Sleipner landed in the driveway, and Gerard and Muka barked.

"Thank you for carrying me," Holli said to the horse as she climbed off his back.

"My pleasure," he said.

FEHU

For the next year Holli's true wealth came from watching her children grow.

EPILOGUE: DAGAZ

The lights went out. A reverberating sound spread throughout The Egan Center, more a feeling, a shaking like a mini earthquake, striking the coast of Alaska, tectonic plates rubbing against each other in slow love making. A lone blue spotlight came on illuminating the keyboardist. Formerly the band's front man, now two years later he stood to the right of the stage at the keyboard with his computer.

The sound from the keyboard shimmered, hovered, the listener could picture dust and wind flying against their bodies as the spaceship finished landing. The keyboardist's once colored, now normal black hair hung over his eyes, and he wore a white t-shirt depicting a yellow emoticon.

The bass player stood center stage at the microphone as the current front man. His voice a mix between Linkin Park and Simon and Garfunkel. He played a few slap notes on his newest custom instrument fashioned by Ibanez. His gray bass had steel silver patterns on either side of the strings resembling tribal tattoos. He grinned at the audience.

"And we have landed in Anchorage, Alaska of all places. How the hell are you doing, Anchorage?" He waited for the reaction. Holli screamed loudly along with the rest of the crowd wishing that Lennie were beside her screaming in his two note Norwegian voice. It was a better than expected reaction at the edge of the world for the front man. "My brother wanted to give his vocal cords a rest from the scream-o, so you get me. It is a win, win. I feel you; I wouldn't want to listen to my brother." He looked over at the keyboard player and smiled throwing up his hands as if to say 'what, it is true'. He slapped out a few more notes. A bass playing Jamirquai-esque funk Irish Jig.

"I'm just gonna shut up and play. Play you some music. This one is called 'Amish Striptease'," he laughed. The young man to his left cranked out a heavy crunch grunge chord, and the band exploded into action, a force of energy and sound. The guitarist ran back and forth weaving between the other band members as he played. Drenched in sweat and smiling wide before their first song even finished. He played a classic white colored Gibson Flying V Tremolo. He shredded as he slid to the front of the stage on his knees, and made a warble with his whammy bar.

The band segued into another song called "Garbuldonians." The Flying V lifted up and the strings sang out electric agony. The two brothers with sting instruments at the front of the stage jumped, twirled, and ran back and forth playing smoothly and winking at girls in the crowd.

"Fucking Anchorage Alaska! Ten fucking below outside. Time to heat it up in this bitch. We call this one, 'Resurrecting the Phoenix'." The song began in darkness with a undulating ringing from a hammer dulcimer. A red spotlight glowed around the band's former mandolin player. She stood behind her hammer dulcimer bringing the piece to life as the strings rang out as if rising into the air just like the mythical bird swirling to life again from ashes. The hammer dulcimer was a unique instrument a blending of strings and percussion. Her toes were painted florescent green, but she wore a medieval gown, a collaboration of darker shimmering blues and greens as of the tail of a mermaid.

The keyboard streamed into the song and built more energy. Then the guitars seared in, and the drums began pounding. The energy kept building; the venue couldn't help but actually heat up as the crowd started to dance. The song jammed for eleven relentless minutes as the flying V shredded, the bass slapped funk, the keyboard flapped wings, the drums shock away ash, and the hammer dulcimer soared the living flying bird among the clouds.

The standing crowd screamed, whistled, hooted, and applauded as they danced.

"That's what you get! Are we having a good time, Alaska?" The audience screamed louder.

"Here is a love song Dad wrote for Mom. We call this thing 'Hearts on Fire'," they went into a five and a half minute song about an aging couple. It must have affected the young women in the audience too as they began blowing kisses at the stage.

"All right. We are gonna play one more before our set break. This one is called '75 Bucks and a Shot in the Eye'," he said and began the tune with a deep bass growl. The rest of the band joined in. The song had a happy drunk, galloping horse, feel to it.

"I can do more than play guitar
I can even drive a car
You might have seen me at the bar
Har, Har
And now it's time to get high
Time to drink some sour mash rye
75 bucks and a shot in the eye
For why?"

The band took their set break. Holli went and got two shots of Jack one for herself and one to drink to Lennie's memory. Damn she missed the man. Fucking Loki for taking away her husband. The second set began with the hammer dulcimer. The song seemed to glisten like ice dripping in spring.

"We call that one 'Icicles on Yggdrasil'. This next one is called 'Shoes for Feet'," he grinned at the woman, and she shot him the finger. The song was a short pounding piece.

"As you may know, we have a new album out. We also made new hoodies especially for you Alaska, so check them out!

Now for a couple of your old favorites," and they launched into "Gray in the Goatee", followed by "Freya's Cats", and "Becoming a Valkyrie." The drummer dressed in his customary black, hair in a ponytail, poured sweat as he banged out an amazing three minute solo song.

"We call that one 'Our Pop Song'," the front man said as the drummer bowed. "This next one is called 'The Tears of Ragnarok'," he said. Throughout the course of the song he switched between his bass and a sitar. The hammer dulcimer player switched to a French Horn for a few sections of the song. The young man traded between his flying V and a banjo. The drummer moved from his bongos to a purple drum kit and double bass thumped through the song like Anthrax's "Charlie Benabte." The song lasted about thirteen minutes.

"How are we fucking doing, Anchorage?"

They clapped, cheered, and screamed appreciatively.

"We are going to Fairbanks tomorrow. I hear that it is so cold there that the Eskimos have migrated to Seattle. Just thought I'd let you know in case you want to make the drive. Now we are going to take it down a notch this is called, 'Merfolk'," and he gestured to his brother and mother. The song was a call and answer between the dulcimer and the keyboard. The floods lights flickered through a spectrum of aqua colors.

They played four more songs. When they took a break, Holli made her way through the sea of people to the restroom. When she finished her business, she got a shot of Jack and a bottle of Bass. She downed her shot of Jack.

"Hail Freya, grant me strength," she said. Then she drank some of the beer, "This is for you Lennie, you sexy bastard, you should be here," she drained the bottle; it wasn't so bad after three shots of Jack. The band returned for their encore.

"You want some more?" the front man asked.

The crowd screamed for more. Their throats were sore, but they screamed and whistled as loud as they could.

"Mom talked us into the next few. When I say talked us into, I really mean bribed us when we were under the spell of a certain green plant. Without further ado, we return to the sixties," the front man told the crowd.

The band went into their rendition of "A Whiter Shade of Pale." Then they covered "Here Comes the Sun" by the Beatles. After those two they moved forward through time a bit and played "Wheel in the Sky" by Journey. In the middle of it they stopped. There was silence.

"Someone is going to fucking die if they scratched the CD we have been playing for these people," the woman playing the hammer dulcimer said. Laughter followed and the band continued the song.

"Anchorage, as we are in the land of the Midnight Sun, and we are a family band, we got another by Journey. And yes you can blame this one on Mom," and they played: Faithfully.

"We just want to keep on playing, Alaska! One more cover. Now he may not be up front right now, but this one if for Dad there in the back. Here is Johnny Cash, 'Man in Black'," the front man said. They finished the concert with their own song "Odin's Missing Eye."

Holli bought their new CD titled *Mermaids & Ragnarok* and a hoodie with an image of a Phoenix shaped spaceship on it. She wished that Lennie could have got a matching sweatshirt, but she would think about him when she wore hers.

END

Appendix A: The Runes Simple Meanings

Fehu: Wealth
Uruz: Aurochs
Thurisaz: Thor, Strength
Ansuz: Odin's wisdom
Raidho: Transportation
Kenaz: Torch, Fire, Passion
Gebo: Gift, Exchange of energy
Wunjo: Joy
Hagalaz: Hail
Naudhiz: Need
Isa: Ice
Jera: Year
Eihwaz: Yew Tree, Yggdrasil
Perthro: Cup, Game Piece, Rebirth
Elhaz: Elk
Sowilo: Sun
Tiwaz: Tyr, Spear, Justice
Berkano: Birch Tree, Rebirth
Mannaz: Man
Laguz: Lake, Feminine Influence
Ingwaz: Fertility
Dagaz: Day
Othala: Ancestral Property, Home
Ehwaz: Horse

Appendix B : Widdershins songs

"ODIN'S MISSING EYE"

Plucked from my socket
Thrown like a rocket
I went down the well
Deeper than the realm of Hel
The Well spit me into space
Where I saw her face

(Chorus)

Grinning 'twas the empty socket
Ready for me, a love locket
I swam toward my place
Had to fill that empty space
Fill it up, fill it up
Make it complete, make it complete

Now I watched Odin getting old
Covered with a patch so cold
But he threw me out
The aged Norse lout
He will face his doom
Without me, I assume

(Chorus)

And I rest in her celestial face
Granting her ethereal grace
I wink at all the boys
To give up their toys
And be my special friend
Ever, forever, to the end

(Chorus)

When they turned me down, I cry
Then I fell eons from the sky
Into the mouth of the eight legged horse
Spit out into Odin's waiting hand, of course
Now I watch his mead cellar
For any a strange feller

"FREYA'S CATS"

Slightly blue, slightly gray
Slightly gray, slightly blue
What color it is, is hard to say
Go ahead, try to tell them to shoo

(Chorus)
Freya's cats kick some ass
Freya's cats don't eat grass
Freya's cats are all the rave
Freya's cats send baddies to the grave

Bygul has icy breath of death
Thofnir has the life healing paw
As a pair they're better than crystal meth

Battle magic, tooth & claw

(Chorus)
Freya's cats kick some ass
Freya's cats don't eat grass
Freya's cats are all the rave
Freya's cats send baddies to the grave

They pull mother Freya's magic sled
With paws that are sure
Mess with 'em you're dead
And they will just purr
They fly the Asgardian sky
Mess with 'em, be ready to die

(Chorus)
Freya's cats kick some ass
Freya's cats don't eat grass
Freya's cats are all the rave
Freya's cats send baddies to the grave

"SHOES FOR FEET"

I wish they made shoes for feet
Ones that could walk the street
Ones that could tap a beat
Wouldn't that be neat

"75 BUCKS AND A SHOT IN THE EYE"

I can do more than play guitar
I can even drive a car

You might have seen me at the bar
Har, har
And now it's time to get high
Time to drink some sour mash rye
75 bucks and a shot in the eye
For why?

"AMISH STRIPTEASE"

Have you ever seen an Amish striptease?
Very dainty, if you please
Makes you want to sneeze
Or eat some moldy cheese
Isn't all cheese mold?
Dude that's cold
Dad is getting old
But his drums are still bold
Another Amish striptease
If you please
If you please

"THE LANDING"

(keyboard instrumental--dubstep)

"GARBULDONIANS""''

Ancient relatives of Cthulhu
They live among the stars

On a planet of green mist
Seeing them will turn you into stew
Worse than Martians from Mars
Hate to see them pissed

The Garbuldonians are fear
The Garduldonians are fear

They weren't in any prophecy of Nostradamus
Not in any Egyptian hieroglyphics
Nor in the Christian bible
Some say they are made of fungus
They speak in moans and harmonics
And are immune to sword and rifle

The Garbuldonians are near
The Garbuldonians are near

Some say they lived awhile in Atlantis
Some say they penned the Necronomicon
Others claim they are disguised as Asians
Perhaps they sailed with 'ol Chris Columbus
Maybe we need more Geodon
To help heal our mind abrasions

The Garbuldonians are here
The Garbuldonians are here

"HEARTS ON FIRE"

Now we are getting a little older
You still lay your head on my shoulder
I'm growing into my sage

Hair dye doesn't show your age
We still hold hands when we take walks
Our home has mermaid clocks

Through the seasons of the year
Our hearts on fire
Through this life we steer
Our hearts on fire

We live with our kids and our cats
Wearing many different hats
Our love grows deeper each day
Under sun and moon ray
We may continue to slow down
Living outside of town

Through the seasons of the year
Our hearts on fire
Though this life we steer
Our hearts on fire

When death claims us this time
We will find each other next time
A little sooner in the next life
One with less strife
Again we will handfast
Together in that life as the last

And still our hearts on fire
Our hearts on fire
Our hearts on fire
Ever our hearts on fire

"RESURRECTING THE PHOENIX"

(Instrumental, length varies on amount of jamming band does, approx. 13 minutes)

"ICICLES ON YGGDRASIL"

There are icicles on Yggdrasil
Ratatosk is freezing
As he skitters
Icicles on The World Tree
Ratatosk keeps running
Got a job to do
Got a Job to do
Got a job to do

"GRAY IN THE GOATEE"

I stand before The World Tree
With gray in my goatee
Before me the runes lay gleaming
I took them up, an electric feeling
As Odin did in days of yore
Now I stand on wisdom's shore

(Chorus)
I have the runes with me
And gray in the goatee

The answers are there, you agree
I got gray in the goatee

I draw Gebo, exchange, a little give and take
Then Laguz, feminine influence, lake
Hey baby let's go to bed
Have fun before we are dead
Feel each other under the covers
Drenched in sweat as lovers

(Chorus)

OUR POP SONG
(drum instrumental, 3:00 minutes long)

"MERFOLK"
(instrumental. 7:56 in length a call and answer between hammer
    dulcimer and keyboard/computer dubstep)

"GARDEN OF HERBS"

Chamomile, cloves, and cumin seed
Frankincense, & jasmine flowers I need
Some lavender over there,
And lemon verbena by my old chair,

Mugwort & myrrh
And Julie patchouli for sure
Peppermint and rose hips
Spearmint leaf for my lover's lips

Sage & red raspberry
Star anise, and juniper-berry
White willow bark
Just for a lark

"X-BOX WARRIORS"

Halo & Reach & 4
Call of Duty, Assassin's Creed, and more
Kicked 'em all out the door
The x-box warriors
The x-box warriors

We've beat 'em all
Not a game too big or too small
In the end they all fall
The x-box warriors
The x-box warriors

Zelda and Fable
Played 'em under the table
Better find an independent label
The x-box warriors
The x-box warriors

Grand Theft Auto & Guitar Her-o
Us one, them zero
They should fear-o
The x-box warriors
The x-box warriors

"BECOMING A VALKYRIE"

As you lay dying on the battlefield
Your lifeforce ebbing away
Blood splattered across your shield
Done, wasted, nothing more to say
Knowing you'd never yield
War in your blood, that was the way
You fought, ever valiant
You fought, ever valiant

Chorus
Freya will call you
Freya will claim you
Freya will name you
That is how you will become
Become (echo effect)
A Valkyrie

You fought with sword and spear
Against an enemy you couldn't defeat
But you fought without fear
Never going to surrender or retreat
Knowing that today your end was near

You were one of the elite
You fought, ever valiant
You fought, ever valiant

(Chorus)
Repeat chorus three more times--fade out

"WAIL OF THE BANSHEE"

(Blood curdling scream-o)
Instrumental Dubstep
Ends with mandolin

"SUNFLOWER MEAD"

We are an old couple
We no longer couple
We've grown stronger as a couple
And we still laugh and play
Under sun and moon ray
And love each other more every day

Among the sunflowers
We started drinking some mead
Magic flowed, stirred our ancient powers
And in you I spilled my seed
Thank the sunflowers & thank the mead
Letting us both fulfill our need

John Opskar

Odinsson

Copyright 2012

PROLOGUE

Once I was a man. Now I am a God. I have as many names as people have languages, but my most common name is Odin. I am the Allfather, and I watch the world of men as well as the other eight realms.

My wife is Freya. Freya rides a chariot pulled by her two cats, and she doesn't find it amusing when I ask her which is Rumpelteazer and which is Mungojerrie (thank you Mr. Elliot). My wife is a cat Goddess, and I am a wolf God. We have managed to get along despite this minor difference. Freya the beautiful, she rides into battle with half of the slain.

I do not have my right eye; I gave it up. A small sacrifice for knowledge. There are sacrifices in war and knowledge is a war; don't let anyone claiming to be a professor tell you differently. They only know a fraction of the infinite.

Under the root of the great ash, I went down to see Mimir. He lent me his horn, Gjoll. Using the tip, I dug my right eye out of its socket. Into Mimir's well I cast part of my human sight for a drink of wisdom.

Still I thirsted. I traveled among the three roots. I stood among them, and the smell of earth permeated my nostrils. Damp, moist clean fresh earth. The roots, colored as Heimdall's bridge, glittered all of the colors of the rainbow.

I took my spear and with the razor sharp tip gashed my side. I gave my blood to the roots. They drank it and thrashed.

Asking for knowledge of the tree, I climbed Yggdasill. I climbed and climbed; when I reached the right height, I took my sword and cut my hair. Not my beard, but the locks that hung down from my head. I made a noose with my hair and tied it around my boots. I began to hang head downward. My beard blew in the cosmic wind and my blood splattered the earth.

I swung there for nine long nights. None saw me hanging; none offered me food or drink. I peered down to the deepest depths. At last I spied the runes. They were small on pieces of a black stone, and the markings on them were the crimson of my blood. I roared for joy and seized them.

When I picked up the runes, my noose of hair broke, and I fell. The world swayed and swirled and my vision blurred. When focus returned, I had gained the knowledge of the runes. From a word to a word and from a deed to another deed.

Although I am in this saga, it is not mine. This is the saga of my son, Leonard Asbourn.

KENAZ

A beautiful woman died in childbirth. The male child lived and was sent to an orphanage ran by the municipality. Nobody knew who the father was, but before the mother died she gasped out the surname of "Asbourn." The nurses at the hospital decided the baby's first name should be Leonard.

Eighteen years later, Leonard walked up to the airline counter and presented his ticket. The ticket agent glanced at him; she seemed harried. Maybe it was just his nerves? No, he decided, she was flustered.

"Checking any baggage, Mr. Asbourn? she asked.

"Just my backpack," he answered.

"So, one carry-on then," she typed away at her computer without looking up at him.

"Yes," he answered annoyed with her flippancy.

"Here is your boarding pass," she handed him the ticket.

"Thanks," he said walking away and feeling a bit sorry for the lady. Work was work, but in her job he thought she might be a little more polite.

Hours later the plane touched down in Minneapolis.

Leonard stepped out into a crazy amount of heat and wondered if he'd just made a huge mistake. The heat hit him, and the length of the flight began to take a toll. His sense of adventure dwindled, but there was no turning back now. It was July 26 and 92 degrees in Minnesota.

Shouldering his tattered white and orange backpack, Leonard began walking south. He had no idea where he was going. Was this what adventure was like? Maybe he should have stayed in Norway. He stopped and looked up at the energy-zapping sun.

"Shit," he said wiping the dripping sweat from his forehead onto his faded ripped blue jeans. His white t-shirt clung to his body. He took it off, wrung it out, and hung it around his neck like a scarf. There was nothing for it; he needed to keep going. He started walking again.

Two hours later, Leonard watched an old station wagon pull off to the side of the road. He tensed. He didn't have the strength to fight or run. Throwing caution to the wind Leonard approached the passenger side of the car.

"I'll give you a ride if you get a haircut and look like a decent young man," said the wrinkled man behind the wheel. He had immaculate silver hair and a bulbous nose. The interior of the car smelled of apples.

"I will. Thanks for the lift, a bit warm out," Leonard said getting in the Buick.

"My name is Irvin. Do you know how to drive?"

"No sir," Leonard answered.

"Okay, I'll teach you how," Irvin said.

"You will?"

"Of course. Not rocket science you know. Mostly you just keep it between the ditches. What's your name son?" Irvin asked.

"Leonard Asbourn."

"Your accent is unmistakable. What part of Norway are you from?"

"Oslo," Leonard answered.

*

I am Leonard's Mother. I did not die in childbirth; although, I made it look like I did. I am a Goddess, and my name is Freya. One might say that I guided Irvin to the side of the road. My baby looked so miserable. I know that he needs to become a man and all that, but I couldn't help myself. A mother is a mother, after all.

Irvin left Leonard at his cabin in Pelican Rapids. A few months passed, and my son was lonely. Part of me wanted to leave him be, but there is that more powerful part of me that wouldn't leave me alone so I went to see him and to give him some company.

*

A knock at the door startled Leonard awake. What time was it? It was pitch black outside. Who in the hell could that be? Leonard grabbed a log that sat by the fireplace and padded toward the door wondering if he'd imagined the knock. It came again.

"Who is it?" Leonard asked.

"I'm a realtor. My name is Lucina," Freya answered drawing on Roman mythology.

"A realtor in the middle of the night? I didn't know the place was for sale," Leonard said opening the door with his free hand. He gripped the log harder ready to strike. Was this Lucina the decoy for the band of burglars?

Before him stood a short woman in a navy blue suit. She held a briefcase. Her short hair styled to be businesslike and recently dyed red to hide her gray roots. While taking her in, Leonard listened for noise from the rest of the thieves but didn't hear a sound.

"Are you going to invite me in? I'm not a vampire," Lucina asked.

"Please do come in," Leonard said searching the darkness behind her for signs of movement. He didn't see any. Once she entered, Leonard closed the door.

"Let me get the fire going again for some better light. There is no electricity here yet. I would hope as the realtor you knew that though," Leonard said playfully as he stoked the fire back to life. The flames flared upward and brightened the cabin illuminating the glossy magazines strewn in front of the hearth.

"Interesting reading material," Lucina said indicating the 60s *Playboys*. Embarrassed, but nonplused as he had literally read them, Leonard replied,

"They were the only books in the cabin. Now how can I help you, Realtor Lucina?"

"Show me the place so I can make a brochure for the listing," she answered.

"Irvin hired me to renovate the place," Leonard began. "Let me give you the tour and explain my plans," Leonard said wondering if Irvin had hired the woman to see about his progress or if he'd run off? He'd told Irvin that he'd work on the place if he could stay there. He hadn't lied. The past few weeks, he'd been busy fishing so he could eat and chopping wood so he could stay warm, but he wasn't going to renege on his work. He might as well show the woman posing as a realtor his plan and have some fun with this.

"Let us call the space where we are standing now the living/dining room. Where I have this makeshift counter covered in fish scales, I am going to build a real counter serving as a divider between the living room and the kitchen. Behind the kitchen will be a small guest bedroom. Are you with me so far?" Leonard explained. Lucina nodded, understanding. Leonard walked forward so he stood slightly to the right of the hearth.

"Where I am standing now will be a hallway," he moved forward a few steps. Lucina followed. Leonard wondered if she might be crazy. The whole realtor in the middle of the night story wasn't washing.

"Why are you here again?" he asked.

"I've told you," she replied.

"Right," Leonard answered sarcastically shaking his head. He took five more steps forward. The woman followed. Leonard figured that the only course of action at this point was to continue. If she were a lunatic, he did not want to set her off; so far this had been a peaceful visit.

"In this space to the right here, I am going to build in a pantry/washroom," he recited. The realtor took out a yellow legal pad and began sketching. Leonard watched her for a few seconds. When she seemed finished, he took up where he'd left off.

"Behind this wall with the fireplace, I am going to put in two rooms. There will be a small bathroom, and the master bedroom, does that make sense?" he asked. She showed him her floor plan. It matched the one in his head.

"Should work fine for your pamphlet, Lucina," he grinned.

"That should do it," she confirmed putting away her sketch. When she left, Leonard didn't follow her.

That was odd. Well, the company had been a nice diversion. Realtors in the middle of the night, not likely. Leonard pinched himself. Not dreaming.

*

When my son answered the door, my heart leapt for joy! My little boy wasn't a baby anymore. A well muscled, well endowed man with rockstar hair opened the door. After his haircut a few months back it now hung over his eyes, and he flicked his head to get it out of the way. Oh, and his eyes. I am surprised that the women were not just melting over him. Eyes like tanzanite.

Still I needed to give him something different to read than 60s Playboys for Asgard's sake. What mothers do for their sons. Time to send him some books.

*

A week later, there was another knock on the door. Leonard put down his pencil from where he'd been measuring a board for cutting and answered the door. There was a delivery driver holding a box.

"Leonard?" he asked.

"I am," he answered.

"If I could get you to sign here," the delivery man indicated the spot. Leonard signed. The driver left.

Leonard opened the box. Inside were three paperback books. *Crime and Punishment*, *The Martian Chronicles*, and *The Lion, the Witch, and the Wardrobe*. There was a note which said: Better reading material. Love Lucina. That night, Leonard burned most of the *Playboys*.

While he worked on renovating the cabin, Leonard read. He found that he wasn't lonely when he read. He had friends in the stories.

The autumn leaves gave way to snow. Not as much snow as Norway but pretty close. During the winter, Leonard ice fished, and hunted rabbits with spears he'd fashioned.

His muscles were like iron, and he had stacks of firewood piled on all sides of the cabin and the shed. When Irvin returned, Leonard would have to leave. He couldn't stay any longer; there had to be more to life than this. Even as Leonard thought that, a new project formed in his mind.

He began cutting boards five feet in length and sanding them. He cut and sanded boards until there were enough of them that when they were laid out in a line they would stretch twenty feet. Leonard was happy, now Irvin could build a dock.

On February 21, Irvin arrived at the cabin.

"You need a haircut," he said.

"Good to see you too, Irvin," Leonard answered. Then Leonard showed Irvin all the work he'd done.

"Good work. As a reward, I'll drive you into Fargo and get you a haircut and some new clothes."

"Thank you." Irvin got Leonard a haircut and as promised some new clothes.

"Leonard, today I will have one more gift for you. I am going to buy a new car, and you can have my old one and some gas money."

"I can't repay you," Leonard replied.

"What do you think I had you build the rooms in the cabin for?"

"Thank you for all of the things you've done for me, Irvin."

"Welcome. I'll never forget the day I picked up a hitch-hiker who needed a haircut," they laughed and took sips from Irvin's flask. Irvin purchased a brown Buick, and Leonard inherited the old station wagon. Leonard shook hands with Irvin and drove east.

Inhaling the smell of apples, Leonard thought about how generous Irvin had been to him. Irvin was the closest thing to a father that Leonard had ever known. And here he was driving away, but that was how life worked. Still he would miss the cantankerous old man.

*

Ten hours later, Leonard found himself in Janesville, Wisconsin. Irvin had left an old wool army blanket in the back of the car. It served its purpose to keep Leonard warm as he slept in the back of the wagon. In the morning, he checked out the Janesville mall. Leonard cleaned up in a bathroom and applied for a job at a large chain department store.

The manager of the store gave Leonard an interview.

"What can you do?" he asked.

"Anything," Leonard answered.

"What are you good at?" the manager wanted to know.

"I am a carpenter," Leonard answered.

"Great, you're our new janitor," they shook hands and Leonard had his first official job. He wasn't sure how one got from carpenter to janitor, but it was a job. Leonard swept and mopped the floors. He cleaned counters and replaced light bulbs. He vacuumed and replaced supplies in the bathrooms.

Two weeks later, Leonard received his first paycheck. The store cashed it for him because he spent three quarters of it on more clothes and bedding.

Leonard smiled looking at the red and white striped pole signifying the barber shop. Leonard thought about Irvin; the old man sure had a thing about haircuts. Leonard stepped into the shop; he could get a haircut and keep up the clean-cut appearance in honor of the man who had taught him how to drive.

"I would like a haircut," he told the barber.

"How short?" the skinny man asked ushering Leonard to a stool.

"Just a little longer than a military cut," the Norwegian answered.

"Never heard it put like that," the barber commented putting a cloth around Leonard's neck.

"Now you have," Leonard closed his eyes.

Leonard worked for another month. When his checks came, he bought books in the mall and groceries at the store at the end of the mall. He moved his station wagon every few days, but it wasn't good enough.

One morning a manager knocked on his car window. Leonard answered.

"Do you sleep in your car?" the manager demanded.

"Yes," Leonard answered truthfully.

"Consider yourself fired," he said red faced.

"Why?" Leonard wanted to know.

"No vagabonds on my watch," he said and stalked off.

"Your loss," Leonard said to the empty air and started his car. The spring air felt good as it went through Leonard's short haircut. The road carried the Norwegian toward Chicago.

*

I watched Leonard as he worked with the wood and hunted and fished for his food. I was already proud of the young Asatru. He had mastered the virtue of industriousness. I took a sip of black raspberry mead and fed my wolves.

I was not concerned that Leonard had not yet found religion; it would come in time. My son needed a guide. I could have sent one of my own wolves or ravens, but that wouldn't have been fun, and it might have been too much for him to handle so quickly, but I would send him a different sort of guide. The dog will work.

*

Leonard nearly caused an accident as he changed lanes to pull off to the side of the road. There was a hurt dog trying to limp along with a broken leg. Once the wagon stopped, Leonard hopped out and went over to the dog.

"Looks like you could use a lift feller," he said. The dog cocked an ear and lifted its head to regard Leonard. His dark eyes were pleading.

His mangy, matted, clumped gray fur was covered in filth and road dust. One of his ears was torn, and he had fleas. Leonard dug his oldest shirt out of his bag and ripped it into strips. He bandaged the leg as well as he could. He placed the dog on the passenger seat, and together they traversed into the heart of the windy city.

The dog whimpered.

"Bet you're hungry as well as in pain. I'll find you some food and then a doctor," Leonard assured the canine. The dog let out a woof that seemed to say okay. Leonard found a supermarket. He picked up a big bag of Kibbles'n Bits and went to the checkout lane.

"Hungry dog?" the Asian looking woman asked.

"You could say that. Hey, do you know where I could find a dog doctor?" Leonard asked.

"You mean a vet?" she asked. Leonard looked at her.

"Stacy," she called. Another woman came over.

"I need to find a dog doctor?" Leonard repeated.

"I get off work in ten minutes; you can follow me to the clinic," Stacy said.

Waiting for Stacy to come out of the store, Leonard opened the bag of food and poured a large amount of it in front of the dog. The dog devoured it and looked up as if asking for more. Leonard poured out some more. The dog ate that too.

"I guess you were hungry. Greedy seems to fit you. Your name is now Greedy," Leonard declared stowing the remainder of the bag in the back seat.

"He sure is a handsome man, isn't he?" Stacy said scratching behind his wounded ear.

"His name is Greedy. Greedy this is Stacy. Stacy, Greedy," Leonard introduced them.

"Where did you get this relic of a car?" Stacy asked.

"A friend gave it to me. Can I follow you to the clinic?" he asked.

"Yup. I drive that green Ranger," she indicated her truck.

"Thanks." Leonard followed her to the veterinarian clinic. The veterinarian did everything he could for Greedy including a flea treatment.

"That will be four hundred sixty two dollars," the receptionist said.

Leonard counted out two hundred seventy eight dollars and handed it to the woman named Brenda.

"That won't cover it," Brenda said.

"It is all I have," Leonard explained.

"Steve!" Brenda yelled.

"What seems to be the problem?" the vet asked as he emerged from within the building.

"He can't pay the whole bill," Brenda explained.

"I like Greedy," Steve said, "Work out an arrangement with Leonard; it's all right with me." Steve returned to the bowels of the building.

"Leonard, when can you pay the remainder of the balance?"

"Can I keep the grounds or do something to work off the rest of it?" Leonard asked. Grasping the fact that Leonard didn't have a job, Brenda's eyebrows about shot off of her head.

"I guess you are gonna be our new groundskeeper even though we don't need one," she sighed.

He worked as the groundskeeper for a month. With his debt settled, Leonard looked at Greedy.

"Well boy you are a handsome one, but I don't like this huge city. Are you ready to move on?" he asked his dog.

Greedy barked in agreement. Leonard waved goodbye to the clinic, and they drove west into the setting sun.

A few hours later they drove into Carmel, Indiana. Leonard pulled into a church parking lot to spend the night. He covered himself with blankets, and Greedy curled up next to him.

"I'm glad we got your leg fixed," Leonard mumbled. Greedy licked his cheek, and they fell asleep.

Find out how to keep reading *Odinsson* at
http://www.wordbranch.com/odinsson.html

For a limited time, you can get a 10% discount on any Word Branch Publishing book from the WBP website. Enter CD10 at the checkout.

Also written by John Opskar. *Odinsson: Book One of the Rune Told Series*

You can purchase John's books at:
http://www.wordbranch.com/book-shop.html

About John Opskar: John likes writing fantasy stories and has a Creative Writing/English Literature degree from Western Michigan University. He lives in Wasilla, Alaska with his wonderful wife, and four cats who think they should be fed at three A.M.

You can email John with your questions and comments at **johnopskar@wordbranch.com.**

If you liked *Loki's Laughter*, please leave feedback.

Loki's Laughter is published by Word Branch Publishing, an independent publishing company located in the heart of Appalachia. We represent talented new and up and coming authors who need a venue to make their voices heard. We offer unique titles in both paperback and e-books in a variety of genres including science fiction, fantasy, young adult, and spiritual.

http://wordbranch.com

See more of Word Branch Publishing's books at http://wordbranch.com/book-shop.html

Made in the USA
Charleston, SC
09 June 2015